Dogged
by
Death

Also available by Laura Scott

Dogged by Death

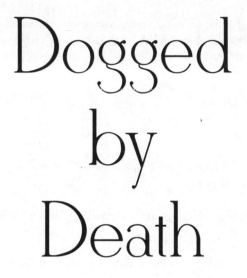

A FURRY FRIENDS MYSTERY

Laura Scott

CROOKED LANE

NEW YORK

Published in the United States by Crooked Lane Books, an imprint of The Quick Brown Fox & Company LLC.

Crooked Lane Books and its logo are trademarks of The Quick Brown Fox & Company LLC.

Library of Congress Catalog-in-Publication data available upon request.

ISBN (hardcover): 978-1-64385-657-5
ISBN (ebook): 978-1-64385-658-2

Cover illustration by David Malan

Printed in the United States.

www.crookedlanebooks.com

Crooked Lane Books
34 West 27th St., 10th Floor
New York, NY 10001

First Edition: July 2021

10 9 8 7 6 5 4 3 2 1

This book is dedicated in loving memory to my paternal grandparents, Harriet and Frank Wanke, my Great Aunt Tillie and my maternal grandparents Lydia and Peter Valerio. Wonderful childhood memories inspired this story.

Chapter One

Ally Winter parked in front of the Willow Bluff Legacy House, the modest assisted living ranch home her grandfather had moved into two months ago after undergoing hip replacement surgery. The regal Lannon stone-wrapped home had aged well, just like her grandfather. She picked up the container of brownies she'd made earlier that morning, slid out from behind the wheel, and approached the front door.

"Are you deaf? I told you to get outta here!"

Gramps' raised voice drifted through the open windows of the Legacy House, named for being located on Legacy Drive. *What in the world was going on? Who was Gramps yelling at?*

"I can stay, Lydia invited me," came another, somewhat whiny, voice.

"Well, I'm uninviting you! Get out and stay out!"

Ally quickened her pace, anxious to get inside to see what was happening, but before she could lift her hand to knock, the door opened, revealing a paunchy bald man wearing thick glasses with dark tufts of hair poking out around his ears. He looked harried as

1

he edged past her. His leather briefcase banged against her thigh, but he didn't appear to notice.

She stared after him for a moment, wondering what had just transpired. The paunchy guy made a beeline for his tan sedan, tossed the leather briefcase on the passenger seat, then wedged himself behind the wheel. Seconds later, he was gone.

"Ally!" She turned back to see a tall, large-boned rectangle-shaped woman with a halo of tightly wound gray curls framing her face. Harriet Lehmann always wore brightly flowered dresses, support hose, and sensible sturdy black shoes, and today was no exception. Harriet beamed from her stance in the doorway. "It's lovely to see you!"

"Hi, Harriet." The woman's enthusiastic greeting made it sound as if Ally hadn't been there in months, when in fact she'd stopped by the day before yesterday during her Saturday lunch break from the Furry Friends Veterinary Clinic she had recently purchased from the previous owner, Gregory Hanson. This time she'd own and operate the business all on her own.

At least, attempt to operate. Lack of clientele was a bit of a problem at the moment.

"Who was that guy?" Ally asked.

"No one important, dear. Come in, come in." Harriet opened the door wider. "Oscar is in the kitchen. Oh, you brought dessert." Her smile faltered. Ally knew the older woman believed her sole purpose in life was to keep Gramps fed, and she didn't take kindly to anyone else cooking or baking for him. "Well, now, that wasn't necessary. I made a delicious apple crisp for tonight, and you know that's one of Oscar's favorites."

"Gramps likes brownies, too." Ally glanced past Harriet to see the other two residents, Tillie Carbine and Lydia Schneider, sitting near her grandfather. Both Tillie and Lydia had white hair, Lydia's curly and Tillie's straight. All four elders were widowed and shared the three-bedroom ranch that had been turned into an assisted living space by the owner, Beatrice Potter. Tillie and Harriet were sisters who shared the large master bedroom, while Lydia and Gramps each had their own rooms.

Gramps privately referred to the three women as the Willow Bluff Widows. They were constantly trying to outdo each other in getting Gramps' attention. Harriet cooked and baked, Tillie played a mean game of cribbage and poker, while Lydia knitted him anything from hats to sweaters. Despite all the female attention, he'd privately confided to her that no one could replace Amelia, his late beloved wife of fifty-five years. Granny had been gone for two years now, but Gramps insisted he'd never love anyone else.

No matter how hard the Willow Bluff Widows tried to convince him otherwise.

"Ally!" Gramps didn't get up from his seat at the table but glanced at her with a smile. He wore his usual attire of khaki slacks and a short-sleeved blue button-down shirt, with a white T-shirt underneath. In the winter the short-sleeved shirts would be replaced with long-sleeved flannels. But never once in her entire life had she seen Gramps wearing blue jeans. "I'm glad you stopped by."

"Always for you, Gramps." She crossed over to squeeze his shoulders in a hug, pressing a kiss to the top of his military cut silver hair. "I brought brownies."

"I'll take those." Harriet whisked the container away and Ally wondered if the widow might toss them in the garbage rather than serve them to Gramps. "We'll have the apple crisp for dessert tonight, Oscar, and save the brownies for tomorrow."

"Sure, Harriet." Gramps winked at Ally, and she knew that was his way of saying he'd have both a brownie and an apple crisp for dessert. He had a crazy sweet tooth, which she'd inherited, but unlike herself, Gramps never seemed to gain an ounce. Her grandfather was tall, about six feet in his prime but having lost an inch or so along the way, with a lean frame and a handsomeness that couldn't be denied. At seventy-eight, he'd been the picture of health until he'd slipped and fallen on a patch of ice, breaking his hip. After his surgery in April and a stay at the rehab facility through May, Gramps had ended up here at the Willow Bluff Legacy House as his doctors didn't want him left alone for any length of time. Gramps considered this move a temporary solution, but Ally suspected it was likely permanent.

Even if Gramps didn't decide to marry one of the widows—and in her opinion the jury was still out on that—her schedule at the veterinary clinic was too unpredictable for her to care for him the way the widows could. Plus she lived in an upper-level apartment, and the stairs would be impossible for him to navigate.

"Who was that guy you were yelling at?" Ally swept her gaze over the four retirees. "What did he want?"

"Nothing important," Gramps waved a hand, downplaying the interaction.

"We're just fine, nothing for you to worry about, dear," Harriet assured her. Lydia and Tillie just glanced at each other without saying a word.

"Let's go into the living room." Gramps reached for his despised walker.

Knowing Gramps couldn't be rushed into telling the story, she helped him stand, then followed him into the living area. The three widows whispered in the kitchen, no doubt bickering over who was going to do what for Gramps once Ally was gone.

Gramps gingerly eased down onto the sofa. "You're a sight for sore eyes, young lady."

"I told you I'd come by this afternoon." She dropped onto the sofa beside him. "Unfortunately, I can't stay too long, I have an appointment at five thirty."

"A client!" Gramps blue eyes twinkled. "That's good news."

"Yes." She raked a hand through her dark curly hair that was constantly springing out of control. She often thought of herself as having poodle hair, naturally curly and untamable. "One of the locals needs me to do some dog walking for him the rest of the week."

"Don't worry, your veterinary business will pick up."

Ally had known small-town Willow Bluff wouldn't be as busy as Madison when it came to needing veterinary services, but the current pace was slower than she'd expected. She'd been there for six weeks but it felt more like six years. Having grown up in Willow Bluff, she thought maybe some of the townsfolk still saw her as the walking teenage disaster they once knew, rather than the experienced thirty-one-year-old veterinarian she was now.

Two previous incidents—one where she'd accidently set the chemistry lab on fire, followed a few months later by inadvertently sitting on a nest of fire ants, which had sent her screaming, yanking off her denim shorts, and jumping into Lake Michigan—had given her the dreaded nickname. *Hot Pants.*

The memory still filled her with embarrassment. Returning home to Willow Bluff under scandalous circumstances didn't help her image any. Her former veterinary partner and fiancé, Tim Mathai, had embezzled from the Mathai-Winter Veterinary Clinic they'd owned jointly in Madison, Wisconsin. She hadn't realized what Tim had done until after he'd taken all the money out of their joint business account and fled the country to Mexico with Trina, the sweet young veterinary assistant he'd been sleeping with on the side. Ally had managed to sell the building to break even, then had to sell her home to pay off her credit cards, leaving her just enough money to buy Hanson's business and start over here in Willow Bluff.

Some of the local pet owners had come around, which was good. She'd had a client come in earlier that morning who had been satisfied with her services. More would trickle in, she was sure. And she preferred running the business herself, accounting for every nickel, dime, and penny she earned. Not that it amounted to much. Yet. But on top of offering veterinary services, she offered grooming services—thanks to learning the skill during her college days—boarding, and now dog-walking services for extra income.

No job too small was her new motto.

"This town is lucky to have you, Ally." Gramps patted her knee.

"Thanks." She leaned closer and dropped her voice. "How are things going with the WBWs?"

Her grandfather grimaced. "Drives me crazy the way they hover over me like flies on red meat."

"Maybe you shouldn't be so charming." The statement was mostly a joke, as her granddad was not known for his charm.

Gramps tended to be blunt and to the point, but apparently the widows didn't need much, if any, encouragement. "Hey, they keep you fed, warm, and entertained."

A ghost of a smile played across his face. "Can't deny it. Harriet is a good cook, although your grandmother was much better."

"Aw, that's sweet." She should have realized a long time ago that Tim wasn't anything like her father and grandfather. Men who were strong and smart, dedicated and faithful to the women they'd loved.

Tim Mathai was the antithesis of her grandfather in every way.

"You remind me of Amelia," Gramps voice dropped, a wistful expression in his blue eyes. "Smart and sassy."

She grinned. "I'll take that comparison any day. Now seriously, Gramps, tell me what happened with the guy you kicked out. I heard you yelling, so don't tell me it was nothing."

He let out a huff. "That idiot lawyer was trying to get the widows to change their wills into some sort of trust, for a fee, of course. I didn't like him, so I booted him out."

"You think he was trying to pull a fast one with the widows?" Her protective instincts flashed on full alert. The older generation were often a target for those trying to scam them out of their hard-earned retirement funds. "You should have told me he was coming. I'd have been here with you."

"Think I can't take care of myself?" Gramps's tone was testy. "He wasn't here to talk to me. Lydia invited him." He waved a hand in a dismissive gesture. "Not saying he was up to no good, but I don't see a reason for Lydia, or any of the widows, to change their wills into trusts at this point. He was slimy, like a used car

7

salesman. Nothing to worry about, though. The way he scuttled out of here proves he's harmless."

She wasn't reassured. "Okay, but I could check him out a bit, if you think that would help."

"Nah. Don't think he'll come back any time soon." Gramps puffed out his chest. "I'm telling you—those widows would be lost without me."

That made her smile. "Yes, they would."

"I warned them to be careful or they'd end up as the next murder victim featured on an upcoming *Dateline* episode."

She worried a bit about her grandfather's preoccupation with crime. Gramps was a Vietnam vet and had owned a construction company for years before he'd sold the business and retired. He'd never worked in law enforcement, not that his lack of experience in the field seemed to stop him from speculating. He scoured the news for the latest stories and ventured to the library on a weekly outing to pick up large-print true crime novels.

"I've told you before, you need better hobbies. Speaking of which, what time are you and Tillie playing cribbage?"

He glanced at his watch and looked glum. "After dinner, but there's no rush. I got more time than I know what to do with."

"I know." She leaned over and hugged him. "How about I drive you to the library on Wednesday? We'll have lunch at the Lakeview Café."

Gramps brightened, his blue eyes, older and wiser replicas of her own, sparked with interest. "Deal. I look forward to it."

"Great." She slowly rose to her feet and placed his walker in front of him. "I have to run, but I'll check in with you tomorrow, too."

"You don't need to come every day," he protested. He let her help him up to his feet. "I know how to call you on that pocket thingy you bought me."

"It's a cell phone, Gramps." One which he did not know how to use correctly, as he always yelled into it. "And the point of me coming back to Willow Bluff in the first place was so I could stop in to see you all the time. It's no trouble."

"Bah." He sounded cranky again, and she knew part of that was related to the ongoing pain in his hip when he walked. But he didn't complain. Gramps was a proud man and refused to be thought of as anything less than the soldier he once was. "You need to find a young man to spend your time with, not an old geezer like me."

"I prefer spending time with you, Gramps." She'd glossed over the details of her broken engagement and Tim and Trina's betrayal, but her granddad was sharp. He'd no doubt put the puzzle pieces together. "Men are highly overrated."

"Some men," he agreed. "But not all."

She let it go. As they entered the kitchen, there was a hint of bacon in the air, along with a variety of other enticing scents. Her mouth watered. "Harriet, something smells amazing."

"I'm making an Old World German recipe handed down to me from my mother. Beef rouladen."

She sniffed the air appreciatively. "I've never heard of it."

"I pound round steak until it's thin, and then roll it into balls with steamed carrots, celery, bacon. and dill pickles tucked inside." Harriet smiled mischievously as if she possessed the secrets needed to entice her grandfather into being the next Mr. Harriet Lehman. "Then I braise them in my own special wine sauce to add a bit of extra flavor."

"You're welcome to join us," Gramps offered.

It was beyond tempting; lately she'd been eating more ramen noodles than she cared to admit, but she shook her head. "No, as I mentioned, I have a client coming in."

The meal sounded incredible, but she knew that if she began eating Harriet's meals, the woman would use that as favoritism to make even a bigger play for Gramps. It was the same reason she'd resisted Tillie's request to join them for cribbage and Lydia's offer to teach her to knit. Safer to stay out of the widows' way.

"Maybe next time. Bye!" Ally lifted a hand as she headed to the door.

The ride from the Legacy House back into town didn't take long. She'd just unlocked and entered her clinic when another car pulled up. She stopped short when she recognized the guy sliding out from behind the wheel. It was the same paunchy bald man with thick glasses. He wasn't holding a briefcase this time, but rather a dog leash attached to a beautiful golden-brown female boxer with a dark face and wide curious eyes.

The idiot lawyer? Interesting—she wouldn't have pegged him as a dog owner. Normally she felt as if pet owners were trustworthy, but maybe not in this case. She forced a smile. "Good afternoon, I'm Dr. Winter."

"Marty Shawlin." He didn't seem to recognize her as being at the Legacy House earlier. Had he been too flustered by Gramps yelling at him to pay attention? Then again, some people didn't look past the white lab coat. "And this is Roxy."

"Hey, Roxy." She grinned when Roxy wagged her stubby tail in greeting. Ally didn't like the tradition of cropping tails but knew it was still a common practice. She offered Roxy her hand, letting her give it a good sniff, before attempting to pet her silky fur. "She's a beauty."

"Yes. I agreed to watch her for the week my ex-wife is traveling out of town." Marty met her gaze. "I really could use your dog-walking services. Maybe an hour each day at lunchtime?"

"Of course." She loved dogs, so that wasn't a problem. And there was no denying she was curious to learn more about Marty Shawlin. "Will I need a key to get in?"

Marty hesitated, then shook his head. "I'll give you my address and the code to my garage. I keep Roxy crated in the kitchen while I'm at work."

She jotted the information on a notepad, then held out her hand for the leash. "I'd like to take her out for a quick minute, just so that she gets used to me and isn't surprised when I show up tomorrow."

"Okay." Marty seemed glad to hand Roxy over.

She led Roxy outside and down the street. The boxer gazed around with interest. "What's a nice girl like you doing with a guy like that?"

Roxy didn't answer, but that was okay. She didn't mind her one-sided conversations with pets. Besides, as Roxy's dog walker for the rest of the week, she'd have plenty of time to snoop around a bit.

Maybe she'd find out what Marty Shawlin was really up to when he'd made that appointment with Lydia.

Like Gramps, she didn't take kindly to anyone messing with the Willow Bluff Widows.

Chapter Two

The next morning, Ally dragged herself into the kitchen for coffee. She hadn't slept well, her thoughts bouncing between the sleazy lawyer and his attempt to do business with the widows, to her less than optimal volume of veterinary clients.

She'd have to go through Hanson's client list again; she had a feeling he might have padded it a bit. But since there wasn't any way to change the past, she needed to stay focused on the future. There had to be something she could do to increase her business, but her creative muse seemed to have taken a hiatus. Maybe it had flown away to Ireland and Scotland with her parents. They were both professors at a private university located about twenty minutes outside Willow Bluff. Over the past few years, they'd taken to traveling every summer. Ally was happy for them, even though she would have liked to talk things through with her mom right about now.

Breakfast consisted of instant oatmeal, heated in a microwave that was older than she was. Looking out the window, she could see pedestrians meandering up and down Main Street. She was temporarily living in the small apartment above the clinic, a space that the former owner used to rent out for additional income.

Maybe one day she'd make enough money to get a place of her own and could do the same.

For now, she needed to find a way to come up with the next mortgage and business loan payment, which included the building housing her clinic and the upper-level apartment, along with the money she'd paid Hanson for his client list. Based on Hanson's client list and his balance sheet, she should be doing okay. Her only competition was a clinic over in Sheboygan, a good twenty-five minutes away on a good day with no traffic. She couldn't imagine the townsfolk preferring to travel that far for services conveniently offered right here in town.

Dog walking was fine, but she'd been hoping for a busier clinic day to day. At least Marty had paid for her services up front.

She wasn't due to walk Roxy until noon, so she finished her breakfast and headed downstairs to the clinic. The emptiness of the place hit hard.

For a moment she thought about how busy she and Tim had been in Madison, with furry patients slotted in every hour from open to close, with the occasional emergency call coming in.

A far cry from the vacant space surrounding her now.

Had coming here been a mistake? Picking up a rag, she began to clean. After finishing the two exam rooms, the third having been turned into a grooming suite, she began wiping down the front desk. When the door opened, she turned and glanced over in surprise. A young girl roughly ten years old with tears in her wide brown eyes held an oddly colored black and white speckled cat that appeared to be having some trouble breathing.

"Can you please help Pepper?" The child's tone was full of fear and worry. "She's sick."

13

"Of course, come this way." She led the little girl and Pepper to the first exam room. "What's your name? Where's your mommy or daddy?"

"At home."

Yeah, so not helpful. But there was no way to ignore the poor cat's plight. The animal was breathing fast and needed immediate care. "Here, let me take Pepper into the back room, I need to give her some oxygen."

"Okay." The girl handed Pepper over, and it was a testament to how badly the cat must have been feeling that the animal didn't struggle or dig in with her claws.

Asthma? Pneumonia? Or a foreign object lodged in her throat? There were several possible causes, but she needed to stabilize the animal before she could properly examine her.

Pepper calmed down with the administration of oxygen, giving Ally enough time to listen to her heart and lungs. There was no evidence of fluid in the lungs or around her heart. Pepper's airway sounded tight, making Abby lean toward a diagnosis of asthma.

She held the cat with one arm and used her right hand to palpate her throat. Thankfully there was nothing stuck in her airway. The cat's gums were pink, so no anemia either.

She brought Pepper back into the exam room. "I'm going to give her something to help her breathing get better, okay?"

"Okay."

After placing Pepper back in the young girl's arms, she went back to find a low-dose steroid and bronchodilator. Pilling cats wasn't easy, even for a vet, so she decided to give the first dose of each medication via injection. Once she had Pepper stabilized, she could switch the cat over to oral meds. But that also meant finding out who the girl's parents were.

"I'm going to need you to hold Pepper really tight for me." Ally waited for the girl to nod before preparing the syringes. "This is medicine to control her breathing."

As she spoke, she inserted the needle into the cat's flank. She began injecting the medication, when the animal screeched and leaped out of the girl's arms.

"Pepper!" The girl chased after her cat with Ally hot on her heels.

They found Pepper hiding under the front desk, thankfully not breathing nearly as rapidly as she had when she'd first arrived. The girl hunkered down on the floor, reaching for Pepper. Ally crouched next to her, offering a hand.

Together they gently pulled the frightened feline out from beneath the desk. As the little girl cradled the cat close, a stunning woman a little older than Ally, wearing a pink dress with matching pink heels, entered the clinic.

"Amanda! How many times have I told you not to leave while I'm working an open house?"

Relieved to have a name for the girl, and a parent, Ally smiled and stepped forward.

"Hello, I'm Dr. Winter. I'm sorry if Amanda left without telling you, but poor Pepper was having an asthma attack. I just need to give Pepper another dose of medication and she'll be ready to go."

The woman lifted her chin with a sneer. "I didn't authorize any treatments for that cat. It's not even ours, just a stray that Amanda picked up."

"Oh, but, I'm sure . . ." Her voice trailed off as Amanda pushed Pepper into Ally's arms and moved away.

"Sorry, I hav'ta go with my mom." Amanda looked dejected as she followed her mother out of the clinic.

Stunned speechless, Ally could only stand there holding the cat. Pepper curled against her, content now that she wasn't being poked with a needle. At least her breathing was better. The partial dose of medication Ally had given her must be working.

Now what? Take the cat to the local shelter? Or keep her?

She blew out a frustrated sigh and returned to the clinic. This time, she decided to try pilling the cat, hoping that would work better than the injections. Still no easy task, but after two attempts, Pepper had ingested both her bronchodilator and steroid medications.

Still holding the cat, Ally dialed the number for the local shelter. Maybe Jeri Smith, the owner, knew all about Pepper. Maybe the animal wasn't a stray but simply lost. She could make posters with a picture of Pepper and hang them around town. The owner would show up, grateful to have her cat back, offering to pay for the animal's treatment.

Sure, and maybe Tim would walk in after having dumped Trina to return the money he owed her. *Not.*

"Clark County Animal Shelter, this is Jeri."

"Jeri? Ally Winter. Are you familiar with a black and white speckled stray cat, possibly going by the name Pepper?"

"No, can't say that I am. Why, what's going on?"

"A girl named Amanda brought her in because the animal was having an asthma attack. I treated her, but Amanda's mother claimed the cat wasn't theirs and left Pepper with me." *Without paying for any services.*

"Amanda?" Jeri sounded as if she were trying to place the name. "What did her mother look like?"

"Pink. Pink dress, pink shoes. Straight blonde hair. She said something about an open house."

"Ah, yes, Ellen Cartwright and her daughter Amanda. Ellen is a real estate agent, and her daughter is likely at loose ends being home for the summer. And Ellen's right about one thing, the cat isn't theirs. That woman wouldn't tolerate having an animal in the house under any circumstances. I'm sure it's a stray the little girl picked up." There was a pause, then Jeri added, "You want to bring her in? I'm pretty full, as always, but could try to make room for one more."

Ally looked down at the cat again and sighed. Who was she kidding? She couldn't add to Jeri's cadre of unwanted animals. As it was, Ally offered free treatment services to the shelter, why add more? "No, that's okay. I'll keep her. But if you hear of someone looking for their lost cat, will you let me know?"

"Sure."

"Thanks. I'll see you later."

Ally hung up the desk phone and carried Pepper around back to the stairs leading up to her apartment. "Looks like it's just me and you, Pepper. Two lost souls bonding in Willow Bluff."

Pepper didn't respond.

"At least I have food and a litter box, thanks to my boarding services." Yet she also knew that, without knowing anything of Pepper's history, she'd need to vaccinate the animal.

Cha-ching.

In her apartment, the June sun shone brightly in through the window overlooking Main Street. When she released Pepper, the cat walked cautiously across the wooden floor, as if unsure how she felt about these new surroundings. Ally wondered where Amanda had found Pepper, then decided it didn't matter.

Back in the clinic, she went to the medication cabinet and pulled out the asthma medication doses she'd need for Pepper. When her phone rang, she tripped over her own two feet in her haste to answer it.

"Furry Friends Veterinary Clinic, may I help you?"

"Is Dr. Greg Hanson available?"

She sighed, wishing the citizens of Willow Bluff would catch on already. She forced herself to answer politely, "No, I'm afraid he's retired and living in Florida. This is Dr. Winter, may I help you?"

"Oh, I thought Dr. Greg was coming back." The female voice turned petulant, as if she had known Hanson on a personal basis. Was this one of his former girlfriends? Or did he have a habit of being overly friendly with his clients?

"No, he's not. I'm Dr. Ally Winter, and I'm happy to help take care of whatever your pet needs are."

"Well, Maurice is due for his rabies vaccination. When is your next opening?"

Ally hesitated, wondering how to respond. If she told this woman that she was fairly wide most of the week, it might send the wrong signal. On the other hand, she desperately needed a paying client. "I have an opening this afternoon at three from a last-minute cancellation, would that work? If not, just let me know what works for you and I'll make the necessary arrangements."

Another long pause. "I can come this afternoon at three."

Yes! She did a quick silent fist pump. "Will you please give me your name and number? Oh, and what type of breed is Maurice?"

"My name is Paula Crandle." Paula rattled off her phone number. "Maurice is a purebred English cocker spaniel."

"Thank you. I have you and Maurice down for an appointment at three o'clock this afternoon. See you then."

After disconnecting with Paula, she did a quick search through Greg Hanson's old records. She found Paula Crandle and Maurice easily enough, but Greg didn't provide any helpful notes about how to handle the dog. Her practice was to take notes, so that she was always prepared, especially since she often only saw pets on an annual basis. Apparently, Greg hadn't bothered to keep track of problems with his four-legged clients. Hoping things would go well, she set the information off to the side, so she could add to it for future reference.

Another paying customer!

The next couple of hours passed by slowly. Pepper had become acquainted with her litter box, reinforcing the fact that she must not have been living out on the street for long. The food Ally had bought remained untouched, but she hoped Pepper would begin to eat and drink soon.

At a quarter to twelve, Ally once again locked up the clinic and walked the short distance to Marty Shawlin's home. He lived on Appletree Lane, two blocks off Main Street, not far from the grocery store.

Approaching the house, she discovered it was a tiny Cape Cod with white siding and black shutters framing the upstairs windows. Smaller than she'd have expected from a lawyer. Then again, people thought veterinarians made a lot of money, and she was living proof of that fallacy.

Besides, it was entirely possible Marty had lost half his assets along with half his income to his ex-wife. Wisconsin was an equal marital property state, another mistake she'd made with Tim. They hadn't been married or signed any sort of contract when they'd gone into business together, which is how she had ended up dealing with everything alone. It was embarrassing to admit now how naïve she'd been.

Not anymore. She was determined to make it on her own and to be taken seriously as a vet.

It was nice to know Marty and his ex-wife were on amicable terms. Enough so that he'd agreed to watch Roxy for her.

She approached the house and the attached single-car garage. Roxy began to bark from inside the home, obviously aware Ally was out there. After punching in the code, she waited a long minute for the rumbling garage door to open. The interior held some lawn equipment tucked along the back wall, but nothing more. Ducking underneath the rising door, she entered the house.

A horrible smell made her recoil in disgust. She covered her mouth, trying not to gag. What in the world? Had Roxy soiled her crate? Or was Marty Shawlin that bad at housekeeping?

Breathing carefully through her mouth, Ally made her way through the kitchen to the dog crate tucked in the corner. Roxy's frenzied barking only grew louder as she got near.

"What is it, girl? You look distressed." The leash was on the table, so she held it ready as she opened the gate latch.

Woof! Woof! Woof! Roxy threw herself out of the crate and plowed into Ally. Knocked backward, she didn't have time to grab

Roxy's collar as the boxer took off through the house barking like mad.

"Roxy! Come back! Roxy!" Ally ran after her but came to a shuddering halt when she saw the animal standing over the source of the horrific smell.

The supine body of Marty Shawlin was stretched out on the floor, his head matted with blood. A heavy glass paperweight, also covered in blood, was lying on the floor beside him. His eyes were staring vacantly into space, his skin pale and waxy. Moving forward, she forced herself to check for a pulse.

It was too late. He was already very cold and very dead.

His briefcase was open, legal papers scattered around him, as if someone had searched through them in a big hurry. Her gaze landed again on the paperweight. It was a glass globe, the base appearing to be made out of marble.

No way was this some sort of terrible accident. Marty Shawlin had been murdered.

And from what she could tell, Roxy was the only witness.

Chapter Three

"Roxy." Ally's voice was hoarse and shaky. The dog looked at her without moving. Avoiding any further contact with the dead body, Ally grabbed Roxy's collar and dragged her away back to the kitchen. Then she clipped the leash to Roxy's collar and pulled the animal outside.

Gulping deep breaths of blessedly fresh air, she fumbled for her phone, her mind swirling with questions. What had happened in there? And when? She dialed 911 and listened as the phone rang in her ear, trying to calm her racing heart.

"This is 911, what's the nature of your emergency?"

"Dead body." Her voice was little more than a croak. She tried again, willing herself not to babble. "I'm at the home of Marty Shawlin and—and he's dead."

"What's the address?"

Feeling desperate, she turned and looked at the Cape Cod. It took a moment for her to focus her gaze on the black numbers mounted on the white siding. The address clicked into her befuddled brain. "Um, 1506 Appletree Lane."

"1506 Appletree Lane," the operator repeated. "Please stay on the line while I dispatch an officer to your location."

"Okay." Ally held the phone in a death-like grip with one hand, the leash in the other. Roxy didn't seem to be disturbed; she went about doing her business and then looking up at Ally as if waiting impatiently for the promised walk.

"I'm sorry, girl. We can't go right now." Talking to the dog helped calm her nerves. Frankly, she generally preferred animals over people. It occurred to her that she couldn't return Roxy to the house now that Marty was dead. Which meant she'd have to bring Roxy home with her. Blowing out a heavy sigh, she wondered how Pepper would get along with Roxy.

Probably not very well.

That was the least of her problems. Marty Shawlin was *dead*. Who could have done such a thing? And why? She wanted to call Gramps to see what he thought about what had happened. Knowing her grandfather, he'd have a theory. So much for her harebrained idea of looking around inside the house. A shudder rippled over her and she tugged Roxy farther from the scene of the crime as if a couple of yards would make a difference.

Which, of course, it didn't. The image of the dead man was permanently etched in her mind. The awful stench lodged in her sinuses.

"An officer and detective will be arriving shortly."

"Thanks." Ally disconnected from the 911 call. Two vehicles, one a black SUV, the other a dark blue squad car, arrived at the same time. The squad's lights were flashing but no sirens. A tall, dark-haired man with a chiseled jaw emerged from the SUV, looking lean and young, roughly her age. The cop from the squad remained behind the wheel.

Roxy was growling low in her throat, her gaze locked on the two vehicles.

"It's okay, girl." Ally patted the boxer's head.

Turning back to the guy she assumed was the detective, her jaw dropped as she recognized the former quarterback of the Willow Bluff high school football team.

Noah Jorgenson.

Her insides fluttered, but she attributed that insane reaction to the stress of stumbling upon the victim of a murder. Noah's eyes widened with awareness, and she was surprised to realize he recognized her, too.

"Hey, Hot—I mean, Ally." He glanced at the squad parked at the side of the road, then turned back to her. "I heard you were back in town."

"Noah." She narrowed her gaze to let him know the Hot Pants nickname needed to stop right here, right now. Noah was dressed in black dress slacks and a navy blue shirt, and she found herself keenly aware of the woodsy scent of his aftershave. "This is Roxy."

He lifted a brow and looked down at the dog standing at her side, still growling. Noah glanced at the squad, then scowled. He walked over, tapped the window and leaned down. "Officer Roberts, I need you to secure the scene."

"In a minute, as soon as I finish this call." The cop sounded disgruntled.

"Hurry up." Noah backed away and came back to where Ally and Roxy waited.

Was it her imagination or was there an undertone of tension between the two men? Not that it was any of her business.

"You found the body?" Noah asked.

"Yes." She shivered and glanced at Roxy who continued to growl. "Really, the dog did."

He glanced again at the growling dog. "She doesn't bite, does she?"

"No." At least, Ally didn't think so.

"Okay, stay here, I need to go inside."

She gave a jerky nod. Noah and the cop went inside the house together. While waiting, she decided to take Roxy for a mini-walk up and down Appletree Lane. The animal finally stopped growling as they moved away from the crime scene. The cop must have stayed inside, because only Noah returned, approaching with a serious expression carved in his face. "I need you to start at the beginning. Why are you here?"

"Marty Shawlin stopped by the clinic yesterday. He paid me to walk Roxy each day at noon for the week. Today was my first day. He gave me the garage code, and when I went inside, I knew from the smell something was wrong. After I let Roxy out of her crate, she ran straight to Marty."

"How well did you know the deceased?"

"I didn't." Should she mention Marty's visit to the Legacy House? She decided to stick to answering Noah's questions. "I never spoke to him until yesterday, when he came to the clinic to hire me as a dog walker."

"What time did he come to your clinic?"

She frowned at his question. "Five thirty, why? Does it matter?"

"I need to understand his actions prior to this event."

"The event?" She shivered. "It's a murder, isn't it? The paper-weight shaped like a globe didn't hit him in the head by accident."

Noah sighed heavily. "I prefer not to leap to conclusions. How about you leave the investigating to me, okay? I just need you to answer my questions. Now, what time did you arrive here at the house."

"Around noon, maybe a few minutes early." She gestured toward Main Street. "I walked from the Furry Friends clinic."

He took note of the current time, and then jotted something in a notebook. She craned her neck in an attempt to see what he'd written down, but he was too far away.

"What did you touch when you were inside?"

She had to think about that. "The garage keypad, the door handle coming in and going out, the crate, Roxy's leash. Oh, and I checked Marty for a pulse."

"That's all?"

"Yes." It was more than enough. "Marty mentioned Roxy belongs to his ex-wife, who is out of town for the week. Any chance you could track her down for me? I mean, I can take Roxy in temporarily, but I just adopted an asthmatic stray cat."

"I'll do my best. How can I reach you?"

Again, her heart gave a betraying thump. *Ridiculous reaction. You're through with men, remember?* Especially Noah, who was one of the football players who'd laughed at her when she'd jumped into Lake Michigan to drown the biting fire ants that had crawled up her shorts. Best to keep her distance. Noah was a detective with a job to do. She was nothing more than a reluctant witness.

Too bad Roxy couldn't talk; the boxer could likely point out the murderer in a heartbeat. Ally recited her cell number. "Any calls coming into the clinic are automatically forwarded to my cell too."

"Okay, thanks." Noah slid his notebook into his pocket. "I appreciate your cooperation."

"Of course." She glanced down at Roxy again. "I don't suppose you could bring her crate out for me, along with her dishes and whatever food and treats might be in there."

The words were barely out of her mouth when Noah shook his head. "Nothing goes out until we finish processing the crime scene."

Yeah, that's what she'd thought. Although it seemed silly. The murderer had obviously been after legal paperwork, as evidenced by the open contents of Marty's briefcase, which had nothing to do with dog food or a crate. Noah walked up to the house, leaving her and Roxy standing on the sidewalk.

Stifling a sigh, she looked down at Roxy. "Okay, girl. I'll take you to my place. You'll have to be nice to Pepper, understand?"

Roxy glanced up at her, then back toward the street as if anxious to go. The boxer stopped frequently to sniff various scents during their walk back to the clinic. As Ally brought the animal up to her apartment, she braced herself for the inevitable confrontation.

Roxy barked. Pepper jumped off the sofa, arching her back and hissing with annoyance. Ally hoped all this excitement didn't bring on another asthma attack.

"Easy, Pepper, be nice. Roxy, you too. Both of you are in need of a temporary home."

Pepper swiped at Ally's jeans-clad leg, her sharp claws raking the denim, then ran off toward her bedroom, no doubt searching for a spot to hide. Roxy sniffed the floor of her apartment, clearly following Pepper's scent, Then Roxy let out several loud barks.

"Shh. Not so loud." Roxy looked at her, tilting her brown face inquisitively. Should Ally take one of the animals down to the clinic to board them? It wasn't as if she didn't have the room—she did. Yet keeping them boarded up didn't sit well with her.

Not when they'd both been recently traumatized.

Heck, she had been traumatized too. Never in her life had she seen a dead body up close. Animals? Yes. Humans? No.

She headed down to the clinic to get dog dishes and food. When she returned, things seemed relatively calm. Roxy met her eagerly at the door.

"I'm here, girl. Everything's fine." Once she gave Roxy a treat, she checked on Pepper.

The cat was still hiding under her bed. Ally stretched out on the floor and peered at the feline. "You okay, Pepper? How's your breathing?"

Pepper didn't answer, but her breathing sounded normal. Ally stood and sighed. So far, so good. Deciding to leave the bedroom door open this time, she returned to the clinic for her afternoon appointment.

In reviewing Maurice's file, she learned the spaniel was due for the rest of his annual shots, too. Ally prepared those doses along with the rabies shot, which was only given every three years.

When Paula arrived, she glanced around the vacant clinic with open curiosity.

"Hi, Maurice." Ally focused her attention on the animal. "This way, please. So I see from Dr. Hanson's records that Maurice is also due for his annual coronavirus, leptospirosis, and parvovirus vaccinations next month as well. It would be cheaper to give them all today and save you another trip."

"Oh, uh, sure. That will be fine." Paula seemed flustered as if she hadn't realized she'd had immunizations scheduled a month apart. Had the woman made it a practice to make frequent visits to the vet on purpose, as a way to get Greg Hanson's attention? Ally estimated Paula to be in her early sixties, not far from Hanson's age, and wondered again if she'd had some sort of personal relationship with the former veterinarian.

Not her business one way or the other.

Maurice tolerated the injections better than Pepper had. When she was finished, Ally walked Paula out to the front desk.

She'd half expected Paula to balk at paying the fee, but the woman didn't blink and thankfully the charge went through on her credit card without a problem.

Feeling encouraged, Ally cleaned up the exam room, then decided to take Roxy out to visit her grandfather. Harriet didn't like it when she brought animals over, but it was nice enough outside that she and Gramps could sit on the patio.

Besides, she wanted to tell him about Marty Shawlin's murder. Not just because he loved hearing about crimes, but because she knew that Noah would eventually stop by to visit Lydia and Gramps at the Legacy House.

Better that Gramps be prepared ahead of time.

"Hey, Roxy, ready to go for a walk?"

The W word sent Roxy into a tailspin, making Ally laugh. This was why she loved animals. They were always happy, which in turn made her happy.

Ally hoped that taking Roxy out for a bit would encourage Pepper to come out of hiding long enough to eat some food. She checked her phone, hoping to have a message from Noah about Marty's ex-wife, but no such luck. Was he still out on Appletree Lane, processing the crime scene? It was tempting to swing by to sneak a peek.

At the crime scene. Not at Noah.

After walking Roxy up and down Main Street, Ally opened the back hatch of her Honda so the dog could jump in. The Legacy House was a ten-minute ride. Roxy pressed her nose against the wire crate in an attempt to sniff the air. Ally grinned. The boxer was a great dog. Under different circumstances she wouldn't mind having one just like her. She and Tim had planned to get a new puppy after their wedding, had even purchased the wire partition for the back of her car, but that had obviously never happened.

Now, taking in a dog permanently wouldn't be fair to Pepper. The poor thing was barely tolerating Roxy.

She pulled into the driveway, Roxy shaking her entire body with excitement, eager to explore her new surroundings. Holding tightly to Roxy's leash, Ally approached the door.

Tillie was the one who answered her knock. "Ally, what a nice surprise." Her gaze dropped to Roxy. "Harriet is going to pitch a fit if she sees that dog."

"I know the rules." Ally peered beyond Tillie to the interior of the house. "Tell Gramps to meet me outside on the patio, okay?"

"Sure, dear. Oscar?" Tillie shouted at the top of her lungs. "Ally's here with a dog! Meet her out back."

"Eh? What did you say?" Ally could hear Gramps clumping through the house with his walker. "All I need is a frog attack?"

"No. *Ally* is here with a *dog*! Meet her out *back*!"

Good grief. Roxy whined under her breath, no doubt her ears hurting from all the shouting. "Easy, girl. It's okay."

"Ally." Gramps' crabby expression cleared when he saw her. Today his shirt was green rather than blue. "Come in."

"Harriet will pitch a fit," Tillie warned.

"Gramps, meet me out on the back patio, okay?" She didn't want to upset Harriet; besides, it would be easier to talk to him without the widows overhearing every word.

"Okay. But I live here too, and can visit with a strange dog if I want to."

Ally shook her head good-naturedly as she led Roxy around to the back patio and waited for Gramps to make his way through the house. When he appeared at the patio doors, she placed her arm under his to assist him down the single step. Then she grabbed his walker and brought that outside.

"Hrmph." Gramps dropped into the closest patio chair. "Since when does Harriet rule the roost?"

"It's okay, some people don't like dogs. I don't get it myself, but whatever." She wrapped Roxy's leash around the arm of her chair and sat beside Gramps. "I wanted to talk to you in private, anyway."

"It's about that dead lawyer isn't it?"

She stared at him in shock. "How did you know?"

A sly grin creased his features. "Lydia got a call from Anita Jones, who saw the police outside Marty's house."

"Who's Anita Jones?"

Gramps waved a hand. "Haven't you been paying attention? Anita is the one who suggested Lydia should meet with Marty to change her will into a trust. Anita lives two houses down from Marty."

Ally was pretty sure Gramps hadn't mentioned Anita the first time but nodded anyway. "Okay, so she saw the police, but how did she know he'd died?"

Gramps scoffed. "The coroner's van came to pick up the body. Who else would it be?"

"I see. Well, I'm the one who found him."

"You?" Gramps' eyes widened in surprise. "Anita didn't say anything about seeing you there."

At least she had something new to share with him. After Ally explained about walking Roxy and finding Marty Shawlin with his head bashed in from a glass and marble globe, her grandfather's expression turned thoughtful.

"I knew he was up to no good. I wonder who else he tried to swindle?"

"Gramps, helping someone write a will or create a trust isn't exactly swindling."

"It is if he's charging people money to do something they don't need. Maybe he even includes himself in the trust, did you think of that?"

"I doubt anyone would let him do such a thing," she protested.

"They may not notice. You know how difficult it is to get through all that legal mumbo jumbo." Gramps absently reached out to pet Roxy. "Besides, I think there's more to the story."

"I ran into Noah Jorgenson. He's a detective for the Willow Bluff Police Department."

Gramps frowned. "I vaguely remember that name. Didn't you go out with him back in high school?"

She blushed, hoping he wouldn't notice. "No, never. He dated the cheerleaders, not science nerds like me." Especially one who started a fire in the chemistry lab and then sat on a nest of fire ants. "But I wanted to warn you that he's investigating Marty's murder."

"Warn me? Why?" Gramps spread his hands. "All I did was to kick Marty out of here."

"Yeah, well, Noah might have questions for you and Lydia. Try not to draw too much attention to yourself."

Gramps feigned innocence. "Who, me?" He paused, then frowned. "Tell me again how you found him?"

Ally repeated what she'd told Noah. "I entered the garage code and went inside. Poor Roxy was barking like crazy, then she bowled me over to go find him." She rubbed Roxy's soft pelt. "If only you could talk, huh, girl? I bet you'd find whoever did this without a problem."

Roxy rested her chin on Ally's knee, enjoying the attention.

"I'm surprised you didn't notice his car sitting in the garage, since that's how you entered the house. That would have been an indication that he was still home." Gramps idly tapped his fingers on the arm of the patio chair.

She straightened. "It wasn't in the garage."

"It wasn't?" Gramps blue eyes gleamed. "Maybe the murderer took it."

"Why would he—"

"—or she," Gramps interjected.

"—do something like that? For what purpose?" She could have smacked herself for not thinking about the missing car earlier. Should she call Noah to let him know?

"Maybe the murderer walked there and wanted a quick getaway. Anyone seeing Marty's car leaving would assume it was the lawyer behind the wheel, rather than the killer."

Gramps' theory made sense. Before she could say anything more, Roxy lifted her head and began to bark. Ally swiveled in her chair, looking for whatever had caught the boxer's attention.

"There you are." Noah's tone was terse as he rounded the corner of the Legacy House. "Mr. Winter? I need a moment of your time."

"Wait, why?" Ally jumped to her feet, standing protectively near her grandfather. "What's going on?"

Noah's gaze narrowed. "You should have told me your grandfather had an argument with the deceased, Ally. I spoke to Anita Jones, Shawlin's neighbor, who heard about it from someone named Lydia. Withholding evidence in a murder investigation is a crime."

"He didn't have an argument with Marty," she protested.

"Yes, I did." Gramps struggled to his feet, leaning heavily on his walker. If she didn't know any better she'd think her grandfather relished the thought of being a murder suspect. "Before I talk to you, I need to call my lawyer."

Noah's mouth dropped open in surprise, then he scowled. "Why? You have something to hide?"

Gramps scowled, too. "It's my right, isn't it?"

"Fine, you do that, Mr. Winter. You get yourself a lawyer and meet me down at the station."

"I will," Gramps shot back. "I'm an old man, I'll need an hour."

The two men—decades between them—exchanged ominous glares. Finally, Noah Jorgenson muttered something incomprehensible under his breath, turned, and crossed the yard, leaving just a hint of his woodsy aftershave behind.

Ally dropped her head in her hands. What in the world was Gramps doing? Being under suspicion of murder was no picnic.

No way was she letting him go to the station alone. Lawyer or no lawyer, she was going with him.

Someone had to keep her grandfather from being tossed in jail.

Chapter Four

Ally dropped Roxy off at her apartment before driving Gramps to the police station. He'd used the phone in the clinic to make calls while she was taking care of the dog. When she'd returned, he was sitting with his arms folded across his chest, his expression mulish. "Come on, Gramps, let's get going."

"Fine." He slid into the passenger seat. The way he stared out through the passenger window made it clear he wasn't happy with her.

Well, fine. She wasn't happy with him, either.

"How many lawyers do you know? And which one did you call?"

Gramps' scowl deepened. "Just one. Reggie Sanders."

"Reggie?" She searched her memory, trying to place the name. "Isn't he a divorce lawyer? Not helpful when you're being questioned in a murder investigation."

"He's smart enough to deal with the cops."

She tried hard not to roll her eyes. "Gramps, why are you doing this? There's no reason to get a lawyer to discuss what happened at the Legacy House. I highly doubt Noah believes you're a suspect."

Gramps snorted. "Shows what you know. All the murderer's friends and family, along with other potential suspects on *Dateline* start out cooperating with the police, yet they always get tripped up and then find themselves being arrested. I'm not that stupid."

Debatable, at least in this instance, but she didn't voice her thought. "But you don't have anything to hide. There's no way you killed Marty Shawlin."

"Of course I didn't. Anyone with half a brain could figure that out. Apparently that old boyfriend of yours isn't very smart."

She clenched her jaw. "He was never my boyfriend."

Gramps shrugged. "I can barely get around on my own, much less find a way to get from the Legacy House to Marty's place long enough to bash his head in, then get back without being seen."

Gramps was right about that, and the longer she thought about it, the more irritated she was with Noah for making it seem as if her grandfather was really in trouble.

She parked in the spot closest to the front door of the police station, then went around to help Gramps. He'd refused his walker but leaned heavily on his cane and her arm as they made their way inside.

A man who looked about ten years younger than her grandfather waited for them inside. "Oscar, it's great to see you again."

"Reggie, thanks for coming." Gramps shook the lawyer's hand.

"It's not a problem, but what is this all about?" Reggie glanced at her, but she grimaced and shook her head, unable to explain Gramps' convoluted logic. "I'm not a criminal lawyer."

"I know. But I'm sure you can knock some sense into that detective's head."

As if on cue, Noah Jorgenson came out to meet them. "Mr. Winter, Mr. Sanders. This way, please."

"I'm coming, too." Ally didn't budge from Gramps' side.

Noah pinched the bridge of his nose as if seeking patience from a higher power, then let out a sigh. "Fine, you can all come this way. We'll be in Interview A."

Ally led Gramps into the room, leaving Reggie to follow. Gramps glanced around with frank interest and she narrowed her gaze at how much he was enjoying this.

"Looks in better shape than some I've seen." Gramps eased himself into one of the hard metal chairs.

"Really? How many police stations have you been in?" Noah's tone was dry.

Gramps sat back and gave him a bland look without answering.

Reggie took a seat on the right and she took the left, so that Gramps was sandwiched protectively between them. Reggie cleared his throat and she wondered how many *Dateline* episodes he had watched. "Detective, I'd like to know exactly what crime you're accusing my client of committing?"

"I haven't accused him of anything, *yet*." The emphasis on the last word made her frown. "But I am interested in hearing about the argument Mr. Winter had with the deceased yesterday afternoon."

Reggie glanced at Gramps, who still looked as if he wasn't interested in talking. Ally tried not to groan. At this rate they'd be here well past dinnertime.

"Go ahead, Oscar. Tell the detective what you told me."

Gramps hesitated, then gave a brief nod. "Marty Shawlin was invited to the Legacy House by Lydia Schneider. He was trying to talk her into rewriting her will and creating a trust. I told him the widows didn't need his help and to get out."

There was a pause as Noah waited for Gramps to continue. When it was clear her grandfather had no intention of saying anything more, Noah asked, "Okay, so then what happened."

"He left." Gramps stared at Noah. "End of story."

Noah's gaze was skeptical, and she couldn't blame him. Even she had heard the two yelling and was certain there had been more said before she'd arrived, but her grandfather remained stoically silent.

"Any other questions you'd like to ask my client?" Reggie asked.

Noah narrowed his gaze. "Why did you tell Shawlin to get out?"

"Because I didn't trust him." Gramps was trying to follow his own advice about not saying too much to the police, but Ally could see he wanted to spill his guts. After another pause, her grandfather added, "You might want to focus your attention on other elderly clients he may have swindled."

"Like who?" Noah asked.

Gramps shook his head. "I don't know, but I don't think his meeting with Lydia was his first. He had his whole song and dance routine rehearsed a little too well, if you ask me."

"You believe he was swindling elderly people like yourself?" Noah persisted.

"Not me." Gramps' denial was swift. "Weren't you listening? Lydia had a meeting with him, I didn't."

Reggie put a warning hand on Gramps' arm. "Okay, Detective, do you have any other questions? If not, we're leaving."

"Where were you this morning between six and nine?"

There was no mistaking the gleam in Gramps' blue eyes. "Why? Am I still a suspect?"

"Gramps." Ally wanted to bang her head on the metal table. "Would you please answer Noah's question?"

There was a long pause, before Gramps replied, "At the Legacy House. I live with three women, in case you didn't notice. I got up at seven, Harriet made breakfast at eight, Tillie and I were playing cribbage by ten."

Noah nodded thoughtfully. Then he surprised Ally by meeting her gaze. "And where were you?"

"Me?" her voice came out in a high squeak. "At the veterinary clinic."

"Alone?" Noah persisted.

"Yes, alone."

Gramps waved a hand. "Ally, don't say anything more. This interview is over."

While she appreciated her grandfather looking out for her, she didn't agree with his tactics. "Gramps, I have nothing to hide. Noah, I already told you I went over to the Shawlin place to walk his dog. Why on earth would I hurt him?"

Noah glanced between her and Gramps, as if imaging them as a criminal team, Ally doing the legwork of killing Shawlin because he'd tried to swindle her grandfather. Craziness. It was too ridiculous to contemplate.

"Okay, that's all I have for now." Noah rose to his feet, looming over them. "But if you remember anything else, I would appreciate you letting me know."

"Hrmph." Gramps clearly wasn't so inclined.

"Have you found Marty's car?" Ally asked.

Noah paused at the doorway, then turned back toward her. "What do you know about his car?"

"I know it's a tan sedan, and it wasn't in his garage when I came in. I was just wondering if you'd found it yet."

Noah stared at her for a long moment, his green eyes seeming to penetrate deep into her brain. "No, we haven't."

"Need the license plate number?" Gramps asked.

Ally gaped at her grandfather. "Why do you have his license plate number?"

Gramps shrugged, the corners of his mouth tipping upward as if he was pleased with himself. "I didn't like him, remember? I wrote it down, right after he arrived."

Noah looked just as shocked as she felt. "No, I already have the plate number. But I think it's interesting you felt compelled to write it down."

Gramps glared at him. "Some people might try to take advantage of an old woman. I served in Vietnam, and while I might be old, I'm not stupid."

"Trust me, I never once thought that about you." Noah lifted a hand in surrender.

"Apology accepted." When Gramps moved to stand, Ally tucked her arm under his to help lever him upright. Gramps reached for his cane. It wasn't until they were back outside in her car that Gramps said, "Maybe he's not as dumb as I originally thought."

"Who? Noah?"

Gramps nodded. "He's probably still new in his detective role, but he'll learn."

The about-face was almost as surprising as finding out that Gramps had written down Marty Shawlin's license plate number.

She wondered if there was more that Gramps knew about the dead lawyer than he was letting on.

*   *   *

Once again, Ally didn't sleep well, but this time the problem was Pepper and Roxy. Over the course of the evening, Pepper had learned to swipe and hiss at Roxy, making the large dog back up comically. Pepper was clearly the one in charge, and Roxy wasn't sure what to make of it.

As she enjoyed her breakfast, she was relieved Pepper had finally eaten a little food—not as much as Ally had hoped, but better than nothing. At least Roxy had maintained a good appetite, scarfing her food in record time.

Ally took Roxy for a quick walk outside, then decided to keep the boxer downstairs in the clinic for a while to give Pepper a break. Hopefully, Marty's ex-wife would be in touch soon about picking Roxy up. Not that Ally didn't enjoy spending time with the boxer—she did. But a full night's sleep would be nice.

There was a grooming appointment set up for nine o'clock, and that was it. Other than taking Gramps to the library and out for lunch, the rest of her day was wide open.

"Roxy, you need to convince your friends to come visit."

Roxy tipped her head inquisitively.

"Yeah, I know. What was I thinking? There isn't a pet out there that likes to visit the vet." Ally sighed and did a quick wipe-down of the clinic before her grooming appointment arrived.

The door opened at exactly nine, a harried mother with two kids holding the leash of an adorable goldendoodle named Clover. The frazzled woman appeared to be at her wits' end, the two kids arguing nonstop from the moment they arrived.

"Thanks for doing this. Can you keep Clover here until later this afternoon?" Grace Hicks raised her voice loudly, to be heard over her kids' bickering. "Trish has soccer camp and Andy has baseball tryouts. I'll come back to get Clover after all the running around is finished for the day."

"Sure, no problem." Ally could tell the poor woman needed a break, even from the family pet. "How short would you like Clover's hair to be cut?"

"Shave him all the way down to a half inch. I only do this once a year every summer. In the winter, I figure he needs the additional fur coat."

"Sounds good." Ally took Clover's leash. "See you later this afternoon."

"Thanks."

Ally took Clover into the grooming room, thinking that a once-a-year job was better than none. Maybe Grace had friends with dogs who'd be willing to bring them in for grooming services? She could only hope.

Clipping Clover didn't take long, he was well behaved and lovable. When she was finished, she tied a red, white, and blue bandana around his neck in honor of the upcoming Fourth of July holiday and stepped back to survey her work.

"You look marvelous." If she did say so herself.

Clover wagged his tail in agreement. Roxy barked from the back room as if jealous of Clover getting all the attention. The sounds of animals provided a hint of what her future could be, once her clinic was in full swing.

She couldn't wait.

For now, she took Clover outside, then crated him in the back. After giving Roxy her turn outside, she took the boxer back upstairs to the apartment.

Remembering her promise to Gramps, she headed over to the Legacy House to drive him to his weekly visit at the local library. She looked forward to sharing lunch with him at the Lakeview Café afterward.

When she pulled into the small parking area at the Legacy House, her heart sank when she noticed a familiar black SUV parked in front of the door.

Detective Noah Jorgenson.

What was he doing here? Talking to Lydia? It made sense. Imagining the fireworks going off inside the house, she quickly slid out from behind the wheel and walked up to the door. She knocked loudly, then paused to listen.

No yelling, from what she could tell. At least, not yet.

When no one came to answer the door, she knocked again. "Gramps! Harriet! Lydia! Tillie! It's me, Ally!"

The door opened, revealing a harried-looking Tillie. "Hi, Ally."

"Is Gramps okay? And Lydia?" She crossed the threshold, glancing around with concern.

"They're in the living room." Tillie gestured with her hand. "Oscar isn't letting Lydia say much."

Of course he wasn't. Did he fancy himself some sort of lawyer now, too? Ally suppressed a sigh and walked through the kitchen to the living room. "Hey, Gramps."

"Ally." Her grandfather didn't take his beady blue gaze off Noah. "I was just explaining how Lydia doesn't know anything."

"If you don't mind, Mr. Winter, I'd like to hear from Lydia herself." Noah's words were spoken politely enough, but the expression on his face reflected intense frustration.

"I don't have anything more to tell you, officer." Lydia held a knitting project in her hands, her knitting needles working the deep blue yarn. Another project for Gramps? Most likely.

"Mr. Winter, please. I'd really like to speak to Ms. Schneider alone."

"She has a right to have an attorney present while talking to the police," Oscar shot back.

"Gramps, you're not a lawyer." Ally crossed over to rest her hand on his shoulder. "You're making this a bigger deal than you need to."

Noah's green gaze reflected gratitude. "I promise Ms. Schneider isn't a suspect. I just want to hear from her how this appointment came about."

"It was Anita Jones who mentioned Marty Shawlin to me," Lydia said, her fingers continuing to work the yarn. "He'd visited her a couple of days before, and she was referring him to her friends and neighbors." Lydia paused her knitting to lean forward. "He'd been through a rough divorce, you see, and needed some new business to help pay the bills."

Noah nodded encouragingly. "Anita gave Marty your name and number?"

"She did." Lydia picked up the dark blue yarn again and resumed her knitting. "But when Marty came, Oscar had a lot of questions for him. Marty was charging a flat fee of eight hundred dollars for his services, but Oscar didn't like that. When Oscar began asking more questions about why the trust was needed, and why our current wills had to be changed, Marty got mad and told Oscar to mind his own business." Lydia dropped her yarn again, reaching out to place her hand on her grandfather's forearm. "Oscar takes such good care of us."

Noah's curious gaze landed on Gramps. "I'm sure he does."

Lydia leaned against Gramps for a moment, then sighed. "That was it. Oscar told Marty to leave and never come back. Marty left, and that was the last we saw him. Right, Oscar?"

"Hrmph." Gramps grunted in what might have been agreement.

Noah smiled. "Thank you, Ms. Schneider. I really appreciate hearing your side of the story."

"You're welcome." Lydia batted her eyelashes in a flirtatious manner.

"By the way, have you heard from Marty's ex-wife about Roxy?" Ally asked.

"I left her a message, but she hasn't returned my call." Noah shrugged. "I'll keep trying, hopefully we'll connect soon."

Ally hoped Roxy's owner showed up before Pepper caused more trauma to the poor animal. Forcing a smile, she looked down at her grandfather. "Gramps, are you ready to head to the library?"

"Soon," her grandfather replied, still glaring at Noah as if the detective was somehow the enemy here.

Noah must have decided he'd gotten enough information, because he stood. "Thanks again, Ms. Schneider. Mr. Winter." He moved away, catching her gaze. "See you around, uh, Ally."

"Sure." Her cheeks went pink, and she hoped Noah hadn't noticed. Bad enough he still thought of her as *Hot Pants*.

She waited until Tillie let Noah out before pinning her grandfather with a narrow gaze. "You have to stop watching so many true crime shows on TV."

Gramps shrugged. "There's a new series on now called *The First Forty-Eight Hours*. Most crimes are solved in the first forty-eight hours and, if they're not, the odds of solving them go down exponentially." Gramps used his walker to stand. "That detective of yours better get a move on. He's already twenty-four hours into his investigation and doesn't have squat."

Great, just what Gramps needed, another crime show. "He's not *my* detective." Ally walked Gramps into the kitchen. "Do you want to take your cane or walker?"

"Cane." Gramps set the walker aside and picked up his cane. She positioned herself on his other side to offer additional support.

The Willow Bluff Library was housed in the same building as City Hall. The front of the municipal building faced Main Street, but there was a decent-sized parking lot along the back.

Ally drove up and down the rows of cars looking for a spot close to the building so Gramps wouldn't have to walk so far.

"Stop!" Gramps grabbed her arm in a tight grip.

She instinctively hit the brake, glancing around frantically. "Why? Was I about to hit something?"

"No, but look. That's Marty Shawlin's car."

She looked in the direction he indicated. Gramps was right. Tucked between two other vehicles was the familiar tan sedan. She stared for a moment. "Are you sure it's the right one?"

"See the license plate? Edward Mary Joseph 252. That's Marty's car."

Ally sighed. She should have known better than to expect a normal visit to the library with her grandfather. Reaching for her phone, she decided to call Noah's cell phone directly, rather than going through the local police.

At this rate, she might as well have his number on speed dial.

Chapter Five

As usual, Noah did not look happy to see them. She wasn't sure why—after all, Gramps was helping him solve the murder. If Gramps was right about the first forty-eight hours being critical to solving a crime, the clock was ticking.

"You just happened to drive through the library parking lot and found Marty's car?" Noah's tone dripped with sarcasm.

"Yep." Gramps looked smug.

"Gramps comes to the library every Wednesday," Ally added in an attempt to smooth things over. "And we drove around a bit because I wanted a closer parking spot so Gramps wouldn't have to walk as far."

Noah's green gaze bored into hers. "I thought I told you to leave the investigating to me?"

"I am!" Ally spread her hands. "It's not my fault I found the body and then drove past the dead man's missing car." From their vantage point, she could just barely make out Appletree Lane behind the grocery store, located kitty-corner from the municipal building. "I'm surprised you didn't check here earlier, after all, it's within walking distance of Marty's place."

"The killer likely drove the car here, figuring it's close to the center of town." Gramps squinted and gave a nod of satisfaction. "From here, he or she could walk just about anywhere without capturing anyone's attention."

A tiny muscle twitched near Noah's left eye and, for a moment, she thought he might lose it. To his credit, he didn't. Instead, he leveled each of them a stern look. "Listen, both of you need to butt out of this. It's a murder investigation, not a hobby."

"We're not trying to be involved," Ally hastened to reassure him. "Right, Gramps?"

Gramps grunted in a way that indicated he'd do whatever he pleased. And if that meant butting in, he'd do exactly that.

"Noah, do you need anything else? I'm sure Gramps is anxious to get into the library."

Gramps let out a snort. "I'm fine right here. You going to look inside the car? Search for clues?"

Noah sighed again. At least the corner of his eye had stopped twitching. "The crime scene techs are on their way. It would be a huge help if you would go inside. I don't want any chance of the crime scene becoming contaminated."

Ally knew Gramps would prefer to stay out here and watch, but she put her hand firmly under his arm. "We're going."

Her grandfather reluctantly walked beside her. "If the killer was smart, he or she would have wiped the car clean of fingerprints."

"But criminals aren't always as smart as they think. Besides, there could be other evidence besides prints. Hair fibers, that kind of thing." It made her smile to think that the interior was likely full of short golden-brown hair from Roxy. "Not our problem, right?"

"It is if I'm still a suspect."

"You're not a suspect, Gramps." *And probably never were, until you got all hyped up and called a lawyer.* For being so smart, Noah had played right into that one.

They crossed the parking lot and headed inside the blessedly cool building. The library was a two-story structure with an elevator that led up to the children's section, which had a play area surrounded by children's books. "What do you feel like reading today?"

"True crime." Gramps didn't hesitate to thump his way straight over to the section of the library where the crime novels were located. Shaking her head with frustration, she decided to go check out a couple of romantic suspense books. Back when she'd lived in Madison, she'd been too busy to read. Considering her lack of appointments at the clinic, it appeared this would be a good time to get caught up with her favorite authors.

Ally found two books and quickly checked them out. Since she didn't have a library card, she went through the process of signing up and received a temporary card until the real one was ready.

Gramps was still perusing the shelves, no doubt having trouble finding something he hadn't already read. She took a seat in a chair off in the corner of the room and opened her book.

"Can you believe someone murdered Marty Shawlin?"

"It's terrible, isn't it? I heard his ex-wife walked away with a lot of money after their divorce."

"Really? She took him to the cleaners?"

"Yes. I also heard they have a potential suspect."

A pair of female voices caught her attention. Glancing up from her novel, Ally scanned the area. A group of ladies who looked to be about her mother's age stood in a cluster at the end of an aisle. When Ally looked in their direction, they all quickly shut up and averted their gazes.

Having only been back in Willow Bluff for the past six weeks, there were many locals she didn't know. None of the three women looked familiar, but clearly they had opinions about Marty's murder. Seeing her, they quickly moved out of earshot.

It took all Ally's willpower not to follow them so she could keep listening. Sounded as if the divorce had been more acrimonious than she'd originally believed. And who was the suspect they'd mentioned? Hopefully not Gramps. Although as far as she knew, Gramps was the only one Noah had interviewed down at the police station. But that was only because Gramps was stubborn down to the bone.

"Found one!" Gramps made his way toward her, leaning heavily on his cane. He flashed the cover of his book.

"*The Evil Within*? Really, Gramps? Won't that give you nightmares?"

"Bah. There ain't nothing worse than 'Nam." He jutted his chin toward the checkout desk. "Are you ready to go? I'm hungry."

"Of course." Ally rose and helped Gramps over to the library checkout counter.

"Hello, Oscar." The woman behind the desk greeted him warmly. She had to be at least twenty years younger than her grandfather but acted as if they were old friends. "I see you found another true crime story. There's a new one that should be here within the next couple of days. I'd be happy to put a hold on it for you, if you'd like."

"I would, indeed." Gramps' blue eyes twinkled. "I appreciate you always keeping an eye out for something I enjoy reading. Thanks, Rosie."

"You're very welcome." Rosie quickly checked the book before handing it back. "See you next week?"

"Of course." Gramps tucked the book under his arm. "I'm looking forward to it."

They left the library, stepping into the warm June sun. Ally shortened her stride for Gramps' sake. "Do you have all the single women in this town running after you?"

"What can I say? I'm a catch." Gramps preened a bit as they walked toward the Lakeview Café.

"More like the local heartbreaker," Ally retorted.

Gramps shrugged, not looking a bit repentant. "Not my fault. But it doesn't matter. Not a one of them can hold a candle to Amelia."

Shaking her head, Ally found herself wondering if Noah's team had finished processing Marty's car. Since the parking lot was located in the back of the building, she couldn't see if they were still around.

Reminding herself that they had agreed to stay out of it, she pushed her curiosity aside and focused on sharing a nice lunch with Gramps.

"So, who do you think killed Marty?" Gramps asked after their server had taken their order and brought their raspberry lemonades.

She eyed him over the rim of her glass. "We're supposed to leave it alone, remember?"

"Bah." Gramps waved a hand. "Where would that detective be without us?"

Ally silently admitted that Gramps had a point. How long would poor Marty have lain there on the floor if she hadn't agreed to walk Roxy? She shivered and tried not to focus on the gory details. "I'm sure Noah is doing a fine job. We have no idea what he's accomplished already, since he isn't about to confide in us."

"I was thinking that maybe the events unfolded in a different way," Gramps mused.

Intrigued in spite of herself, she leaned closer. "What do you mean?"

"Like maybe Marty parked his car here because he was meeting someone in town. Maybe they ended up going back to his place to get something, some paperwork or something he'd forgotten, only that's when the murderer knocked him over the head and then slipped out the back."

Ally eyed her grandfather thoughtfully. "That would make sense, since Roxy was in her crate when I arrived. I thought it was odd for the dog to be crated while Marty was still at home."

"Exactly." Gramps' blue eyes gleamed.

"I'm sure Noah has considered that possibility."

"Maybe. Regardless, I think we should talk to Anita Jones about what other poor unsuspecting souls she sicced Marty on." Gramps looked far too excited about the prospect. "We might pick up on something to help your detective figure out whodunit."

"He's not *my* detective." Ally glanced around the café in search of their server, hoping their lunch would arrive soon. "Besides, what do you know about questioning a witness?"

"I read." Gramps tapped the library book sitting on the table between them.

"Yeah, a little too much." Ally took another sip of her tangy raspberry lemonade. "Enough talk about murder. What are your plans for the rest of the day?"

"Tillie wants to play cribbage, but I'd rather you drive us over to chat with Anita."

"Gramps." She sighed. "I just don't think that's a good idea. Noah will be upset if he finds out we did that."

"Who cares? He'll get over it." Gramps sat back in his seat. "Especially if we help him solve the case."

Their meals arrived, and the conversation turned to less morbid topics. As Ally finished with her salad, her phone rang.

The number wasn't familiar, maybe a potential client? She answered in a professional tone. "Hello, this is Dr. Winter."

"Where's Dr. Hanson?"

Good grief, would anyone in this town ever figure out Hanson was gone and not coming back? "I'm sorry, he's retired. I'm Dr. Winter and am happy to help."

There was a slight pause, then the caller said, "I have a problem. My black Lab, Smoky, ate my sock."

Ally stood and moved away from the table so there was less background noise. "A sock?"

"Yes." The poor girl sounded as if she might cry. "It's not a large sock, just goes up to my ankle, but I caught a glimpse of the red toe part hanging out of his mouth as he ran away. By the time I caught him, he'd already swallowed it."

"I see." Fortunately, she'd been through this scenario before. "Okay, listen, fabric like that isn't good for dogs, it will glom together and cause a bowel obstruction, which in turn will require

55

surgery. My advice is that you give him some hydrogen peroxide right away, to make him throw up."

"How much hydrogen peroxide?" There were sounds in the background that made Ally think the caller was rifling through the bathroom closet.

"How much does Smoky weigh?"

"Seventy pounds."

"Okay, no more than forty-five milliliters of peroxide, then, that's the max. Do you have a syringe like for giving animals liquid medication? It will work better if you can get the peroxide way into the back of his mouth, he won't drink it voluntarily. If that doesn't work, call me back, you'll need to bring Smoky in."

"I will, thanks." The girl hung up.

Ally hurried back to the table. "I have a possible emergency coming into the clinic, so we'll need to leave." She glanced around for the server to pay their bill.

"I already took care of it." Gramps pushed himself upright.

"Gramps, I wanted to pay." It didn't feel right to have her grandfather buying her meal. She might not be swimming in cash, but she wasn't so bad off she'd mooch off her grandfather.

"Next time." He tucked his book beneath his arm, then turned back to glance at their empty table. "You know, I can just sit here for a spell and wait for you."

She narrowed her gaze. "Why, so you can go talk to Anita?" The flash of guilt in his gaze made her roll her eyes. "Yeah, no. I don't think so. Besides, I have a grooming pickup later this afternoon anyway but don't have a specific time, so it would be better if I drove you back to the Legacy House now."

"Okay, fine." Gramps heaved a heavy and thoroughly disappointed sigh.

The walk back to the municipal building parking lot took longer than the drive to the Legacy House. There was no sign of Noah or Marty's car, which she imagined had been towed away. Gramps looked thoughtful, and she couldn't help being worried about what new scheme he was cooking up. It wouldn't surprise her that he might find a way to talk privately with Anita Jones.

The more she thought about it, the more she realized it might be better if she was the one to take Gramps over to speak to Anita. At least that way she could make sure he didn't get too far out of line.

Noah couldn't tell them who they were allowed to talk to, right?

Right.

"Tell you what, Gramps. When I finish up at the clinic, I'll drive you over to see Anita Jones."

He glanced at her in surprise. "Oh yeah? What made you change your mind?"

She didn't dare tell him the truth. "I owe you for lunch, this is the least I can do."

"Okay, that would be great." His blue eyes gleamed again, and heaven help her, she could tell he was already creating a list of questions to ask the woman.

Yep, much better to go along with him than leave him on his own.

"I'll call you later," she promised as she walked Gramps up to the door.

"Oscar! You're just in time for lunch." Harriet beamed at him, as Ally helped him over the threshold.

"I already ate but wouldn't mind having some of Ally's brownies for dessert," Gramps said.

"Of course! And I have leftover apple crisp, too."

"Perfect." Gramps grinned. "They were both very tasty."

Harriet blushed and closed the door behind him.

Ally smiled and hurried back to her car. As she was driving back to the clinic, her phone rang again. She recognized the number from earlier. She pulled over to the side of the road and answered. "Hello, this is Dr. Winter."

"He won't throw up," the girl wailed. "I shot the peroxide into the back of his mouth the way you said, but Smoky still hasn't thrown up!"

"I'm sorry, but you'll need to bring him to the Furry Friends Veterinary Clinic." Ally hoped the girl was old enough to pay for the Lab's treatment. "Bring your mom or dad with you, okay?"

"They're out of town." The girl sniffled loudly. "But I have their credit card."

"That's fine, then. See you soon." Ally tossed her phone back in her purse and pulled back into traffic. Not that she wanted bad things to happen to people's pets, because she didn't. But all things considered, this was turning out to be a decent day for her business.

She had just enough time to take Clover and Roxy out for quick bathroom breaks before Smoky arrived.

The girl holding Smoky's leash was older than Ally had guessed, in her late teens or early twenties. "Hi, I'm Rachel Turks, and this is Smoky."

"Hi Rachel, Smoky." Ally held out her hand for the black Lab to sniff. He seemed friendly enough, not showing any discomfort after having eaten a red sock for a midday snack. "This shouldn't take too long, why don't you have a seat in the waiting room?"

"Okay." Rachel looked as if she wanted to cry but left Smoky in Ally's capable hands.

Ally took Smoky into the back, where she'd already prepared a syringe of apomorphine. She tied Smoky's leash to a pole and set him in the oversized sink. Then she donned gloves, a paper gown, and a face mask to protect herself. When she was ready, she wrapped her arms around him and quickly injected the medication into his flank.

The dog yelped and tried to squirm away, but she held tight. Then she prepared herself for the inevitable results. Over-the-counter supplies like hydrogen peroxide to make a dog vomit weren't nearly as powerful as apomorphine.

Sure enough, it didn't take long for poor Smoky to begin to vomit. She felt bad for him but knew it was for the best.

"Good boy," she encouraged. "Yes, you're a good boy. We need to get that nasty sock out of there, don't we? Yes, we do."

The sock came out amidst other stomach contents.

"There, see? You'll feel much better in the long run."

Smoky convulsed and vomited again, and she was horrified to find there was another ball of fabric in the bottom of the wash tub. Another sock? She picked up a scalpel and tweezers to pry the ball of fabric open.

Two socks stuck together for a total of three.

What in the world?

Smoky threw up again, heaving up yet another balled-up hunk of fabric. By the time he'd emptied his gut, she had six socks of various colors yet all roughly the same size.

Not a single matching pair among them.

"Good thing Rachel brought you in today, Smoky, or we'd have been operating on you for sure." Ally cleaned up the mess, including the dog, before walking him back out into the waiting area.

"How is he?" Rachel tossed the six-month-old *People* magazine aside and jumped to her feet.

"He's fine, but do you realize he'd eaten six socks?"

"Six?" Rachel paled. "I had no idea. I assumed they were lost in the dryer."

"Yeah, well, they weren't. You need to keep your dirty clothes off the floor or anywhere he can get them." Ally kept her tone stern. "Next time, he might need surgery."

"I'm sorry. I didn't mean to cause him harm." Tears welled in Rachel's eyes as she crouched down to put her arms around the Lab's neck. "I love you, Smoky."

Ally felt certain Smoky would be in good hands from this point forward. "Let's get you checked out, okay?"

Rachel and Smoky followed her over to the desk. Ally printed an invoice and showed it to Rachel. The girl winced, but readily handed over the credit card that must have belonged to her parents, because the name Richard Turks was printed on the front of the card.

Ally ran the card through her machine. After a moment there was a beep, along with a message that flashed on the screen.

Declined.

Ally took a deep breath and tried again. Credit card machines could be finicky.

Declined.

"Are you sure this is the only credit card you have?" Ally frowned. "This one is being declined."

"It is?" Rachel looked surprised. "But—I don't have another card."

Of course she didn't. Ally fought the urge to bang her head against the counter. "How much cash do you have?"

"I'm not sure." The girl rummaged in her purse. "Twenty-four dollars and eighty-one cents."

Ally tried not to groan. "Okay, I'll take the twenty dollars as a down payment, but you'll need your parents to pay the rest when they return."

Rachel reluctantly pushed the bill across the counter. "I will. They'll be home tomorrow."

"Tomorrow is fine." Ally ignored the stab of guilt as she took the money. Was there more food in Rachel's house than in hers? Probably. Unless you counted the dog and cat food she had for Pepper and Roxy.

How else had the parent's credit card gotten maxed out?

Her optimism faded. She could only hope and pray Richard Turks would actually come in to pay the rest of the outstanding veterinary bill.

If this trend didn't turn around soon, she might have to move into the Legacy House with Gramps.

Chapter Six

Ally watched the clock, waiting for Grace Hicks to come pick up Clover. At a quarter past four, she began to worry.

At four thirty, she grew desperate. What if the woman didn't come at all? Would she be forced to take in a second dog, on top of Roxy? Poor Pepper was already traumatized enough; adding another dog might give the poor thing another asthma attack, or worse, a full-blown heart attack.

At four forty-eight exactly, the door opened, and the harried woman walked in. She looked a tad calmer without the kids fighting at her side. Ally figured the extra time must have meant Grace had dropped the kids off at home before coming in. "Hi, I'm here to pick up Clover."

"Of course, Ms. Hicks. I have Clover ready for you." Ally breathed a sigh of relief and fetched Clover. He was an easygoing dog, as goldendoodles often were. He smelled good and pranced out with his Fourth of July scarf around his neck, as if he were king of the world. Clover enthusiastically greeted Grace. She smiled, but then frowned.

"Down, Clover. Behave." Grace reached into her purse for her wallet. "How much?"

Ally printed the invoice and slid it over. Grace nodded and paid the amount in cash, adding a modest tip. "Thanks."

"You're welcome." Ally waited until they were gone before opening the cash drawer and pulling out the twenty Rachel had paid. Sixty bucks total. Not too bad.

A step in the right direction.

Tucking the cash into the front pocket of her jeans, she headed upstairs to the second-floor apartment. The boxer barked like mad when she heard Ally on the steps.

"I'm coming, Rox," she called. "Don't get your boxers in a twist. Ha! Get it? Boxers? In a twist?"

Chuckling at her own lame joke, Ally opened the door. Roxy greeted her like a long-lost friend, although Ally had taken the canine outside several times already that day.

"Are you behaving yourself with Pepper? Huh? Are you?" As always, talking to animals made Ally relax. If only people could be more like dogs and cats. The world would be a much better place, that was for sure.

"Meow!" Pepper strolled out of the open bedroom door, keeping her yellow eyes peeled on Roxy.

"I suppose you're feeling neglected, poor kitty. Sorry about that. I'm sure Roxy's mommy will be here to pick her up soon." At least, that was the plan. Surely Noah would have to talk to the ex-wife sooner rather than later. After all, wasn't the former spouse always the main suspect in a crime like this? And those women had mentioned how Marty's ex had taken him to the cleaners.

She'd have to remember to mention that tidbit of information to Noah.

After spending a few minutes with Pepper, she took Roxy back outside to do her business. It was tempting to bring Roxy along for the meeting with Anita, but she reluctantly decided against it.

She'd have her hands full with Gramps alone. No need to add the stress of bringing a dog.

By the time Ally had fed both Roxy and Pepper, and driven to the Legacy House, it was five forty-five. As usual, Harriet answered the door. "Hello, Ally. You're just in time for dinner."

"Oh, but . . ." Rats. She probably should have anticipated this. "I really shouldn't."

Her stomach growled at the enticing aroma wafting from the kitchen. Gramps was seated at the table, and from the looks of it had no intention of leaving before he'd eaten.

"Come sit down, Ally." Gramps patted the chair beside him. "We can't go see Anita at dinner time, it wouldn't be polite. We'll have to wait until afterwards."

"I can come back later," Ally said. Her resolve weakened when she took another deep sniff. "Harriet, what are you making this time?"

"Wiener schnitzel." Harriet beamed. "It's another of my mother's recipes."

"It smells incredible." Ally put a hand over her rumbling stomach. She should go back to her apartment, but the thought of another dinner that consisted of ramen noodles or boxed macaroni and cheese wasn't the least bit appealing.

"I've also made oven-roasted red potatoes and broccoli." Harriet sure knew how to make a meal.

64

"Join us," Gramps urged. "This way we can leave as soon as dinner is over."

"Are you sure you don't mind?" Ally glanced at Harriet, who looked pleased as punch. The German woman sent knowing glances toward Lydia and Tillie, as if to say, see? My cooking beats all.

And she might not be far off in that assessment. Heaven knew the way to Gramps' heart could very well be through his stomach.

"Of course not! I'm happy to set another place." Harriet moved from one cupboard to the other, getting another plate, glass, and silverware.

Ally dropped into the seat to her grandfather's right, knowing she would live to regret this, but unable to find the strength to walk away. Maybe if she ate Harriet's meals, allowed Lydia to teach her to knit, and played cribbage with Tillie and Gramps, they'd all remain on equal footing.

Better that than having the WBWs think she was currying favor with one of them over the others.

"What's this about talking to Anita?" Lydia asked, patting her snow-white curls as she entered the kitchen.

"Nothing for you to worry about," Gramps said with a wave of his hand. "We're just going to have a friendly chat, that's all."

"About Marty?" Lydia's sharp gaze cut from Gramps to Ally. "You're investigating this murder, aren't you?" When Gramps didn't deny it, she sighed and drilled Ally with a look. "Why are you encouraging him?"

"Me?" Ally did her best to look innocent. "I'm not encouraging him, Lydia. But let's face it. Gramps is going to talk to her with or without me."

"Tsk-tsk." Tillie took the seat across from Ally. "I'm sure that handsome detective of yours has already spoken to Anita. What more could she possibly have to offer?"

"He's not my detective." Ally wondered if she should have that sentence painted in neon pink across her forehead. "And I'm sure you're right. Still, Gramps insisted, so here I am." Her mouth was watering at the scents of the schnitzel, roasted potatoes, and broccoli.

Several minutes later, Harriet placed a heavy platter of fried and breaded meat in the center of the table. Then she added a bowl of roasted red potatoes and a smaller bowl of broccoli. "Dig in," she said as she took a seat on the other side of Gramps.

Apparently cooking for her grandfather gave her the right to sit beside him.

Gramps picked up the platter and held it out for Ally, then sent it around the table. Then did the same with the potatoes and broccoli. Ally took a bite of the Wiener schnitzel and nearly moaned out loud. It was so good. She ate another bite, savoring the flavor.

"Ally, I was thinking, if you need someone to help answer the phone at the clinic, I could sit there for a few hours each day," Lydia offered.

Ally inhaled in surprise, then choked on a piece of meat. She coughed and sputtered, her eyes watering with the effort.

Gramps thumped her on the back. "Are you okay?"

"You would?" She managed in a hoarse voice.

"Of course." Lydia beamed, making Ally wonder if this was another attempt to curry favor with her grandfather. "I'd love to help."

"Me, too," Tillie piped up.

Harriet frowned, as if not liking this new development.

"Uh, well, thanks. I appreciate your offer." There was no denying she could use a receptionist, but she hadn't anticipated the widows offering to do the job. Had her grandfather put them up to it? Maybe. She couldn't think of a reason to refuse their kindness. "Let me look into that and come up with some sort of schedule, okay?"

"Perfect." Lydia beamed.

"Sounds great," Tillie added.

When they were finished eating, Ally jumped up to help clear the table.

"Sit down," Harriet admonished. "We still need to have dessert."

Maybe it was a good thing Ally didn't eat here often, or she'd need bigger jeans. As it was, her figure was curvier than most. "I don't need dessert, but thanks anyway. I insist on helping with the dishes."

"Oh, but we still have your brownies." Harriet smiled. "We need to finish them up before they get stale."

"No need to worry about that, we can always add vanilla ice cream to soften them up," Gramps pointed out. "Frankly, I prefer them that way."

Ally gave in and ate a small square of brownie, topped with ice cream and a sliver of Harriet's apple crisp. Both were delicious, but even she had to admit the crisp was better. It was close to seven o'clock by the time she and Gramps were able to head out to Anita Jones' house. On the way, they discussed strategy.

"What are you going to do? Ask if you can question her about Marty's murder?"

"Of course not." Gramps huffed. "I'm going to ask her if that detective of yours put her through the wringer the same way he did me. That should soften her up and encourage her to talk."

HE'S NOT MY DETECTIVE! She shouted the words silently in her mind but didn't bother voicing the sentiment again.

Reminding him the last several times certainly hadn't done any good.

She pulled in and parked in Anita's driveway. The windows were open, allowing the cool breeze off Lake Michigan to come in. Ally figured the woman must be home.

"Is she married?" Ally whispered as she helped Gramps slide out of the passenger seat.

"I don't think so. I believe she's a widow."

What was with all the single middle-aged women in town? And so many of them widows? Ally told herself that she was only noticing them because they were people Gramps knew, and that there had to be younger people who lived here too.

Someone besides Noah. Maybe she should look up her old friend Erica Logan, the one who'd saved her from further humiliation by bringing over a beach towel the night the fire ants had sent her into the lake. She hadn't spoken to Erica after their freshman year of college, and it would be nice to catch up.

Gramps knocked on the door. Anita stepped forward, eyeing them through the screen door with apprehension. "Oscar? What do you want?"

"Hello, Anita." Gramps smiled. "I was hoping to talk to you, if you have a moment. I'm just so shaken up by being questioned by Detective Jorgenson that I wanted to see if he put you through the same round of questions. I could use your help if you have time."

Ally must have been wrong about Gramps' charm, because apparently, he could turn it on and off like a hot water spigot.

"Oh, Oscar." Anita's gaze softened. "You poor thing. Come in, both of you."

"This is my granddaughter Ally. She's been a gem standing by my side through all of this. It's been so upsetting."

Ally coughed to hide her smile. Gramps was really laying it on thick. And Anita was lapping it up, despite the nearly twenty-year age gap between them.

Apparently, Gramps really was Willow Bluff's most eligible bachelor.

Anita led them into the living room, gesturing toward the sofa. Ally helped Gramps sit down, then took a spot beside him. "Can I offer you something to drink?" Anita asked.

"No, thank you. I wouldn't want to put you out." Gramps offered a weary smile. "Please tell me that detective came to talk to you. I would hate to feel like I was the only one."

"Yes, of course he did." Anita sat back in her overstuffed chair. "I knew he would, since I live two doors down from Marty's place."

Gramps nodded encouragingly. "Did you mention how you referred Marty Shawlin to Lydia as a potential client?"

Anita stiffened, but her expression remained neutral. "Of course, why wouldn't I?"

"Oh, I know you would do whatever was necessary to help the police." Her grandfather's tone oozed sympathy. "It's all so shocking, isn't it? Marty gone, just like that."

"Very much so." Anita leaned forward in her seat. "I feel partially responsible, you know."

Ally's pulse kicked up. She wanted to ask why but decided to let Gramps do the talking.

"I'm sure that's not true," Gramps assured her. "Why would you think such a thing?"

"It's just—if I'd have looked out my windows earlier, maybe I would have caught the murderer leaving the house." Anita's expression was earnest. "I'm usually so in tune with what's going on in this neighborhood. After Joey passed away, I took it upon myself to keep a keen eye out for any sign of trouble. I'm like the neighborhood watchdog."

Oh brother. Now who was laying it on thick?

"You're doing a wonderful job of keeping the town safe, Anita." Gramps smiled. "I'm sure you also gave the detective a list of all the other people you referred Marty to as potential clients."

Anita looked taken aback. "What do you mean, a list?"

This time, Gramps didn't back down. "I know Lydia wasn't the only friend you referred to Marty, there were others as well. Marty spoke about them the night he came to see Lydia."

"Oh, uh, yes—I mean, I may have mentioned a few other names to Marty. You know, just as a way to help out a neighbor." Anita gathered herself. "The poor man was going through a rough divorce, and frankly he needed all the help he could get. I felt it was my duty to assist in any way possible."

"Understandable," Gramps agreed. "Who else did you refer him to?"

Anita flushed, not liking being put on the spot. "I don't know, just a few of the other neighbors. The Ryersons, the Whites, Kevin Kuhn." She pretended to think. "Oh, and Rosie Malone."

The same Rosie that worked at the library? From the slight narrowing of Gramps' gaze, Ally guessed so.

"I see. You were his client and liked his services so much you then referred him to Lydia, the Ryersons, the Whites, Kevin Kuhn, and Rosie Malone. Is that right?"

"I was never Marty's client," Anita responded in a tart tone. "Joey left me in perfectly good shape, bless his heart."

That made Gramps frown. "Why did you refer Marty to others if you weren't his client?"

Flustered, Anita glanced away. "I just told you, the poor man needed a break. His ex-wife was mean and took him for everything she could. He needed some extra money to get back on his feet. Why wouldn't I refer him to my friends?"

Ally put a hand on Gramps' arm, sensing he was getting worked up. It wouldn't do any good to yell at Anita Jones at this point.

"I'm sure you were just being kind," she said soothingly. "I'm a little surprised you didn't hear Roxy barking in her crate, though."

Anita frowned and crossed her arms over her chest. "Well, I did hear the dog barking, but that isn't anything new. Dogs bark all the time. Now, if you don't mind, I'd like to get ready for bed."

At barely seven thirty in the evening? Strange, but Ally knew that was their cue to leave. "Thanks again," she murmured, helping Gramps to his feet.

"Yes, thanks, Anita." Gramps didn't sound nearly as sincere.

As they left, she thought it very interesting that Anita had recommended Marty Shawlin's services to her friends and neighbors without knowing anything about those services.

Out of the kindness of her heart? Or was there something more going on here?

Ally was forced to admit Gramps had been right to come here tonight.

Something wasn't quite right in Willow Bluff. And whatever was going on had led to murder.

Chapter Seven

"I don't believe it." Gramps buckled his seat belt, then glanced at her from his position in the passenger seat. "Anita had to be Marty's client. It's the only thing that makes sense."

"Not necessarily." Ally put the car in reverse and backed out of Anita's driveway. She drove slowly past Marty Shawlin's place. The house looked the same as the day before, except for the yellow crime scene tape Officer Robertson had stretched across the front door. "Why is it so hard to believe she'd been giving him a helping hand with his business?"

"Bah." Gramps grunted with annoyance. "If that's true, it just makes it worse. That goofy woman had no right sending Marty to talk to Lydia if she had no idea what he was trying to sell at eight hundred bucks a pop."

"Not sell, exactly, but create." At least, that's the impression she'd gotten regarding Marty Shawlin's business. Although what did she know? Too bad she hadn't gotten a closer look at the paperwork scattered around his dead body. "Wills and trusts, right?"

"Supposedly." Gramps was skeptical. "It all sounded hokey to me."

Since her grandfather didn't use a debit card, or log into his bank via his computer, she wasn't sure he was the expert on wills and trusts. "You don't know that, Gramps. I'm pretty sure the cops on *Dateline* don't make hasty assumptions."

"You have a point," he conceded. "I'll keep my mind open to all possibilities."

Okay, encouraging him was not what she'd intended. "Do you think she gave the client information to Noah?"

Gramps shrugged. "Not sure. It seemed clear she didn't want to tell me, but maybe that's just because I caught her off guard." He arched a brow. "Maybe you should call your detective to make sure he knows about the list she provided to us."

She sighed and ignored his comment. "Maybe I will."

"Not sure I believe her about the dog barking, either," Gramps said slyly. "Roxy must have barked more than normal, indicating something was wrong."

"You never know, and you need to keep all possibilities in mind, remember?"

After dropping Gramps off at the Legacy House, Ally returned home. Roxy was thrilled to see her, but Pepper was once again hiding under the bed. Ally took Roxy outside for a walk.

"I have to say, there was something off about Anita," she confided to her canine friend. "At first she was all sweetness and smiles, but as soon as Gramps pushed a bit, she became flustered and shut down. Do you suppose she's hiding something?"

Roxy sniffed the ground, then squatted to pee.

"Or maybe I'm letting Gramps' penchant for crime mess with my head. Who wouldn't be flustered after finding out your neighbor was murdered? Heaven knows, I would be. Finding Marty with his head bashed in was bad enough."

Roxy looked up at her with wide adoring eyes, then went back to sniffing her surroundings.

Ally glanced around, noting how her apartment above the clinic was the only residence along all of Main Street. Most of the homes were in neighborhoods that fanned out from the center of town. Except to the east, where there was nothing more than large beautiful weeping willows and sandy bluffs overlooking Lake Michigan.

She enjoyed watching the water and was tempted to walk all the way down to the shoreline to listen to the waves but decided against it. Pepper deserved a little time and attention too.

Turning around at the grocery store, she walked Roxy back to the clinic. Upstairs, she spent twenty minutes cajoling Pepper from her hiding spot. Once she had the cat in her arms, she cuddled her close. "There now, you're being so good with Roxy, aren't you? Yes, you are."

The cat didn't purr, and less than five minutes later, dug her claws into Ally's arms and jumped down.

Ally sighed, rubbed at the surface scratches along her forearms, then headed to bed.

*   *   *

The next morning, she brought Roxy down to the clinic for some company. The dog sniffed all along the various exam rooms, then followed her toward the front desk area. When the phone rang, she dove for it. "Furry Friends Veterinary Clinic, this is Dr. Winter. May I help you?"

"Uh, yes. This is Richard Turks. I understand we owe you some money."

Ally lifted her gaze to the ceiling in silent gratitude. "Yes, sir. The credit card Rachel brought in with her was declined. How is Smoky, by the way? I hope he's feeling better."

"He's fine. I can be there in ten minutes, if that works for you?" Richard Turks was all business.

"Absolutely, thank you." Ally hung up the phone and spun in a circle, nearly tripping over Roxy, who jumped up to join her. She rubbed the boxer's fur. "Finally, another paying customer, Rox. Yes indeed."

Once the clinic was again wiped down with bleach, she sat at her computer with Roxy at her feet and tried to come up with an idea to spur more customers. Advertising her grooming services might help. She'd already added the information, including her prices, on her Furry Friends website. She created a flyer and printed out several copies on the color printer. Rosie might allow her to hang one at the library, and maybe she could advertise at the grocery store. Even the Lakeview Café might display one.

It was worth a shot.

Richard Turks arrived as promised. He didn't look at all happy as he handed over a different credit card. She ran it through the machine, and this time the amount, less the twenty dollars cash she'd taken from Rachel, went through.

She handed the card back to him with a smile. "Thanks again, Mr. Turks. I hope Smoky is feeling better."

"He's perfectly fine." The curtness in his tone indicated he felt as if her services hadn't been needed.

"I reinforced with Rachel that she shouldn't leave her dirty socks on the floor or anywhere where Smoky might find them. I'll be honest, this is the first time I've seen six socks come from a dog's stomach."

"Six?" He looked surprised and she realized Rachel must have glossed over the seriousness of the situation.

"I'm just glad surgery wasn't necessary." She smiled sweetly. "Take care, Mr. Turks."

"Yeah, you too. Thanks, Dr. Winter." He wore a grim expression when he left that almost made her feel sorry for Rachel.

Almost, but not quite. After all, the socks had belonged to Rachel in the first place.

Her phone rang again. Maybe having Lydia and Tillie working here would be a good thing, especially once she began seeing more customers. "Furry Friends Veterinary Clinic, this is Dr. Winter."

"I hear you have Roxy." The female voice sounded resigned.

"Yes, I do." This must be her lucky day. She glanced down at Roxy. "You must be Mrs. Shawlin."

"I prefer to go by my maiden name of Young. Sheila Young."

"Of course, I didn't realize. Please accept my condolences on your recent loss. I assume you've spoken to Detective Jorgenson about your late ex-husband and learned Roxy has been in my care since Monday."

"Of course. But I'm in Chicago on business and simply can't get away until next Monday. You'll have to keep Roxy until then."

Sheila's tart tone put her teeth on edge. "Of course, that's not a problem. But please know I charge a daily boarding fee."

There was a long silence, as if the other woman wasn't happy to hear about the fee. Finally, she spoke. "I guess I don't have a choice, although it's not my fault Marty got himself killed. He was supposed to take custody of Roxy in the first place after our divorce. This is all very inconvenient."

Inconvenient? Maybe the ex-wife should be moved to the top of Noah's suspect list. "I'm sorry about your loss, truly." Ally tried to keep her tone even, despite this woman's attitude toward her dog. "But I can't offer free services."

"Fine. I'll pay your boarding fee and see you on Monday." Sheila disconnected from the call.

"Wow, wish I could say I'm looking forward to that." She bent down to scratch the dog behind her ears. "You poor thing. Your mommy sounds mean." Hadn't Anita also called Marty's ex mean? Ally hoped Sheila Young was nicer to the dog in person compared to how she'd sounded on the phone.

She wondered what Sheila had told Noah about her relationship with her late ex-husband. Traveling to Chicago for work likely provided a decent alibi. Still, there was clearly no love lost between the two of them.

The more she thought about it, the more she believed Gramps was onto something. The person who'd killed Marty must have been one of his clients. Or maybe the spouse of a client, someone who was upset about whatever transaction Marty had convinced them to take.

Pulling out a pad of paper, she listed the names Anita had given them again. The Ryersons, the Whites, Kevin Kuhn, and Rosie Malone.

Oops. Almost forgot Lydia Schneider.

Ally tapped her pencil thoughtfully. She added Anita Jones to the list, wondering if the woman might have been holding back. There certainly could have been other referrals.

Still, it was a place to start.

Out of pure curiosity, Ally went through Hanson's client files to see if any of the possible suspects had pets who'd been to the clinic.

Eli and Virginia White had a tabby cat, and Kevin Kuhn had a dachshund.

In reviewing the files, she realized Kevin's dachshund, Lola, was due for her annual vaccinations. She picked up the phone and called the number listed on record. He didn't pick up, so she left a message.

"Hello, this is the Furry Friends Veterinary Clinic. Lola is due for her annual vaccinations. Please call back to make an appointment." She rattled off her number, then hung up the phone. If Kuhn brought Lola in, she could try to ask him about his interactions with Marty Shawlin and make some money to boot.

In fact, why not go through all the files to find pets in need of their shots? It certainly couldn't hurt. Back in Madison, they'd had an automated system that provided pet owners with reminder calls.

Her pulse jumped. Why hadn't she thought of this before?

Abandoning her idea of questioning the potential suspects, Ally sat down behind the computer and began going through the records one by one. It was tedious work, but after the end of two hours, she had ten names written down, in addition to Kevin Kuhn.

Eleven potential clients! She could barely contain her excitement.

"This is great news, isn't it, Roxy?"

The dog wiggled her stubby tail in agreement.

Ally was halfway through making the calls when her door opened. Looking up, she was hoping to find another client, but it was Noah Jorgenson who stood inside the doorway, gazing around with interest.

Her stomach knotted with nerves. Roxy stretched and came to her feet, sniffing the air curiously. She must have recognized Noah's woodsy scent from that first day, because she didn't bark or growl this time.

"Hi, how can I help you?"

"Just checking things out." His stance was casual, but she didn't think he'd dropped by without an ulterior motive. Roxy ran around the edge of the counter to greet Noah. He good-naturedly bent down to pet the dog.

Her heart melted a bit as she watched him. She'd always liked men who were good to animals. Then again, Tim had loved animals and look where that had gotten her. Hmm. So much for being a good judge of character. "Do you have a pet?"

"No, I'm not home enough for a dog. And I'm allergic to cats." He straightened and came toward the desk. "Did Sheila Young, Shawlin's ex-wife, call?"

"Yes, but she wasn't happy. Which is odd because you'd think she'd be grateful to hear I've been caring for Roxy while she's out of town."

"Yeah, she was the same way with me." Noah's green gaze caught hers. "What's this I hear about you and your grandfather paying a visit to Anita Jones last night?"

Uh-oh. Busted. She tried not to show her reaction. "It's not a crime to drop in and visit a neighbor."

"You mean the neighbor of a murdered man, because last I checked neither this place nor the Legacy House are located next door to Anita Jones."

She waved an impatient hand. "What difference does that make? Anita knows Lydia, who lives with Gramps. They obviously all know each other. That basically makes them neighbors."

"Ally." His low husky voice saying her name sent shivers of awareness down her spine. "How many times have I told you not to mess with my investigation?"

About as many times as I told Gramps that you aren't my detective, she thought wryly. "We're not." Her protest sounded weak, even to her own ears.

"You are." Noah sounded resigned. "Now tell me what you learned."

"Huh?" His comment surprised her.

"Spill it. I know that sly grandfather of yours got her to say something, and I want to know what it was."

She had to give Noah credit for understanding how her grandfather's mind worked. "Gramps specifically requested the names of other people Anita had suggested Marty meet with, and she told us she referred him to the Ryersons, the Whites, Kevin Kuhn, and Rosie Malone."

His steady green gaze didn't reveal a thing. "Anything else?"

His woodsy scent grew somehow stronger. If he wasn't standing so close, it would be easier to think. She pursed her lips. "Oh, Gramps inferred that Anita herself was one of his clients, but she denied doing any business with Marty."

"Really." A flicker of surprise crossed his features.

"Was that a lie? Because I have to tell you, Gramps and I both felt as if she was holding back from us."

"Anything else?" Whatever Noah thought about Anita's story, he obviously wasn't letting on.

"She claims she heard Roxy barking that morning but that it was nothing unusual. Again, we thought that was odd, as Roxy must have been frantic while Marty was being attacked."

No response from Noah, which made her think Anita had told him the same thing.

"That's all I can remember." She glanced down as Roxy brushed up against her leg. "I hope Sheila treats Roxy well. If she doesn't, I want you to arrest her."

For the first time since their meeting at Marty Shawlin's, Noah smiled. She tried to ignore the way his face lit up. "Happy to. I don't understand why people own pets if they don't want them."

"You and me both." It occurred to her that, if not for Marty's murder investigation standing between them, and the way he'd nearly referred to her as Hot Pants, they might have become friends.

"As long as we're talking pets, I have a stray cat upstairs in my apartment. She's a very oddly colored black and white speckled cat, goes by the name of Pepper."

"Sorry, haven't heard of any lost cats recently. Did you check with the shelter?"

"Yes. Jeri Smith doesn't know of a lost cat matching that description, either. I'll keep her until someone claims her."

Noah glanced around at her empty clinic. "Looks like you're not very busy."

"Gee, thanks for the keen observation." She hadn't meant to sound so snarky. "The fine citizens of Willow Bluff seem to be lamenting the fact that Greg Hanson has retired and apparently don't trust me with their pets."

He frowned. "That's crazy."

She shrugged. "Whatever. I'll win them over eventually, you'll see."

"I'm sure you will." Again, his steady green gaze made her flush.

"Thanks for stopping by." She gestured toward the phone. "I have more calls to make."

"Okay, see you later—*Hot Pants*."

And there it was. She scowled at him. "Knock it off—"

Crack! Something smashed loudly against the glass door of her clinic, causing it to crack and split into thousands of tiny pieces. Noah jumped back in shock, staring in horror at the shattered glass that remained within the frame.

"What was that?" Her voice emerged high and squeaky again.

"Stay here." Noah's tone was authoritative. He strode toward the door and carefully pulled it open. She held her breath, but the glass didn't spill out of the doorframe, maybe because it was shatter-proof. A part of her realized that was a good thing, because she didn't want Roxy or any future clients to step on any glass fragments.

Noah disappeared outside. She sank into her chair, gathering Roxy close. "We're okay, girl. Noah is going to make sure we're okay." She took several deep breaths to calm her racing heart.

Her door was not okay. It would need to be replaced, and soon. The glass bits hadn't fallen out yet, but she expected it wouldn't take much to jar them loose.

What was her insurance deductible, anyway? A thousand dollars? She dropped her forehead to rest on Roxy's soft fur.

She had money, but it was earmarked to make her upcoming loan payment.

The thought of failing at this, the way she had in Madison, was almost too much to bear.

"Ally?" Noah's voice penetrated her pity party. "You okay?"

"Yes, I'm fine." She lifted her head and forced a smile. "What did you find?"

"Someone threw a rock at your door, it's still on the sidewalk outside. So far, I haven't found any witnesses." He frowned. "Have you upset someone lately?"

She thought for a moment about the handful of clients she'd had so far this week. "Not that I'm aware of."

"I have a squad on the way, we'll do our best to find someone who might have witnessed someone going by your clinic with a rock." He set his business card on the counter. "Call if you need anything."

"Okay." She nodded, because what choice did she have? If Noah found the person who did this, they'd have to pay for the damage, right?

When Noah turned away, she called, "Wait."

He turned to face her. "What is it?"

"Do you think this could have something to do with Marty Shawlin's murder?"

His green gaze darkened. "I don't know, anything is possible. You and your grandfather really need to stay out of it, Ally. For real. Whoever killed Marty isn't fooling around."

He left and she sat there, realizing he was right. She needed to warn Gramps, right away.

Before something bad happened.

Losing her business was one thing. She'd *never* survive losing her grandfather.

Chapter Eight

Ally wanted nothing more than to rush over to see Gramps but decided to get in touch with her insurance company first. A shattered door was hardly welcoming, not to mention potentially dangerous, and needed to be replaced as soon as possible.

Her insurance agent called her back and agreed to have someone there to provide an estimate and repair first thing in the morning.

She'd hoped for today, but better late than never.

After taping a sheet of plastic over both sides of the shattered glass door, she clipped Roxy to her leash and headed outside. With a frown, she paused, realizing the broken door might invite looters. The door itself was locked, but one swift kick would likely destroy what was left of the glass.

Catching a glimpse of a uniformed officer made her relax. He was younger, seemingly more energetic than Roberts, the officer who'd responded to Marty's murder. Surely her clinic would be safe as the police investigated.

She'd keep her visit with Gramps short. And maybe sleep on the floor in the clinic overnight, just in case.

"Come on, Roxy. Let's check in on Gramps." She'd only taken two steps when her cell phone rang.

"ALLY?" Gramps' voice boomed loudly in her ear. "I HEARD THE NEWS. ARE YOU OKAY?"

"I'm not hurt, Gramps." She quickly deduced he was using the cell phone she'd purchased for him. How in the world had he heard about her clinic already? The man had more lines of communication snaking through town than NASA had satellites. "You don't have to yell, I can hear you just fine."

"WHAT?"

She glanced at Roxy, who seemed to be listening to Gramps, too. "I said you don't have to yell." She found herself raising her voice to match his. "I'm on my way over to see you. I'll have Roxy, so meet me on the patio."

"OKAY!"

Good grief. She disconnected the call and quickened her pace, Roxy eagerly trotting along beside her. Gramps must have been really worried about her—he rarely used the cell phone.

Which wasn't necessarily a bad thing, considering the way he'd shouted into her ear. Many more conversations like that and she'd need ear plugs to deaden the noise.

She reached Legacy Drive within fifteen minutes and found Gramps sitting outside on the patio, holding the cell phone in his lap. Swallowing a sigh, she quickly joined him.

"Roxy, sit." The boxer dropped to her haunches. "Gramps, it's good to see you." She gave him a quick hug and kiss before settling in beside him. "You need to hold the cell phone up to your ear to have a conversation, just like you did with the old phone receiver connected to a landline."

"I know that." He looked affronted by her suggestion. "But I can't figure out where the microphone is located."

Well, that explained the shouting. "It's part of the phone, so there's no need to yell into it." She decided to drop the issue. "I was headed over to see you when you called. How in the world did you hear about what happened at the clinic?"

"Rosie Malone at the library heard it from Jimmy Landon, who drove by and mentioned it during brunch at the Lakeview Café. Naturally, she was concerned and called Harriet, who filled me in." His expression was full of concern as he idly petted Roxy's fur. "I'm glad you weren't hurt, although I understand your front door is toast."

"Yeah, pretty much." She reached over to take his hand. "I love you, Gramps, and while I'm fine, I'm worried that this incident is related to Marty Shawlin's murder."

Gramps solemnly nodded. "That's exactly what I think. And you know what that means?"

"What?"

"That we're making someone nervous with all the questions we're asking." He bobbed his head in satisfaction. While he gently squeezed her hand reassuringly, she could tell he was excited at the prospect of cracking the case. "You need to be careful, Ally. It's a good thing you have Roxy there with you. Maybe you should see if Marty's widow will let you keep her?"

The boxer's ears perked up at her name. Ally couldn't deny she'd grown attached to Roxy—the dog was really well behaved. She scratched Roxy behind the ears, then turned back to her grandfather.

"I will be careful, and you need to promise me to do the same." She swallowed hard, overcome with emotion. "I love you, Gramps. I don't want anything bad to happen to you."

"Who, me? I'm too cranky to die." His tone was light, but his gaze was serious.

"Gramps . . ."

"Now, now. I was only kidding. I love you, too, Ally. But remember, I survived 'Nam. Besides, I'm pretty sure the door incident was a meager attempt to scare you off, nothing more."

"Maybe, and if that's the case it worked." She narrowed her gaze. "From now on, we leave the investigating to Noah."

"Hmm." Gramps' noncommittal tone was not the least bit convincing. "I was thinking about those people Anita mentioned, the ones she recommended meet with Marty. Could be one of them could give us a little more information on what Marty was up to. And maybe one of them has a reason to want him dead."

"Really, Gramps? What good will come from that? I'm sure Noah will be interviewing each and every one of them, if he hasn't already."

"But what if your detective misses something?" Gramps leaned forward, his expression earnest. "He's good, but we're better."

We? She opened her mouth to argue, then remembered the flash of surprise in Noah's eyes when she'd mentioned Anita Jones's claim that she wasn't Marty's client.

Was Gramps right? Even if he wasn't, there was always the concern that if she didn't help Gramps, he'd simply go off on his own. From what she could tell, Rosie Malone wouldn't hesitate to take Gramps wherever he wanted to go.

She sighed and rubbed her aching temple. "Listen, Gramps. I've already contacted Kevin Kuhn because Lola, his dachshund, is due for her vaccinations. I also left a message with Virginia White, since her tabby cat, Taffy, is also overdue for shots. No need for you to do anything about interviewing these people. I promise I'll let you know what I find out, okay?"

Gramps's blue eyes gleamed. "Good thinking, Ally. But what if the others don't have pets due for shots?"

His persistence was starting to wear on her. "We'll figure out something, don't worry." What she really meant is that she'd figure out something, because she wasn't about to place Gramps in harm's way.

"Maybe I should help you answer the phone in the clinic while you take care of the pets," Gramps mused, staring out at the sliver of lake shore that could be seen from the Legacy House patio. "After the incident with your door, it might be better for me to do that, rather than risk exposing Lydia or Tillie to danger."

He wasn't fooling her the least little bit, but what could she do? For one thing, someone answering phones would be nice, and she totally agreed that having Lydia or Tillie at the clinic after the rock incident was a bad idea. Once Noah arrested Marty's killer, the widows could take turns helping her out.

For now, having Gramps helping out would be a good way to keep an eye on him.

"That's a great idea," she said, injecting enthusiasm into her tone. "We can start tomorrow. I'll pick you up around nine and bring you down to the clinic, okay?"

"Works for me." Gramps looked pleased with himself.

It was all she could do not to roll her eyes. "Oh, and Gramps?"

"Yes, Ally?"

"You really do need to answer the phone. Not just sit there and listen to what's going on."

Without waiting for his response, she stood and tugged on Roxy's leash. As she headed back to the clinic, she hoped she wasn't making a mistake having Gramps come down to the clinic.

He might be old, but he was crafty. And she felt certain that his offer to help wasn't the real reason he wanted to be there.

Knowing Gramps, his main goal was to be smack dab in the heart of the action.

*　　*　　*

Ally slept on the floor of the clinic, with Roxy stretched out beside her. Pepper wandered down during the night, then put up her tail and ran back upstairs. Pepper and Roxy had found some sort of truce, but Ally still didn't sleep well. The floor was hard as a rock, even with the extra padding she'd lugged down from the apartment. The only good thing about the night was that no one had tried to break in.

As promised, the insurance adjuster arrived bright and early, giving her an estimate on the door, and the name of a preapproved glass company to call. Thankfully, the glass guy promised to be there by noon. She was glad it would be repaired in time for the weekend.

Before she could head out with Roxy to pick up Gramps, the phone rang. She quickly reached for it. "Furry Friends Veterinary Clinic, this is Dr. Winter. May I help you?"

"This is Ginny White, you left me a message about Taffy being overdue for shots?"

"Yes, thanks so much for returning my call. I've been going through Dr. Hanson's files and came across Taffy's information. Would you have time to bring her in?"

"I do, how does ten AM today work?"

Ally smiled broadly. Another paying customer! "Ten is perfect. I'll see you and Taffy then."

"All right." Ginny sighed heavily. "It will probably take me an hour to get Taffy into her crate. She doesn't like car rides, you know."

She quickly made a note on Taffy's chart about not liking crates or car rides. "Most of our pets don't, but we need to make sure they're well cared for anyway. See you at ten." Ally disconnected from the call and did a quick little jig. Those phone calls she'd made yesterday were already paying off. At this rate, she'd be able to make her next month's business and mortgage loan payment despite the large dent in her banking account from the door repair.

"Hear that, Roxy? We're in business!" She clipped a leash to Roxy's collar and headed out back to her Honda Civic hatchback. The car was over ten years old and had over 100,000 miles on it but still ran like a dream. She put Roxy in the crated back, then slid behind the wheel.

Gramps was quite the eager beaver, ready and waiting out front for her when she arrived. He was using his cane rather than the walker, which was a little concerning. She pulled up, parked, then ran around to open the door for him.

"Maybe I should grab your walker, too." She helped Gramps slide into the passenger seat. Roxy whined from her spot way in the back of the car. "Might be a long day."

"I'm fine without it," he said testily.

"Okay, if you're sure. Quiet down, Roxy." Arguing with him was useless. As she drove back to the clinic, she told him about Ginny White bringing Taffy the Tabby in at ten.

Instantly his cranky mood vanished. "You did good work there, Ally." He drummed his fingers on the arm rest between them. "We just need to think of a couple of key questions to ask while she's there."

Ally was already regretting the bright idea of having her grandfather helping her out, and they hadn't even gotten to the clinic yet. "You're going to be busy answering the phone, remember?"

"Bah." He waved a hand. "I doubt the phone will be ringing so much that I can't have a conversation with the woman."

Unfortunately, he was probably right about that.

Once she had Gramps settled in a chair behind the counter and taught him how to use the multi-button phone, she took Roxy outside for a quick bathroom break, then put the dog upstairs in the apartment. "Behave," she said to Pepper, who hissed and swiped at Roxy.

In the clinic she began her daily cleaning ritual. As the minutes ticked by toward ten, the phone remained stubbornly silent.

Maybe hoping for more calls like the one she'd received from Ginny White had been a bit ambitious.

Gramps had found paper and pencil and was busily jotting down notes. Ally was relieved Noah wasn't here to witness Gramps' interrogation technique.

The phone rang, making both her and Gramps jump. He snatched up the receiver. "Furry Friends Veterinary Clinic, can I help you?" Gramps listened for a moment, then said, "Hold on a sec." He raised his voice. "Ally? Can you groom a Westie?"

"Yes, of course." Her fingers itched to snatch the phone away. "Anytime is fine. Except for ten," she hastily amended.

"After lunch is fine, thanks." Gramps hung up the phone. "Westie will be here after lunch."

"Great, but did you get a name?"

Gramps frowned. "I forgot. But it's a Westie, can't be too many of them around, right?"

"Right." She forced a smile. This was her fault. It wasn't as if Gramps had ever worked as a receptionist before. She helped herself to the same paper and pencil he'd used, and dashed off a quick script. "From now on, Gramps, when customers call, you get their name, their number, and the name of the pet. That helps me be prepared, okay?"

He frowned at the note and shrugged. "Yeah, I got it."

The plastic-covered door opened, revealing a tall brunette lugging a cat carrier. Ginny White set the crate down with a sigh.

"I made it. Taffy's not too happy about it, though."

"Thanks so much for coming," Ally held out her hand. "I'm Dr. Winter, it's nice to meet you." She bent down to peer into the cat carrier. Taffy hissed and clawed at the screen. Her smile dimmed. "Hi, Taffy."

"I'm glad I only have to do this once a year," Ginny said, smoothing a hand over her hair. "There are times I wonder if it's worth the hassle."

"Trust me, Taffy will be fine. Let's get her into an exam room."

Ginny picked up the carrier, glancing curiously at Gramps.

"Hi, I'm Oscar Winter, Ally's assistant." Gramps smiled and reached over the counter to shake Ginny's hand. "It's nice to meet you."

"Oh, a family business. How sweet." Ginny beamed. "You don't always see family members sticking together these days."

Ally shifted her weight from one foot to the other. She wanted to get Taffy vaccinated before Gramps began grilling Mrs. White about her meeting with Marty Shawlin. "Gramps is a huge help, but let's get Taffy taken care of, shall we?"

"Of course." Ginny reluctantly turned away from Gramps, who scowled at Ally behind the woman's back. Ally narrowed her gaze in warning and quickly followed Ginny and Taffy into the exam room.

"Do you have any other concerns about Taffy?" Ally asked as she pulled a medication syringe out of the cabinet. "She's eating well? No bowel or bladder problems?"

"She seems fine," Ginny said, opening the crate and peering inside. "Come on, Taffy. Time to come out."

The cat didn't move.

"Taffy," Ginny's voice held a note of warning. As if that alone would convince the cat to obey.

"Here's a liver treat." Ally presented several for Ginny to use as bait.

Taffy let out a plaintive meow and inched forward toward the treat. Ginny kept up a one-sided dialogue, urging the cat to come out of the crate. After what seemed like forever, Taffy had most of her body outside the carrier, stretching her neck to get the treat.

Ally moved quickly, catching the cat's scruff and quickly lifting the cat into her arms. Holding her tight, she injected the animal's flank with the vaccination.

Taffy let out a howl, arching and hissing in annoyance. Ally figured the worst was over, when the cat suddenly released a stream of diarrhea down her front.

"Oh, Taffy." Ginny looked horrified, but really, Ally was the one with cat diarrhea covering her once-white lab coat.

And her shoes. Her pretty red shoes.

Ugh.

She summoned a smile. "It's okay." What else could she say? It was hardly the cat's fault. "Wait here, I'll get Taffy cleaned up."

"I told you she doesn't like car rides," Ginny called out as Ally took Taffy out of the exam room through the back door and straight to the wash tub.

Ally gave the cat a quick bath, which Taffy hated even more than car rides, then stripped off her lab coat and cleaned herself up as much as possible.

The red shoes however, were toast. The brown splotches hadn't washed out, and she couldn't wait to get upstairs to find a clean pair.

When she returned Taffy to Ginny, she was nonplussed to find the woman standing at the counter chatting with Gramps.

What was it about him, anyway? When had he become such a woman magnet?

"Taffy is all set," Ally said cheerfully, trying to ignore the stench of cat diarrhea in the air. "Do you want help getting her back into the carrier?"

"Yes, please."

Together she and Ginny managed to get Taffy tucked back inside the crate, only suffering a few scratches along her forearm. Nothing worse than Pepper had done.

"Okay, then, here's the invoice." Ally had the paperwork printed and ready to go. "Will that be cash or credit?"

"Credit." Ginny fished in her purse for her card.

Ally swiped the card, praying it wouldn't be declined. As she waited for the machine to process, Gramps went to work.

"Ginny, Anita told me that you and your husband met with Marty Shawlin before he was murdered." Gramps kept his blue gaze serious. "Just like I did."

"You did?" Ginny looked surprised. "I must say my husband Eli wasn't very impressed."

Gramps leaned forward. "Me either, if you want to know the truth. Did you end up paying him for any services?"

"Oh no, Eli wouldn't hear of it." Ginny suddenly looked suspicious. "Why do you ask?"

"Some people did pay him, and I was hoping that those who did might be able to get their money back," Gramps said. "You know, now that he's been murdered, his estate should reimburse those who paid, right? A real good lawyer could help with that."

"Really?" Ginny seemed a little too interested, considering she'd just claimed she hadn't paid for any of Marty's services.

"Yes, really," Gramps insisted.

Ally eyed her grandfather, wondering if he was telling the truth or had just made the whole thing up.

"Well, we might be interested in something like that," Ginny finally admitted.

"Why don't you give me your number?" Gramps picked up a pencil. "I'll let you know if others feel the same way."

Ginny didn't hesitate to rattle off her phone number. Now that the news was out, she couldn't stop talking. "After we paid the man, we heard nothing from him. Eli grew convinced that Marty was a scumbag swindler, and I have to agree. I never should have listened to Anita, praising Marty as being such a nice guy." Her dark brown eyes filled with tears. "We could have used that sixteen hundred dollars on a new television."

Sixteen hundred dollars? Ally caught Gramps' gaze. That was way more than what Marty had intended to charge Lydia. Unless it was double the eight hundred fee because there were two of them? Maybe.

"There, there," Gramps said, patting Ginny's shoulder awkwardly. "I'll see what I can do to help, okay?"

"Thank you, Oscar." Ginny sniffed and brushed the tears from her eyes. "You're a wonderful man."

Gramps beamed in a way that made Ally want to roll her eyes. These women shouldn't be feeding into his ego.

"Take care now," Ally said as Ginny lifted Taffy's crate and headed outside.

"Don't forget to call me," Ginny said over her shoulder to Gramps.

"I won't." The minute the door shut behind her, Gramps slapped his hand on the countertop. "I knew it! Did you hear that, Ally? Sixteen hundred dollars? As far as I'm concerned, that's motive for murder!"

Chapter Nine

Ally stifled a sigh. "Gramps, that's not necessarily true. I mean, yes, that's a lot of money, but enough to kill someone over? I'm not sure about that."

Gramps waggled a finger at her. "You wait and see. Marty swindled the Whites and maybe others. Could be they all got together and plotted to do him in."

"Well, if they had you'd think they'd have already tried to get their money back." She glared at him. "I hope you didn't raise Ginny's hopes on that front for nothing."

"I didn't!" Gramps tried to look innocent but couldn't quite pull it off. "After all, why wouldn't they get their money back? They paid for services they'll never get. His estate should pay them back plus interest."

As much as she hated to admit it, he had a point. The door opened and a familiar little girl came in, cradling a robin against her chest. Blonde hair pulled into pigtails, scruffy shorts and a pink top.

Amanda Cartwright.

"Please help Robby, there's something wrong with his wing." Amanda's large eyes were just as imploring as they had been when she'd brought Pepper in.

A stray cat and now an injured bird. Where in the world did Amanda keep finding these creatures? The kid was clearly a stray animal magnet.

"Listen, honey, I'm not able to help a wild robin—" She stopped abruptly when the bird suddenly broke loose and flew off, darting around the interior of the clinic.

"Oh!" Amanda exclaimed with joy. "Robby is feeling better!"

Ally ducked as the robin dive-bombed her. The wing was definitely not entirely up to par, but the bird was compensating for the injury with short flights. The robin darted into an open exam room.

Wrong way! She wanted the bird out of the clinic, not in.

"Amanda, open the clinic door so we can flush Robby out." The sooner the better. Bad enough she still smelled like cat diarrhea, she didn't want to add bird droppings to the list.

Ally went into the exam room and tried to convince Robby to go outside. The bird was sitting up on top of the supply cabinet. Ally waved her arms. "Shoo, shoo!"

The bird flapped its wings and took off, flying around the room and landing right back on the top of the cabinet. Probably figured it was the safest place to be.

Now what? She wasn't necessarily an expert on birds. Sure, they covered parakeets, parrots, canaries, and cockatoos in her veterinary studies. Those were all birds that were more likely to become a pet.

Not robins.

Should she run up and get Roxy? Or Pepper? Ally rather liked the idea of getting the cat and dog to chase the bird.

"Shoo! Get out!" Ally jumped up and down, flapping her arms at Robby.

"What's going on?"

The deep familiar voice made Ally pause her efforts to de-bird the room. She wanted to crawl into the corner to hide, but of course she didn't. A glance over her shoulder confirmed Noah Jorgenson was standing there, watching her with a wide grin on his face.

If he called her Hot Pants . . . She ground her teeth together with an effort. Knowing she looked like a crazy woman, and smelled worse, she snapped. "I'm trying to get a bird out of here. Why, is that a crime?"

"No crime," Noah agreed, the silly grin still on his face. That he was enjoying this at her expense only upset her more.

"If you're not here to help, then get out." She knew she sounded crabby, but this wasn't her finest hour. "Shoo!" she yelled, almost as loud as Gramps had shouted into the phone. Robby dive-bombed her again, and then whizzed past Noah into the main part of the clinic. Relieved, she hurried after it, closing the exam room door behind her.

Ignoring Noah, she quickly closed the other exam room door and the one to the grooming suite. Glancing around, she found Robby flying from one corner of the room to the other, clearly trying to find the way out.

Didn't the bird have instincts on where to find the outdoors? Would bringing Pepper down to chase it make things better? Or worse?

"Here, Robby, this way," Amanda crooned. As if mesmerized by her voice, the robin darted past Ally's head, dropped a poop right in front of her, then flew outside.

For a long moment, no one spoke. Risking a glance at Noah, she could see he was trying really hard not to laugh.

And why not? Despite her early annoyance, even she could see the humor in the situation.

She sighed and smiled. Noah bust out laughing, and Gramps joined in. Soon they were all laughing uncontrollably, to the point that Ally had tears in her eyes.

Why did this kind of thing always happen to her? The chemistry lab, the fire ants, and now this. She had no idea, but managed to pull herself together by taking several deep breaths. She stepped around the bird mess toward the little girl.

"Thanks, Amanda, but you'd better go find your mom so she won't worry about you."

"Okay. Bye!" The little girl disappeared back to who knows where she'd come from.

With any luck, the kid wouldn't be back with a new stray anytime soon.

Noah sniffed the air. "Something smells . . ." He stopped when she glared at him. "Like a veterinary clinic."

"Good one," Gramps agreed with a wink.

Ally shook her head and opened the exam room doors. She found the cleaning supplies and went to work on the bird mess. "Did you come for a reason?" She asked Noah.

"Yes, I was going to give you an update on our investigation into the vandalism to your door."

"Did you find the person responsible?" She could only hope.

"Not yet," Noah admitted.

"Then what's the update?" She tried not to show the extent of her frustration.

Gramps cleared his throat loudly. "Uh, Ally? The door guy is here."

She sat back on her heels, and looked up at the man standing there, regarding her plastic-covered shattered glass door. Considering yesterday she was rambling around in the clinic by herself, today the place felt downright crowded.

He was early, but who was she to argue? She rose to her feet and set the cleaning supplies on the counter so she could join the door guy. She hoped he didn't smell the cat diarrhea on her shoes. "Hello, I'm Dr. Winter. I appreciate you coming to fix this for me."

"Sure, no problem." The guy was roughly the same age she was but looked at Noah and Gramps with frank curiosity. "Name's Max Joiner. I'll get to work replacing the door, if that's okay."

"Perfect." She turned back to Noah, ignoring Gramps' keen gaze. "Thanks for stopping by, Detective. I appreciate the update."

"You didn't let me finish," Noah protested. "We did get a couple of witnesses who heard the crash, followed by the sound of a loud car."

"Like one with a muffler problem?" Gramps asked.

Noah lifted a brow and nodded. "Yes, exactly like that." He turned toward Ally. "I came here to ask if you know of anyone who drives a car that needs a new muffler."

That information made her frown. Had she heard the loud muffler? She couldn't remember. Had Noah heard it? He'd been here inside the clinic when the door had been hit by the rock.

Max Joiner had taken the old broken door down and carried it away. She looked through the open space to the street outside but couldn't come up with anything.

"No, sorry." Ally shrugged. "I've only been back a few weeks now, I don't know that many people, especially not their cars."

Noah turned to Gramps. "What about you, Mr. Winter? You've lived in Willow Bluff for a long time. Any particular car you remember as having a bad muffler?"

Gramps stroked his chin, looking thoughtful. "I can't think of one at the moment," he admitted. "But it's something for us to keep an ear out for, isn't it? If I come across a car with a bad muffler, I'll be sure to let you know."

Noah frowned. "Mr. Winter, as I told Ally, it's best that you both leave the investigation to me."

Gramps sat back in the chair and folded his arms across his chest. "I'm disappointed, Detective. I'd think you'd be interested to know what we've found out about a couple of Marty's clients."

The corner of Noah's left eye began to twitch, and this time it was Ally who had to swallow the urge to laugh. Poor Noah was no match for her grandfather.

"Okay, Mr. Winter," Noah said, the words seemingly forced through a tight throat. "You're right. I *would* like to know what you've found out."

Gramps' blue eyes gleamed and he nodded. "Tell you what, Detective. I'll tell you what I've found out if you reciprocate. I'm sure you've already interviewed Marty's clients."

The muscle twitched faster now, and Ally found herself stepping forward, putting herself between Noah and Gramps while holding her breath. At some point, Noah was going to lose his temper with her grandfather.

Not that she could entirely blame him. Gramps was walking along the edge and enjoying himself far too much.

"Just to be clear, Mr. Winter, interfering with a police investigation is a crime," Noah continued. His tone was even, but his green eyes flashed fire. "I don't care how old you are, if you continue to interfere, I won't hesitate to lock you up for the duration of this investigation."

"Enough," Ally said, shooting a warning look at her grandfather. Max Joiner brought in a new glass door, fitting it onto the hinges. He was clearly listening, so she lowered her voice. "Tell him what we learned, Gramps. Or I will."

Gramps sighed and filled Noah in on how Ginny White had initially denied paying Marty Shawlin anything, but then eventually confessed to forking over sixteen hundred dollars. Ally watched Noah's gaze carefully, and once again caught a flicker of surprise in the green depths.

"Anything else?" Noah persisted when Gramps fell silent.

"No, that's all." Ally winced as the door guy hammered the pin through the hinge. "Right, Gramps?"

"Right."

Noah gave a curt nod, spun on his heel, and edged past Max through the open doorway.

She let out a heavy sigh. "You better behave, Gramps. I don't think Noah was joking about locking you up."

"Bah." Gramps flashed an impish grin. "Your detective is too smart for that. Look at all the help we're giving him. Trust me, he'll keep coming around to find out what we know."

"Gramps." Ally stared at him. What could she do? Other than keep protecting him.

"Oh, and by the way, Kevin Kuhn is bringing Lola in for her shots at two o'clock tomorrow afternoon." His eyes gleamed with keen anticipation as he rubbed his hands together. "I can't wait."

She sighed. "You know tomorrow is Saturday, right?"

Gramps shrugged. "Who cares? A client is a client, you can't be picky about that. And the clock on this investigation is ticking."

* * *

Ally ran upstairs to change her clothes and her shoes. The shoes went straight out to the garbage, but she tossed her clothes and lab coat into the laundry before grabbing Roxy and returning to the clinic. Roxy greeted Gramps as if he were a long-lost friend.

Of course, now that she looked and smelled better, Noah was nowhere to be found.

"Did you decide on lunch?" She'd given Gramps the takeout menu for the sandwich shop two doors down.

"Meatball sub," Gramps said. "You know, if we asked Harriet nicely, I'm sure she'd make us lunch. No need for us to eat out every day."

"Maybe tomorrow." Ally used the phone to order their meals, then glanced at Gramps. "Are you sure you're up to working here two days in a row?"

"Ha! Trying to keep me away from Kevin Kuhn, are you?"

"No, Gramps, I just don't want you to get worn down. Let me know if your hip starts bothering you. I can always run you back to the Legacy House."

"Hurts whether I'm here or there, so what's the difference?" He sounded cranky about it. "I'm fine staying in the clinic with you."

She should have known he wouldn't want to leave early. "Okay, listen, I'm going to pick up our lunch so that we're finished by the time the Westie arrives." She hesitated, not liking the idea of leaving Gramps here on his own. "You want to walk with me?"

"Nah. But take Roxy with you."

"I'll take her out for a quick bathroom break but leave her here with you for protection." She liked that idea better. Roxy wouldn't let anything happen to Gramps.

As Ally walked into the sandwich shop, she nearly collided with a man in his forties with brown hair. "Oops, sorry," she said, trying to step around him.

"You're the new vet, right?" The guy asked.

Was he a pet owner? She smiled brightly. "Yes, I'm Dr. Ally Winter, it's nice to meet you."

"Eli White, heard my wife brought Taffy in for a visit."

"Yes, she did." Her smile dimmed. Hopefully, Ginny hadn't told him what a disaster that was. She eyed him curiously, wondering just how upset Eli White was about paying Marty Shawlin sixteen hundred dollars.

Was Gramps right about that being motive for murder?

"What happened to your door?" Eli asked. "I noticed it's being repaired."

Nothing stayed secret in a small town for very long. "Oh, someone threw a rock at it, but it's no big deal. I'm sure it was an accident." She didn't want the townsfolk to think she was being targeted on purpose. "Well, it was nice meeting you, Mr. White," she said, edging around him.

"Nice to meet you, too, Ally."

She frowned as she watched Eli White walk outside. He didn't seem upset about the money he'd paid Marty, so maybe they should cross the Whites off the suspect list. The way he'd used her first name seemed a bit familiar, but then again, this was Willow Bluff, not Madison.

Whatever. She picked up the sandwiches and returned to Gramps. They ate behind the counter. The phone didn't ring the entire time, but Ally decided to keep thinking positive. After all, she'd already had more business in the past few days than she'd had in the previous few weeks.

The only setback being the stupid vandalism.

Ally was grateful Max Joiner had the door repaired by the time Sophie, the Westie, arrived for her grooming appointment. The Westie was too cute for words, and very well behaved. Ally had grown up with a Westie and had a soft spot for them. If only all her four-legged clients were as sweet as Sophie.

Ms. Christman, Sophie's mom, was pleased with how Sophie looked and rewarded Ally with a very generous tip.

Despite the minor incidents of Taffy's untimely diarrhea and the frightened robin, this was turning out to be a fantastic day.

Ally took her phone upstairs to the apartment and coaxed Pepper out of hiding. She managed to get a decent picture of Pepper and went back downstairs to make flyers.

She didn't mind hanging around with Roxy and Pepper, but if the cat was truly lost, it was only right she attempt to find the owner.

Leaving Roxy with Gramps, she went out and put up several flyers with Pepper's photo big enough to grab someone's attention:

Found black and white speckled female cat, going by name Pepper. Call 555-2798 to claim her.

Feeling better, she returned to the clinic. Gramps was still seated behind the counter with Roxy at his side.

"Any more appointments?" She tried not to sound overly hopeful.

"Nah." Gramps shot her a look. "But the word is getting out, right? That Westie woman sang your praises."

"Thanks, Gramps." He was sweet to be so supportive. She bent over to stroke Roxy's fur. "Ready to call it a night?"

"Sure." Gramps winced as he stood and reached for his cane. "We could stop at the Lakeview Café, see if anyone interesting might be around."

"No, Gramps." She wasn't falling for that trick. "Harriet will have dinner waiting for you, and besides, we already have Kevin Kuhn coming in tomorrow with Lola. No need to go out and find the other clients."

"Hrmph." Gramps scowled. "Remember what I said about the first forty-eight hours? If we don't find some leads soon, we'll never solve this thing."

She decided not to remind him that they weren't the ones responsible for solving Marty's murder, Noah was. "I know, but hopefully we'll get something good from Kevin Kuhn tomorrow."

"We better." He looked annoyed. "We need to help that detective of yours find the murderer, and soon."

It was all she could do not to roll her eyes. It was wrong to encourage him, yet it was clear Gramps had a way of making people open up to him. He'd proved that with Anita Jones and again with Ginny White. It might be interesting to see how Gramps did interrogating a man. She felt certain his charm wouldn't work the same way on Kevin Kuhn that it seemed to with women.

Still, she didn't have the energy to spend the evening wandering around Willow Bluff looking for the rest of Marty's clients.

How was it possible her grandfather had more energy than she did?

Gramps and Roxy stood outside as Ally locked her new door. As they headed down toward Ally's ancient Honda, Roxy began to growl.

A shiver snaked down Ally's spine. She glanced around apprehensively, wondering what Roxy had scented. "What's wrong, girl?"

The low, deep growling continued. Ally slowed to a stop, trying to identify what on earth had caught the boxer's attention.

It was your average summer Friday in Willow Bluff. Nothing at all out of the ordinary.

When they reached her car, Ally helped Gramps in first, then put Roxy in the back. Sweeping her gaze over the street one last time, she still didn't see anything amiss. A couple of cops were standing in front of the sandwich shop, and a young family complete with two adorable twin boys were devouring ice cream cones.

"It's okay, girl," she soothed the animal. "Nothing for you to growl at."

But as she headed down Main Street, she recognized Officer Roberts as one of the two officers standing in front of the sandwich shop. Remembering how Roxy had growled that first day outside Marty's house when Noah and Roberts had shown up made her wonder.

Did Roxy have some reason to dislike Officer Roberts? Or was she just being overly protective?

Hard to know for sure. She was about to mention it to Gramps but then thought better of it.

Gramps would have them heading right back to Officer Roberts to test her theory.

And she wasn't up for more sleuthing today.

"Are you going to stay for dinner?" Gramps asked.

Lunch was hours ago, but she shook her head. "I don't think so, Gramps. I need to get back to Pepper."

"You don't know what you're missing. Harriet is a great cook."

She sent him a sideways glance. "But not as good as Granny."

"True, very true." Gramps suddenly straightened in his seat. "Wait, hear that?"

"No, what?" She had no idea what had garnered his attention.

"The muffler." Gramps twisted in his seat, craning his neck to glance around. They were approaching the Legacy House, and there wasn't exactly bumper to bumper traffic. "Take a right turn up ahead, let's see if we can find it."

"Really?" She eyed him warily, wondering if those true crime novels had messed with his head. "Maybe it was your imagination."

"Turn, turn!" He shouted.

She turned. And listened.

Nothing.

Neither of them spoke as she drove down one street and the next, looking for a car with a loud muffler that was likely nothing more than Gramps' imagination.

"Where did it go?" Gramps muttered as he peered out the window.

"You know, there's probably more than one car in town that could use a new muffler."

"I know what I heard," Gramps repeated stubbornly. "And I'm telling you, the murderer could be living somewhere close by."

Great, that was just peachy.

She didn't want to think of Marty Shawlin's murderer living within a few blocks of Gramps.

What if her grandfather became his or her next victim?

Chapter Ten

Ally spent another restless night and couldn't blame Pepper and Roxy for her lack of sleep.

The blame rested solely on Gramps and his persistence in being involved in Marty Shawlin's murder investigation.

After taking Roxy outside, she poured herself a large cup of coffee and tried to think of a way to deter Gramps from coming into the clinic that day. Normally she closed early on Saturdays, but if there was work to be done, she'd gladly stay open. She rather liked having company, and heaven knew Gramps had a way of convincing people to talk. Ginny White was proof of that. Deep down, she felt Gramps might have the best chance of getting key information from Kevin Kuhn.

But all of that aside, ensuring Gramps' safety was the most important thing.

The real question? Was Gramps safer at the clinic with her? Or back at the Legacy House with the widows?

She sighed. Likely here with her, where she could watch over him.

Okay, then. She showered and did her best to tame her unruly hair into some semblance of control. As she headed downstairs with Roxy at her side, she thought about calling Noah before heading out to pick up Gramps.

Noah needed to know that Gramps had heard a car with a loud muffler near the Legacy House. For all she knew, Noah might have a suspect in mind, one who might live near Gramps and the widows.

She had Noah's personal cell number, but hesitated before calling. She had no idea what hours Noah worked—did he have Saturdays off? With a shrug, she punched in his number.

It rang several times before Noah's husky voice invited her to leave a message. She did, mentioning the fact that she had more information related to the case.

She didn't want Noah to think she was calling for a personal reason.

"Come on, Roxy. Let's go get Gramps." She clipped a leash to Roxy's collar and led the animal out back where she'd left her ancient Honda. Hoping she wasn't making a huge mistake, she backed out of the parking lot and headed toward the Legacy House.

As she drove, she kept a sharp eye, and ear, out for a vehicle with a bad muffler. Had Gramps imagined the sound? Despite his age, and spending time in Vietnam, he had decent hearing.

If Gramps had been wrong, he likely wouldn't admit it. Not that it was her problem to solve. She'd pass the information along to Noah and leave it at that.

Too bad Gramps likely wouldn't do the same.

When Ally knocked on the door, Harriet answered, wearing another of her brightly flowered dresses. She smiled broadly. "Ally! Oscar is still eating, why don't you come in and have some breakfast?"

"Oh, well," she hesitated, glancing back at Roxy, who was stuck in the crated section of the car, her nose pressed against the wire bars as if begging to be let free from prison. "I can't leave Roxy out here alone."

Harriet glared at the dog, then sighed. "Fine, bring her inside, then. But you have to clean up any mess she makes."

"She's well trained and won't make a mess, but of course I'd clean it up if she did. Thanks, Harriet." On impulse she gave the older woman a hug then went back to get Roxy.

By the time Ally had taken a seat at the table, with Roxy stretched out at her feet, her plate was heaped with bacon, eggs, and hash brown potatoes. She thought only for a second about her tight jeans, then dove in. "Delish, Harriet."

The woman beamed, even though she seemed to keep a wary eye on Roxy. "Thank you, Ally. Oh, and I made lunch for you and Oscar today."

Despite the pinch in her waistband, she nodded. "Great, thanks."

"Ally, dear, don't forget my offer," Lydia said sweetly. "I'd love to come down to the clinic to help out." She leaned forward, resting her hand on Ally's arm. "I used to be a receptionist at my husband's dental office, you know."

"Really?" Ally chewed and swallowed a mouthful of eggs that tasted better than anything she'd ever cooked. "I'll work out a schedule for next week, to have you and Gramps take turns at the reception desk."

"I would like that, dear." Lydia patted Ally's arm.

"Who said I can't work every day to help my own granddaughter?" Gramps asked with a frown. "Doesn't take any skill to sit and answer the phone."

"And what am I, chopped liver?" Tillie asked. "I offered to help Ally before Oscar decided to join the fun."

Oh boy. Ally stalled by eating a piece of bacon. Then frowned when she caught Gramps slipping Roxy a piece as well.

The WBWs were driving her crazy. If she had the money, she'd hire someone to be a veterinary tech/receptionist. But at the moment, that was impossible. When Lydia opened her mouth to argue, Ally held up a hand. "Enough. Stop fighting, or I won't have any of you come down to help." She narrowed her gaze at her grandfather. "Even you, Gramps."

The three elders fell silent, leaving Harriet to preen a bit, as she had no intention of coming to the veterinary clinic. Her prowess was clearly in the kitchen. "More bacon, Ally?" Harriet asked. "Oscar, would you like more coffee?"

Since Gramps had finished eating, Ally quickly finished the last of her eggs and pushed her plate away. "No more, thanks, Harriet. Everything was delicious." She stood and gave Roxy's leash a gentle tug, encouraging the animal to come out from beneath the table. Roxy licked her chops and looked adoringly up at her, making Ally smile. "Ready to go, Gramps?"

"Yep." Gramps reached for his cane, and she helped him stand.

"Don't forget your lunch!" Harriet handed Ally a grocery bag filled with plates of food. No chance of going hungry with Harriet around.

"Thanks, Harriet. And I appreciate breakfast, too." Ally led the way outside, pausing so Roxy could water the grass in a few spots before jumping into the open hatch of her Honda.

Five minutes later, they were on the road. Gramps held the grocery bag of food on his lap, while Roxy once again had her nose pressed against the wire in a meager attempt to sniff the contents.

"Are you really going to let Lydia come in, instead of me?" Gramps sent her a wounded look.

"I love you, Gramps. If you want to come next week, that's fine. But you can't just come on days when you get to interrogate my clients." She eyed him sternly. "I'm running a business."

"I know that." He averted his gaze and sighed. "Fine, you made your point. But tomorrow I'm thinking of heading over to the Lakefront Café."

It was all she could do not to pound her forehead against the steering wheel. "To do what, Gramps?"

"To have lunch with Rosie Malone." He smiled broadly, then suddenly said, "There it is again!"

"What? Where?" It took a moment for her to realize he was referring to a car with a loud muffler. She caught a glimpse of a car turning a corner, followed by a truck. "Which one? The red Chevy truck?"

"Huh?" Gramps peered out his window. "I thought it might be the green Ford sedan."

After a moment both vehicles disappeared from view. Ally was going too fast to safely turn in an attempt to follow. "Did you get a license plate?"

Gramps sighed. "No. I must be slipping."

"You're not slipping, Gramps." She made a mental note to add both vehicles as possibilities when Noah returned her call.

As if on cue her cell phone rang. She glanced at the screen. Not Noah, but the clinic. She pulled over to the side of the road and answered. "This is Dr. Winter."

"Taffy has been having diarrhea all night," Ginny White wailed. "Something terrible is wrong with her."

"Bring her into the clinic, I'll be happy to check her out."

"Okay, but could the shot you gave cause this?" There was an underlying note of suspicious accusation in Ginny's tone.

"Not likely, especially since she had diarrhea seconds after I vaccinated her. That wasn't enough time for the medication to get into her bloodstream."

"Okay." Ginny didn't sound convinced. "Although I'm not happy about needing to have my carpets cleaned."

Gee, welcome to the world of owning a pet. But she kept that thought to herself. "See you soon." Ally disconnected from the line and drove to the clinic. She helped Gramps get settled in behind the counter, then went over to wipe down an exam room. Finally, she pulled her curly hair back into a bushy ponytail, pulled a long plastic gown over her clothes, and slipped booties over her boring black flats.

This time, she was ready for whatever Taffy might dish out.

*   *   *

The poor cat was severely dehydrated, but after a quarter liter of fluid, the feline perked up.

Ginny White was chatting with Gramps when Ally came out of the back area, where she'd given Taffy's infusion. Ally hoped her grandfather wasn't interrogating the woman again.

"Ally, your detective is on his way in," Gramps said by way of greeting. He frowned. "You didn't mention leaving him a message."

She suppressed a sigh. Of course Noah had returned her call while she was tied up with Taffy. Ignoring Gramps, she turned to Ginny. "Taffy seems much better now that I've given her some fluids, but do you have any idea what she might have gotten into?"

"Nothing," Ginny insisted.

"Well, you may want to take a good look around your home just in case. Most of the time when we see animals with bad diarrhea or vomiting it's because they ate something that is toxic to them. House plants, pesticides, anything can be harmful to our pets."

Ginny's mouth made a round O. "I used ant spray in the kitchen, there were dozens of them everywhere."

"Ah, that must have been it, then." Ally was glad to have found the source of the problem. "Taffy can go home with you, but make sure you wash the areas you sprayed."

"I will, thank you."

"Let's get Taffy into her carrier." Ally knew full well it was a two-person job.

Once Taffy was safely in her carrier, she shed the plastic gown and shoe coverings, both of which thankfully hadn't been needed, before following Ginny back to the desk. Ginny paid her fee and left just as Noah came in.

"Hi, Ally. Mr. Winter." Noah eyed Gramps warily. "You mentioned having new information for me?"

Gramps had? Ally raised a brow in surprise. She'd left that message, but her grandfather must have said something as well.

Gramps cleared his throat. "Yeah, well, twice now Ally and I heard a car with a loud muffler not too far from the Legacy House."

"Do you have a description of the car?"

"There are two possibilities," Ally said. "A green Ford sedan and a red Chevy truck."

Gramps scowled. "Either of those belong to one of your suspects?"

Thankfully, Noah's left eye didn't twitch this time. He gave Gramps a bland stare. "Thanks for letting me know about the vehicles that might have muffler problems. Anything else you care to share?"

"Who, me?" Gramps looked downright angelic.

Ally sent Gramps an exasperated look before addressing Noah. "We just wanted you to know about the vehicles, Noah. I'm worried because we've twice heard the loud-sounding vehicle near the Legacy House." She hesitated, then added, "I would appreciate if you would have your officers cruise by the area more often to keep an eye on Gramps."

To her surprise, Noah nodded in agreement. "I can do that. And I'll look into both vehicles, see if I can narrow down which one has a loud muffler." Noah looked directly at Gramps. "Just remember there are many cars in the Willow Bluff area and that there could be more than one needing a new muffler."

"I know that," Gramps replied stiffly. "But you should be glad I'm staying on top of things. If one of those two vehicles leads to the murder suspect, you'll have me to thank for helping you crack the case."

"Trust me, I'll make sure *Dateline* gives you the credit you deserve," Noah shot back.

Ally coughed to hide her smile. "Thanks, Noah. Any other progress on the case?"

"You mean your vandalized door?" Noah shook his head and reached into the pocket of his dress slacks. "No, but I brought the police report along, so you can give it to your insurance company."

He handed her the report, his warm smile making her toes curl. "Figured I'd save you a trip to the station."

"Oh, uh, thanks." She hoped he didn't notice her blush. What was it about Noah doing nice things that made her feel special, as if he might be attempting to make up for the relentless teasing he'd inflicted during their high school days? She'd had a crush on him back then, and this newer version of Noah was much harder to resist.

She gave herself a mental shake. Enough. Time to get a grip on reality. She was through with men, and that included the handsome, attractive, and possibly—but no way to know for sure—single Noah.

"Well, if you don't have anything else for me, I need to go." Noah shot one last look at Gramps. "I hate to say it, but I'm sure I'll be seeing both of you soon."

Ally didn't know what to say in response, so she simply watched silently as Noah left.

"I'm not sure I like that detective of yours, Ally." Gramps scowled and drummed his fingers on the counter. "He's got an attitude."

Before she could point out that Gramps happened to have an attitude of his own, a very thin young woman about her own age came into the clinic. She was dressed in worn clothes, her hair limp. Her skin was so pale, Ally wondered if she'd spent time in a hospital—or a jail cell. "Hi, um, are you Dr. Ally Winter?"

"Yes, how can I help you?" The woman didn't have a pet with her, so Ally wasn't sure what she needed. Other than maybe a job. "I'm sorry, but I don't have any open positions at the moment." Heaven knew she had her hands full with Gramps and the WBWs.

"No, it's just, I saw the flyer. The black and white speckled cat? The one you're calling Pepper? Her name is actually Spot and she belongs to me. My name is Lilly Johnson."

"Oh!" Ally smiled broadly. "I'm so glad you came by to claim her, Lilly. Wait here, she's upstairs."

The woman twisted her hands together. "Thanks."

Ally bypassed Roxy to head up to her apartment. Pepper was in her favorite spot on the sofa, basking in the sun. "Time to go home. Your mommy came to get you, Pep—uh, Spot." In Ally's mind, Spot was a dog's name, but who was she to argue?

The cat's owner had been found, which was all that mattered.

She carried the cat downstairs. When Pepper/Spot saw Lilly, she leaped from Ally's arms, leaving scratches in her wake, landing on the floor and then climbing up Lilly's holey jeans. Lilly nuzzled Spot, who began to purr.

Aww, how sweet. Ally was happy to see the two of them together. Roxy stayed near Gramps without barking, maybe sensing the cat wasn't going to be a thorn in her side much longer.

"A little girl by the name of Amanda brought her in," Ally said, when Lilly didn't say anything more. "Pepper, I mean Spot was having an asthma attack."

Lilly winced and nodded. "I know, she gets them sometimes, but I didn't have enough money to refill her medication."

"Well, I'll give you what's left of the bottle I used, okay?" Ally pulled the medication from her pocket and handed it over. No point in trying to get payment for services rendered. "Take care of Spot, okay?"

"I will. Thanks." Lilly turned and left.

The rest of the day passed slowly. Harriet had sent a feast—chicken salad with homemade bread, fruit, and apple pie for dessert. Ally tried to refrain from sampling the pie, but when Gramps dug in, she couldn't help herself.

Yum.

"You have another vaccination scheduled for Monday," Gramps informed her when they'd finished putting their leftovers away. "And another grooming, too."

"I'll take what I can get," Ally said, meaning it. "No job too small, remember?"

A ghost of a smile creased Gramps' features. "I remember."

She took Roxy for a walk up and down Main Street, removing Pepper's flyers along the way. She kept an eye out for anything unusual, but the town was busy with what appeared to be summer tourists who loved spending weekends up here.

She saw Rosie Malone heading toward the library and thought about her grandfather's plan to have lunch with the woman tomorrow. Since she knew very well it wasn't a date, she made a mental note to tag along.

When she returned to the clinic, she put Roxy upstairs in the apartment and waited a full hour for Kevin Kuhn and Lola.

"You're Dr. Winter?" Kevin asked in surprise. He was of average height, with nondescript brown hair. "I never went to a woman vet before."

Another fan of Dr. Greg Hanson? She did her best to keep smiling. "I'm a good vet, I promise." She dropped to her knees, offering a hand to the dachshund. "Hey, Lola, how are you today?"

Lola sniffed her fingers and wagged her tail.

"You're adorable, yes you are." She glanced up at Kevin. "Let's use exam room number two, okay?"

Kevin followed her into the exam room, and lifted Lola onto the stainless steel table. He spoke reassuringly to Lola, stroking her fur as Ally gave the vaccination. Lola was very well behaved, for which Ally was grateful.

She didn't want to believe someone who appeared to care about animals the way Kevin Kuhn seemed to love his Lola, could possibly be involved in murder.

Then again, she preferred pets over people, so why not a killer having the same perspective?

When they were finished, she handed Kevin the invoice. As she swiped his credit card, Gramps started in.

"Mr. Kuhn? My name is Oscar Winter. I'm wondering if you would share your opinion of the work Marty Shawlin did for you. To be honest, I had some issues with him, myself."

Kevin looked surprised, then glared at Gramps. "I'm not telling you anything! In fact, I never want to hear that man's name ever again, you understand me?" Kevin pounded the counter with his fist. "Never!"

"Oh, but—" Gramps tried, but Kuhn wasn't having it.

Kevin snatched his credit card from Ally's fingers and tugged on Lola's leash, the clinic door shutting loudly behind him.

Chapter Eleven

"Well, that was a bust." Ally glanced at Gramps. "Guess your charm only works with the ladies."

"He was very upset," Gramps agreed, his gaze thoughtful. "Too upset, if you ask me."

"Being upset doesn't make you a murderer."

"No, but it proves he has a temper." Gramps gave a curt nod. "Yes, a temper like that could easily get out of control, causing a man to do something in haste that he might later regret." He paused, then added, "Like smashing a glass and marble globe against a man's skull."

The memory of Marty Shawlin's dead body made her stomach clench. But more concerning was that her grandfather wasn't going to give up on his theory of the murderer being one of Marty's less-than-satisfied clients.

"Well, it was worth an attempt to talk with Mr. Kuhn." Secretly relieved her grandfather hadn't gotten any more information about the murder, she took off her lab coat and hung it on a coat stand near the door. "Ready to head back to the Legacy House? I need to grab Roxy."

Gramps didn't answer right away, and she could practically see thoughts tumbling through his head. This was what happened when you spent too much time watching *Dateline* and reading true crime novels.

Then again, maybe heading over to the library now would serve two purposes. Gramps could talk to Rosie Malone (while she listened in) to get that interrogation done and pick up another book to keep him busy for the next few days.

Her grandfather needed to distance himself from Marty Shawlin's murder. Before anything else happened.

"Gramps, how about we stop at the library before heading back to the Legacy House?" She smiled. "I don't have any other clients coming in, so we have plenty of time before dinner."

That got Gramps' attention. "To talk to Rosie?"

"Yes," she admitted reluctantly. "And to see if that true crime book she mentioned has come in yet. Might be a better read than *The Evil Within*." Even the thought of Gramps reading a book with that title made her shiver.

"You got yourself a deal." Gramps stood and reached for his cane. "Let's take Roxy with us."

"Speaking of Roxy, we forgot to bring her down to check her reaction to Kevin Kuhn," Ally noted. She ran upstairs and brought the boxer back down by Gramps. "You know who came into the house that day, don't you, girl?"

"You're right," Gramps agreed. "Although she didn't growl at Ginny White, but we didn't have her husband here, either. I hate to say it, but could be the killer was someone that Marty knew well and had been there several times before. If so, would Roxy still growl? I mean, I know dogs can be smart, but to make that distinction? Maybe not."

"It's a good point," Ally conceded. "I met Eli White at the sandwich shop but didn't have Roxy with me then, either. It could be that I'm putting too much faith in Roxy's ability to hunt down the killer."

"Probably," Gramps agreed.

Roxy licked her cheek, making her laugh. "Okay, let's go for a walk."

The boxer jumped around in excitement, making it difficult for Ally to clip the leash to her collar. Making sure Gramps was steady on his feet, they made their way outside.

She locked the door and hooked her arm with her grandfather's. "Lean on me, Gramps."

"Bah," he muttered. "I'm telling you Ally, getting old ain't for sissies."

"I know, Gramps." She truly felt bad that he'd broken his hip and now needed a cane or a walker to get around. At Christmas he'd been full of energy and now they were walking slowly toward the library. "If you want to wait here, I can get the car."

"Doc insists walking is good for me." The scowl etched on his features belied his words. "Course it's not his hip that hurts like a son of a gun."

Ally wisely held her tongue. The summer breeze coming in off Lake Michigan was nice, the temperature in the high seventies. She'd missed being here amidst the laid-back atmosphere of Willow Bluff.

Madison has lakes, too, but the beauty was marred, at least in her opinion, with crazy busy traffic, all roads leading to the state capital.

"It's really nice here, Gramps." She shot him a sideways glance. "I'm glad I came back."

"Me too," Gramps admitted. "I think your detective likes having you around as well."

"Gramps," she said on a sigh. "You have to stop calling him my detective. We never dated. And even if Noah was interested—which he isn't—I'm not. I have enough to worry about between keeping my business going and watching over you." *And the widows*, she silently added.

"No reason to watch over me," Gramps shot back.

"Sure, you keep telling yourself that." She gestured toward the Lakeview Café. "You want to stop and rest for a minute before going to the library?"

"No, I want to talk to Rosie."

"All right." They made their way past the café and into the municipal building. The air-conditioning seemed to be on high, making her shiver.

Rosie Malone was at her usual spot behind the circulation desk, chatting with patrons and checking out books. She looked more somber today, and Gramps stayed back until the desk was free.

"Oscar!" Rosie greeted him with a sad smile, then frowned when she saw the dog. "Oh, I'm sorry, but pets aren't allowed in the library."

"He's my comfort dog," Gramps said with a wink. "And we won't be long."

Rosie sighed. "Okay, fine. Did you come to pick up the book I set aside for you?"

"Yep." There was no denying Gramps was interested in the new book. He leaned closer, lowering his voice. "I need to talk to you about Marty Shawlin. Did you know he came to see me and Lydia at the Legacy House the day before he died?"

Rosie's eyes widened as she took Gramps' library card and quickly checked out the book. Rosie's voice was low. "I didn't know that. How awful for you, Oscar. I'm sure that must have been a terrible shock to hear he'd been . . . murdered."

Gramps nodded sagely. "I wanted to talk to you, Rosie, but I heard Marty met with you, too."

"What?" Rosie looked momentarily flustered. "My goodness, Oscar, where did you hear something like that? I never spoke to Marty Shawlin."

Ally tried to keep her expression neutral, but deep down she had the distinct sense the sweet librarian was lying through her teeth.

"Are you sure?" Gramps persisted. "He must have called to try to set up a meeting."

"Never." Rosie pushed his book toward him. "I don't know where you're getting your information, Oscar, but it's inaccurate." She pursed her lips with disapproval. "I never spoke to Mr. Shawlin or met him in person. He never came into the library, at least not while I was on duty."

"I see." Gramps stared at Rosie for a long moment before reaching for his book. "Well, I guess I have wrong information then." He looked chagrined. "Here I was hoping to have someone to talk to about the services he wanted to provide."

Something flickered across Rosie's gaze but was gone so quickly Ally figured she may have imagined it. "I'm sorry, Oscar, but I can't help you. I don't know anything about what Mr. Shawlin was up to." She stepped back from the counter. "If you'll excuse me, I have books that need to be reshelved."

"Sure, sure. Sorry to keep you." Gramps lifted the book. "Thanks again for looking out for me, Rosie. I appreciate it."

"Take care, Oscar." Rosie's smile did not reach her eyes. And there was absolutely no flirtation in her manner toward Gramps, the way there had been the other day.

Interesting, Ally thought, as she took the book from Gramps and tucked it under her arm. Still holding onto Roxy's leash with her left hand, she linked her right arm with Gramps.

Neither one of them said anything until they were back out on Main Street.

"You need to call your detective, Ally. Rosie is lying about seeing Marty." His blue eyes gleamed with satisfaction. "This is definitely a lead that needs to be followed up on."

"We might think she's lying, Gramps, but there's no way to know for sure," Ally argued. "You know as well as I do that Noah will interview all of Marty's actual and potential clients. I'm sure he'll be able to figure out whether or not Rosie Malone had an appointment with Marty."

"It's not just that," Gramps said with a flash of irritation. "I know she's lying."

"What do you mean?"

"Marty did come to the library." Gramps thumped his cane on the ground for emphasis. "I saw him there. In fact, I saw him standing at that very desk talking to Rosie." He looked thoughtful. "I believe it was the Wednesday before his murder."

Ally stared at him in surprise. "I don't understand, why would she lie about something like that? I mean having him come to the library is no big secret. Lots of people come to the library."

"Exactly." Gramps' tone rang with satisfaction. "Don't you see? I made her nervous, so she lied. About something silly. Which tells me she has something to hide."

"Okay, but I'm still not sure how this helps solve the case." Ally gave Roxy's leash a tug when the dog wandered too close to the edge of the road. "Seriously, Gramps, at this point we have more suspects with a grudge against Marty Shawlin than we know what to do with."

"True," Gramps agreed. "But I'm fairly certain only one of them is capable of murder." He paused, then added, "We just need to figure out which one."

*   *   *

Ally's phone rang as they returned to the clinic. "This is Dr. Winter, may I help you?"

"I think there's something wrong with my Lab, Patsy." a female voice said. "Her abdomen is bloated. Do you think she has a tumor?"

"I can't say what might be the cause of her belly distention until I examine her." Ally glanced at her watch. So much for closing early on a Saturday. "If you'd like to bring Patsy in, I'm happy to take a look."

"Well," the owner seemed to hesitate.

"If she's eating well, and is having no trouble going to the bathroom, we can wait until Monday." Ally tucked the phone in the crook of her shoulder and unlocked the door, so Gramps could take a seat inside. "Whatever works better for you."

"I guess I'll bring Patsy now, then. You're—uh, still open, right? I mean, you're not charging me extra because it's an emergency?"

"I'm still open," Ally assured her. She set Gramps' book on the counter and reached for paper and pencil. "What's your name and number?"

"Wendy Granger." Wendy rattled off her phone number.

"Thanks, I'll see you and Patsy soon, then." Ally disconnected from the line and looked at Gramps. "I can't believe how many clients I've seen in the past few days. Business is really starting to perk up, Gramps."

"I'm glad." Gramps grinned. "I told you it would take some time, but soon you'll have more four-legged patients than you'll know what to do with."

Ally nodded, starting to believe he was right. It made her think about possibly hiring a vet tech, then reminded herself not to go crazy yet. After all, she still had to pay her insurance deductible for the damaged door.

Wendy Granger arrived five minutes later. She was an older woman with graying hair and she gazed down at Patsy, a pretty yellow Lab, with clear devotion. "Oh, dear, I really hope Patsy doesn't have a tumor."

"She's young, maybe two or three years old," Ally observed, bending over to greet the Lab. "How long have you had her?"

"Since she was a puppy." Wendy beamed. "Patsy is such a good dog."

"I'm sure." Patsy sniffed her hand and wagged her tail. "Let's get her into an exam room so I can take a look."

Ally led them into the first exam room, and helped Wendy get the Lab up on the stainless steel table. Ally started with looking at the Lab's eyes, ears, and mouth, then moved to her belly.

It didn't take but a second to understand what was causing the animal's distention. "Ms. Granger, didn't you get Patsy spayed?"

"Oh, well, I meant to." She flushed and looked embarrassed. "I just didn't have time. But it's okay, she's never out of my sight."

Ally bit her lip to keep from smiling. "Patsy isn't sick, Ms. Granger, she's pregnant. About four or five weeks along."

"Pregnant!" The woman's expression was horrified. "But—that's impossible!"

"I assure you it's not." Ally stroked a hand over the Lab's fur. "Patsy will likely deliver her pups in the next few weeks."

"But—who's the father?"

Again, it was difficult not to smile. "You must have a dog that lives nearby who is also not neutered." The bane of a veterinarian's existence. "Once Patsy delivers her pups, you may want to make an appointment with me to perform surgery so this doesn't happen again."

Ms. Granger looked upset. "I don't know anything about dealing with puppies."

"Patsy will know what to do. And of course, I'm available to help as needed. There are also library books and plenty of information on the computer if you want to read up before the big event."

"I guess I'll go to the library." She lifted Patsy off the table and onto the floor. "Thanks, Dr. Winter."

"You're welcome." Ally followed her out. "Tell you what, Ms. Granger. I won't charge you anything for examining Patsy today if you promise to bring her in to be neutered a few months after she delivers her pups."

The woman's expression turned grateful. "I'd appreciate that, thanks."

"What was that about?" Gramps asked. "I'm not sure you should be giving away your services for free. First that cat and now this."

"The dog is fine, just pregnant." Ally waved her hand. "I can't charge for that. Besides, it's more important that we take care of any future litters. I'm already worried these mixed-breed pups may not find good homes."

"True." Gramps grinned. "I'd take one, just to watch Harriet have a conniption fit."

Ally shook her head, hoping he was just teasing. "Let's go, Gramps."

"Good timing," Gramps said. "We'll arrive just in time for dinner."

Ally shouldn't have been hungry, but the idea of eating more of Harriet's cooking was enticing. She made a last-minute decision not to bring Roxy along, just in case she ended up staying.

Besides, with Pepper/Spot now with her rightful owner, Roxy would have the apartment to herself. Ally took the boxer upstairs, told her to behave, then went back down to meet Gramps.

The drive to the Legacy House didn't take long. There was no sign, or sound, of a vehicle with a bad muffler, either. She helped Gramps inside, frowning a bit at how tired he seemed to be.

Working two days in a row at the clinic and walking to and from the library might have been a bit too much for him.

"Hi, Ally, Oscar." Harriet beamed at them. "Did you enjoy your lunch?"

"It was amazing, Harriet," Ally told her. "We brought back the leftovers. I have to tell you, that was best lunch I've had since coming back to town."

"I'm not surprised." Harriet apparently wasn't modest when it came to her own cooking. "Come in, both of you. Dinner will be ready shortly."

"Oh, I really shouldn't stay," Ally said, even though her mouth was watering from the delicious scent of Italian food coming from the kitchen.

"I've made lasagna, complete with homemade garlic bread." Harriet preened. "There's plenty for you, Ally."

"Okay." She knew she should have tried harder to resist, but homemade garlic bread sounded incredible. She hoped she wouldn't have to unbutton her jeans after dinner.

"So what time will you be coming by on Monday to pick me up," Lydia asked with a smile. "I'm so looking forward to helping you in the clinic, Ally."

"Nine o'clock too early?"

"I'll be ready."

Lydia's excitement was sweet, but Ally suspected that, like Gramps, the long days would tire Lydia out. Thankfully, they'd all have Sunday off. She'd have to come up with a better schedule next week. Maybe having the widows—Gramps, Lydia, and Tillie—each work one day, Monday, Wednesday, and Friday, wouldn't be too hard on them.

After dinner, and after Ally had been forced to undo the top button on her jeans, Lydia showed off her knitting project while Tillie suckered her into a game of cribbage.

It was late and dark by the time Ally headed for home. It was one of the best Saturday nights she'd spent in a long time, but she battled a wave of guilt as she thought of Roxy being alone for that long.

Bright lights came up fast behind her, making her hold up her hand against the glare. Why did people insist on driving with their high beams on?

The lights were close. Too close. She frowned and squinted, trying to see what kind of vehicle it was. Something high, she guessed a truck or maybe an SUV.

Slam!

Her ancient Honda jolted beneath the pressure of being rear-ended. Ally fought to control the steering wheel, doing her best to stay on the road.

The lights grew brighter, and she knew the vehicle was going to hit her again. She abruptly swerved onto the other side of the road, landing partially in the ditch.

The lights swept past and quickly disappeared. She unclenched her fingers from the steering wheel, grateful the air bags hadn't deployed.

Ignoring the pain in her neck, she fumbled for her phone and called Noah's personal cell phone.

"Ally? What's wrong?"

"A truck or SUV hit me from behind," she said in a quivering voice. "Sent me into the ditch."

"I'll be right there. Don't move, unless you smell gas."

She felt disoriented but sniffed the air. "No gas."

"I'll be right there," Noah repeated.

Tears pricked Ally's eyes as she realized she'd been targeted. Hit on purpose. Because of the murder?

Why else?

The only good thing? Gramps and Roxy hadn't been in the car with her.

Chapter Twelve

Noah's comment about smelling gas, and remembering how car explosions were often replayed on television, sent Ally stumbling from the vehicle. She made sure she had her phone and her keys, the two most important items.

Goosebumps rippled along her skin, despite the warm summer air. She rubbed her hands up and down her arms while watching the road, hoping the driver of the truck or SUV that had struck her hadn't decided to turn around to finish the job.

Gramps' words echoed in her mind.

We just need to figure out which one of them is capable of murder.

Everything seemed so surreal. First the rock striking her door and now this. The first could easily be explained away as a prank.

But not running her off the road. No, that had been a cruel and deliberate act.

A set of headlights made her stomach clench with fear a split second before she noticed the flashing red light on the dashboard.

Noah.

She took a deep breath and squared her shoulders, determined to stay strong. Noah's dark SUV came to a jarring stop, and he immediately jumped from the car and hurried toward her.

"Ally?" The concern in his tone was impossible to ignore.

"I—I'm all right." Except she really wasn't.

Noah put a hand on her shoulder, and the warmth of his fingers made her long to throw herself into his arms. "Your car is on the wrong side of the road."

"I—I did that on purpose." She couldn't seem to speak normally. "T—to avoid being hit a second time."

"A second time? Are you sure?" Noah searched her gaze in the darkness.

"I'm sure."

"Ally." The care in his tone was surprising, but even more so was his abrupt embrace. "I'm so glad you weren't seriously hurt."

"Me too." Her voice was muffled against his shirt, and she couldn't help but cling to him, absorbing his strength. His woodsy aftershave made her dizzy, or maybe it was being rear-ended. Either way, she wanted to burrow closer.

When she was a teenager, she'd fantasized about going out with him.

This was better than anything she could have imagined back then.

She would have stayed in his arms forever, but he gently eased them apart, peering at her with a frown.

"Sure you're okay? I can call an ambulance."

"No need, I'm fine." She didn't mention the soreness in her neck, because no way was she going to the hospital. They didn't do anything for whiplash anyway, did they? "But I'm worried about my car. The air bags didn't deploy, but I'm not sure if I damaged something along the bottom or not."

The thought of adding another insurance deductible to her balance sheet, in addition to her property claim, almost made her burst into tears.

"Why don't we have it towed and checked out, just to be sure. Did you see the driver?" Noah asked. "Or can you describe the car?"

"No and no." She battled a wave of helpless frustration. "The driver had their high beams on, probably trying to blind me." She thought back to when she'd noticed the vehicle coming up behind her. "The car was close, really close, and the headlights were square, not round. Oh, and they were high, like from a truck or SUV."

"Good memory," Noah said with admiration. "I can see you've inherited your grandfather's keen observation skills."

"For all the good it will do," she said, secretly pleased with his kind words. "It was too dark to see the vehicle color, make, or model."

"Square headlights can help me narrow that down," Noah assured her. "Anything else you remember?"

"No." She sighed and looked at her car. From here it looked fine, the tires were good, no dents from what she could see. The hatch worked, which was important for carting Roxy around.

The ancient Honda was old, with over a hundred thousand miles on it, but the car had been a very dependable ride.

She hoped and prayed she wouldn't have to buy a replacement.

"Let me call that tow truck, we'll want to examine your car more closely to see if there's any paint transfer from the vehicle that hit you. And I'll drive you home." Noah must have sensed her despair. "You'll have to call your insurance company on Monday morning."

"Yeah, while I still have one," she muttered glumly. "At the rate I'm making claims, I'm pretty sure they'll drop me like a hot potato."

"This crash wasn't your fault," Noah reminded her. "And there may not even be much damage."

She grimaced. "Maybe not, but unless you find who did this, and who threw the rock at my door, all the repairs are the responsibility of my insurance."

"I'll find the person responsible." Noah's tone rang with confidence.

She wanted to believe him—after all, he was a detective. And she felt certain he was good at his job.

But she secretly feared the murderer might get away with it.

"Come on, Ally." Noah took her hand and led her toward his SUV. He opened the passenger door for her, and she felt certain he would have lifted her up into the seat if she hadn't gotten in under her own power.

Noah slid behind the wheel, then executed a U-turn to take her back into town. "I forgot to ask, where's Roxy?"

"I left her behind, thankfully." She shivered. "Mostly because I knew Harriet would invite me to stay for dinner, and she doesn't like dogs."

"Harriet?" His expression cleared. "Oh yes, one of the widows your grandfather shares a home with."

"Harriet's the cook, Tillie plays cribbage and poker, and Lydia—the one you spoke to about the meeting with Marty Shawlin—knits."

"And your grandfather solves crimes."

"Not really," Ally protested, thinking that he hadn't solved any crime—*yet*. "He watches too much television and reads too many true crime novels, which isn't the worst hobby on the planet." Although she would have given anything for Gramps to pick up a new hobby. Didn't people his age like to play horseshoes? Maybe watch a little golf? Go bowling?

Something safe?

"Hmm." Noah glanced at her. "I'm going to be honest with you. I'm really worried about you and your grandfather, Ally. What happened back there?" He jerked his thumb toward where they'd left her Honda. "That was another warning, a much stronger and dangerous one, telling you to stop asking questions about Marty's murder."

"Yeah, don't need to be a rocket scientist to figure that out," she said dryly. "And what can I do? Besides hogtie Gramps to his bedroom? It's not my fault he fancies himself some sort of amateur sleuth, and no matter what I say, he seems determined to help you solve the case."

It was too dark to see, but she suspected the muscle at the corner of his left eye had begun to twitch again. "I don't need his help, or yours."

Noah pulled over and parked in front of her clinic. She pushed open the door, then glanced back at him. "You don't need or want our help? Fine. Then hurry up and solve this thing, before anyone else gets hurt."

She stepped away from the vehicle and slammed the door, feeling better after venting her frustration. Using her key, she unlocked the clinic door and went inside. Roxy immediately began to bark.

"I'm coming, girl." The poor dog had been left alone longer than Ally had intended, so she hurried up the stairs, and was nearly bowled over by Roxy's enthusiastic greeting.

"Aw, it's good to see you, too. Yes, it is." She lavished the boxer with attention, then found the dog's leash. Ally led her down the stairs and outside. Noah's SUV was gone, and she let out a heavy sigh.

"Tell me this, Roxy, why can't men be more like dogs?"

Roxy didn't answer.

* * *

Nothing much happened in Willow Bluff on Sundays, and that particular Sunday was no exception. Ally left a message with her insurance company, figuring she wouldn't hear anything until the following day but was surprised when her agent called her back.

"You were rear-ended and run off the road." The agent's deadpan voice made it clear he didn't believe her.

"Yes. I notified the police, and they're looking into it."

"I see." Clearly, he didn't. "I'll need a copy of the police report. And I need to know how much damage was done to the car."

"There may not be much damage," she said, hoping fervently that was true. "The air bag didn't deploy, and the tires seemed okay."

"Are you sure you didn't swerve to avoid a deer?"

"Positive." She held onto her temper with an effort. "I'll get a copy of the police report as soon as possible, okay?"

"I can't wait." The agent clicked off without saying anything more.

Idiot. She'd never once gotten so much as a speeding ticket, why would she suddenly lose control of her car? She blew out a heavy sigh and hoped Noah's team found paint transfer or something that would prove she hadn't done this to herself.

The last thing she needed was to go from Hot Pants to Calamity Jane. Then again, she might already have.

She left a message on Noah's work number about needing the police report. No more calling his personal number. She needed to keep a casually friendly relationship between them.

The day passed by slowly. Roxy kept her company, and she found herself wondering if Marty's ex-wife, Sheila Young, would be willing to sell her the dog.

After all, the woman didn't sound very enthusiastic about coming to pick up the animal.

"It's you and me today, Rox." Ally smoothed her hand over her golden-brown fur. "Just you and me."

Funny how quickly she'd gotten used to having someone sharing the clinic with her. She wasn't open for routine hours on Sundays but decided to clean as usual just in case she received another emergency call. She'd had two in the past week, which was promising. After cleaning the exam rooms, she made her way over to the desk where Gramps had worked the past two days.

He'd mentioned something about a grooming appointment and another immunization scheduled for Monday. She searched the area, looking for his notes. She found one, but it was nearly impossible to read.

"T-po at ten." She frowned, looked at Roxy. "Any idea what t-po means?"

Roxy cocked her head, her gaze inquisitive.

She reached for the phone and dialed Gramps' cell phone. Even though she tried to be prepared, she winced when his voice boomed in her ear.

"HELLO?"

"Gramps, it's me, Ally. Do I have a grooming appointment at ten tomorrow morning?"

"ALLY! I'M GLAD YOU CALLED! ARE YOU OKAY?"

She dropped her forehead into her free hand, thinking that her headache from being jostled in the car would be much better without his yelling. She'd called earlier to let Lydia know she didn't have a car and wouldn't be able to pick her up to work at the clinic on Monday. The widow had wasted no time in filling Gramps in on the news. "I'm fine, Gramps. Noah drove me home, and he's working the case."

"GOOD! I'M GLAD YOUR DETECTIVE WAS THERE FOR YOU."

"Gramps, please don't yell. I called because you wrote something on a note, the letter T and a hyphen then the letters P O. What does that mean?"

There was a moment of blessed silence as he tried to remember. "TOY POODLE. SOME WOMAN WANTS YOU TO GROOM HER TOY POODLE."

Gee, why didn't she think of that? "Okay, thanks Gramps. Didn't you also say something about a dog coming in for shots?"

"DID I? CAN'T REMEMBER."

Great. She rubbed her temple harder. "Okay, never mind. You're going to stay at home with the Willow Bluff Widows, today, right? I think we could all use a day of rest."

"I WILL. I'LL CALL YOU BACK IF I REMEMBER WHAT KIND OF DOG IS COMING IN FOR SHOTS."

"Thanks, Gramps, but there's no need. I'll figure it out. Take care and we'll talk later."

"BYE, ALLY."

The rest of the day passed without a single call from anyone needing veterinary services.

She also didn't hear from Noah, but no doubt he had the day off as well. For all she knew, he might be spending some time with a girlfriend. Something she could ask Erica about, yet even the mere thought was far more depressing than it should be.

All the more reason to keep him firmly in the friend zone.

* * *

The next morning, her neck didn't hurt any worse than the day before, which gave her hope the rest of the day would turn out to be a good one as well. After checking her clinic supplies and inventory, she settled behind the desk.

No car meant having none of the widows working as a receptionist. Since she'd be alone with four-legged patients coming in, she took Roxy upstairs.

"Behave, okay?" She gave the dog a good rub, wondering if Sheila Young would show up to pick up Roxy later today as promised.

Ally kinda hoped she wouldn't.

Back at the desk, she went through her client list, searching for poodles. There were several, but two of them didn't specify if they were toy or standard-sized poodles.

A short, rather rotund man entered her clinic at just before ten, holding a white toy poodle in his arms. He glanced around with a frown, maybe wondering where the rest of her patients were. He introduced himself. "I'm Jerry Stevens, and this is Vivian."

"Hello, I'm Dr. Ally Winter." She smiled warmly at him. "I'm also a certified groomer. What would you like me to do with Vivian today?"

He gave her an odd look. "Do with her? I thought you left me a message about her needing shots?"

"Oh, of course!" Ally inwardly winced, vaguely remembering all the phone calls she'd made the previous week. So much had happened since then she'd completely forgotten. "I'm so sorry for the confusion, I have a poodle coming in to be groomed, as well. Yes, Vivian needs her shots. Why don't you take her into exam room number one and I'll be with you in a moment?"

Jerry hesitated, and she wouldn't have blamed him if he'd turned and left, but he didn't. He carried Vivian into the exam room, while she frantically searched her files.

There it was, Vivian, the poodle, belonged to Josie and Jerry Stevens. Again, no notes left behind by Dr. Greg Hanson. She quickly added toy poodle to the description, then went into the back to get the vaccinations that she needed.

Upon entering the exam room she found Vivian on the stainless steel table, visibly trembling.

"Oh, you poor thing," Ally murmured. She offered Vivian a treat, but the dog turned her nose up, leaving it untouched. Better to get this over and done with in a hurry. "Okay, please hold her still, Mr. Stevens. This won't take but a moment."

"I know." He looked so sad as he held onto Vivian. "This is why I tend to put off these appointments."

"Understandable." She quickly gave the injection, causing Vivian to yelp and try to scramble away. Her owner held her firmly, which was a good thing. "Maybe now she'll take the treat?"

Jerry picked it up and offered it to the dog. Vivian daintily took the treat. "She only eats out of my hand," he confessed.

"I see." It was strange, but not the worst thing she'd seen pet owners do.

Jerry Stevens paid cash for his visit and, when he left, Ally found herself wondering if she really had a grooming appointment scheduled for later that day.

Or if Gramps had gotten that mixed up too?

When her door opened again thirty minutes later, she expected another client, but her visitor was Noah.

Her heart gave a betraying flutter. She tried not to look happy to see him. "Hey."

"You look better this morning."

She lifted a brow. "Thanks, I think." She tried not to remember how good he'd smelled Saturday night. "Did you get my message about the police report? My insurance company needs it for their records."

"No, I've been out at the garage checking out your car." His expression turned serious. "They found a very small dark red paint chip embedded in the rear bumper of your car."

Red paint. She thought back to the loud muffler incident. "The red Chevy truck."

"Actually, the mechanic is leaning toward a GMC truck because of the square lights." His green gaze caught hers. "Could the red truck you and your grandfather saw the other day have been a GMC?"

"I—maybe." She tried to remember. "But I honestly thought for sure the logo was Chevy. I know what that looks like, because my former fiancé had one."

Noah nodded. "Just thought I'd ask. Could be the red truck you saw wasn't the one that ran into you."

The blood drained from her face. "You mean, there's more than one murderer?"

"No, I just meant that some people put loud mufflers on their trucks on purpose. Even though they *are* considered illegal." He shrugged. "The one you heard while driving your grandfather may not have anything to do with the case."

The tension eased. "That's true. I guess I never thought of that."

"It's just one possibility." He glanced around. "Made your grandfather stay home?"

"Yes. Although I don't have a car to pick him or any of the widows up anyway. I've walked over there plenty of times, but Gramps and the women can't walk that far. He broke his hip back in April and hasn't been the same since, at least physically." She grinned. "His brain is sharp as ever."

"Can't argue with that," Noah conceded. "But you know, I can help run errands for you if necessary."

Her jaw dropped, and she wondered if she'd imagined his offer. "Um, well, thanks. Does that mean the car needs repairs?"

"There was some minor damage to the undercarriage that they're repairing now. Shouldn't be too bad, though." His intense green gaze seemed to look deep into her soul. It was all she could do not to squirm under his scrutiny. "I don't mind helping you out."

She had no idea what to say. Was Noah simply being friendly? Or, like their brief embrace last night, the beginning of something more?

She didn't want something more. Did she?

No. Been there, done that. Would have rather had the T-shirt.

"Thanks." She needed desperately to get back on a professional footing. The case. They'd only met because of Marty's murder. "Oh, I—um, should probably mention we spoke to both Kevin Kuhn and Rosie Malone, yesterday." She frowned. "I mean, on Saturday."

"Why am I not surprised?" Noah drawled, a flash of annoyance crossing his features. Oddly enough, she found it easier to deal with him when he was irritated with her. "Find out anything interesting?"

"Not really. Kevin Kuhn has a temper." She recounted the brief conversation Gramps had initiated with the man, only to be cut off and yelled at while he pounded his fist on the counter.

Noah didn't give anything away, simply nodding encouragingly. "And what about Rosie Malone?"

"She denied being one of Marty's clients, the same way Anita Jones did. Oh, and she lied about talking to Marty."

"Lied how?" Noah asked.

"Rosie specifically said she hadn't spoken to Marty and claimed he never even so much as came to the library while she was there. But Gramps said he saw Marty there at the library, talking to Rosie the Wednesday before Marty's murder. He thinks she's lying to cover it up."

Noah lifted a brow. "And what do you think?"

"I believe Gramps. The first time I saw Rosie and Gramps interact, she flirted with him. After he brought up Marty Shawlin, she couldn't wait to get rid of us."

Noah nodded thoughtfully, this time keeping his thoughts well hidden.

"Are we right about her lying?" Ally pressed. "I'm sure you've probably talked to all of Marty's clients by now."

"I can't talk about the case with you, Ally. Is there anything else?" Noah asked.

"No, that's all." She frowned. "Does that mean you're not going to tell me if any of Marty's clients drives a red GMC truck?"

"Ally." She took it as a good sign that his left eye wasn't twitching. Maybe only Gramps caused that level of frustration. "When I arrest the person responsible for Marty's murder, and the attack against you, I promise to let you know."

Before she could ask any more questions, Noah turned to leave. At the door he hesitated and looked back at her.

"Call me anytime, Ally."

The door closed behind him and she let out a breath, knowing that calling wouldn't be a good idea.

Noah was nothing but trouble.

Chapter Thirteen

Ally's grooming appointment showed up just after lunch and also turned out to be a poodle. Only this wasn't a little dog but a large standard poodle. His name was Domino, and he had bushy, curly black hair.

Ally fingered her own out-of-control dark curls, instantly feeling a kindship with the big guy.

"I'll be here in two hours to pick him up, if that's okay?" The harried owner was a woman roughly Ally's own age by the name of Kayla Benton. "I have to drive the twins to swimming lessons, which takes an hour, then we'll swing by to pick up Domino."

Twins? Ally couldn't imagine but smiled and took Domino's leash. "Not a problem. Did you want me to do the typical poodle cut for him?"

"No need, just shave him down for the summer." Kayla waved a hand. "Poor thing gets so hot out in the sun with all that thick black fur." She handed Ally the leash, then bent over and scratched Domino behind the ears. "Behave, Domino, and I'll see you soon."

Kayla whirled and quickly left. Ally told herself that not having a husband and kids didn't mean she was missing out. Even if

Noah's handsome face flashed in her mind. Didn't she prefer furry companions to people anyway?

Yes, she did.

"Hey, Domino, let's get you washed and clipped, shall we?" The dog was a good four inches taller than Roxy, and he wagged his tail, sniffing around the clinic with interest.

Good thing she'd left Roxy upstairs. Although a little socialization might be good for both of them.

"You want to meet Roxy? Do you?" She led Domino into the grooming station. "I bet Roxy would like to meet you, too."

Domino was easygoing. He tolerated the clipping without a problem but balked at being washed. By the time she'd finished, she was just as wet as he was and needed to change her clothes.

At least Domino smelled great. And as she had with Clover, she tied a red, white, and blue bandana around his neck.

She placed Domino in a kennel while she went up to change and to get Roxy. The boxer instantly headed toward Domino's crate.

"Behave," she warned as she released Domino.

The two dogs sniffed each other for long moments before beginning to play, chasing each other around the clinic. It was cute, until they tipped over the desk chair behind the counter. Ally ran over in an attempt to grab it, before it hit the window.

Too late. The chair hit the window with a loud whack. She froze, a slight crack forming in the glass. She let out a sigh when the one-inch crack didn't get any larger, the rest of the window remaining intact.

The relief was short-lived as the dogs continued to go at each other, barking, jumping, spinning, and nipping. Roxy latched onto the Fourth of July bandana and wouldn't let go, backing up in an attempt to take Domino down.

"Roxy! No! Stop!"

Roxy was having too much fun to listen. Domino growled and struggled to get away. The bandana ripped in half, sending Roxy flying backward.

Ally lunged for Roxy's collar. "Roxy, no!"

Domino ran in a circle, then came back for more. Ally moved to put herself between the dogs, dragging Roxy toward the kennel.

Domino jumped up and placed his paws on her back. She shrugged him off, managed to thrust Roxy into the crate, then grabbed the poodle's collar.

"I guess socialization was a bad idea," she muttered, taking Domino back to the grooming room. After giving him yet another wash, getting just as drenched as the first time, she replaced the bandana, then stepped back, placing placed her hands on her hips.

"Okay, here's the deal. We're not telling your mommy about this, understand?"

Domino lolled his tongue out, turning his head toward the direction of Roxy's crate.

"No way. Not happening." She eyed the poodle sternly. Taking him by the leash, she went back to the desk and pulled up her client list. Domino wasn't due for his shots for another two months, so she added his name along with Kayla Benton's to her reminder list.

Having two clients in one day was far better than nothing.

By the time Kayla arrived with the twin girls to pick up Domino, Ally had the clinic spotless. The only sign of the doggy disaster was the small crack in the window.

"Thanks, Dr. Winter," Kayla said, taking Domino's leash. The twin girls both smothered Domino in hugs, but the poodle continued to look back in the direction of Roxy's kennel. "Bridgit, don't strangle Domino with his scarf. Brooke, don't try to chew on it, either."

"See you in a few months for his vaccinations," Ally said with a smile.

"Sounds good. Come on, Bridgit, Brooke. Let's go."

Ally waited until the trio and the dog were safe in the car before she freed Roxy from her crate. Roxy instantly dashed around the clinic, picking up Domino's scent, despite Ally having cleaned the place, and trotting along to find him.

"You were naughty," she scolded. "If you want friends to come over, you need to learn to play nice."

Roxy's stubby tail waved back and forth, the boxer clearly not understanding what Ally's problem was.

Her phone rang and she tripped over Roxy while making a grab for it. "Furry Friends Veterinary Clinic, this is Dr. Winter, may I help you?"

"Ally? It's Noah. Just wanted to let you know the police report on your car is finished."

"That's great news, thanks. I'll be there in a few minutes to get it."

"The report will be at the front desk," Noah said.

She shouldn't have been disappointed he wouldn't be there to personally hand it over. "Perfect, thanks again." Disconnecting from the call, she looked at Roxy. "You don't deserve a reward, but you'll get one anyway. Ready to go for a W-A-L-K?"

The police station wasn't far. It was located within the municipal building that also housed the library and the Willow Bluff City Hall.

"So Roxy, what do you think of Gramps' list of suspects?" She paused as the dog took a moment to sniff the base of a tree. "I wonder if Noah has found out whether or not the Whites or Kevin Kuhn own a GMC truck."

Roxy moved on from that tree to the next.

"I know the killer could be a woman, but I'm having trouble picturing Ginny White, Rosie Malone, or Anita Jones ramming my car into the ditch. Throwing a rock at the clinic? Sure, but rear-ending me on purpose?" She shook her head. "Can't visualize that one."

Roxy glanced up at her for a moment, then headed for the next tree. It occurred to Ally that Domino might have marked them all with his scent.

Thank goodness both animals were neutered. Although boxer and standard poodle pups would be adorable.

"And what about that other couple Anita mentioned. What was their name?" She had to think back to the evening she and Gramps had visited her. "The Ryersons. I never did find their names in the clinic's client list."

Not her problem, but she found herself wondering about them anyway. They must live and work somewhere within Willow Bluff.

If she asked Noah, would he tell her anything about them? Doubtful. And she was staying out of the investigation, to protect herself and her grandfather.

The Lakefront Café was hopping with business, all the outside tables full of patrons. Ally kept Roxy close and gave the café a wide berth as they made their way to the police station.

Two squads were parked outside the police station entrance. She wondered how many officers were on duty at any given time. If two squads were here, she hoped there were at least several others driving around the town, keeping an eye out for criminals.

Like the one who had run her off the road.

Ally tightened her grip on Roxy's leash and headed inside.

A woman wearing a police uniform sat behind the front desk, her name tag identifying her as Barbara Sommers. Behind her was a glass wall, through which Ally could see several cubicles. Two officers were seated next to each other, talking. The ones who should be out in the squads, she assumed.

Roxy began to growl, low in her throat. Ally frowned at her. "Behave."

"Dogs aren't allowed in here," Sommers said with a frown.

"I'm just here to pick up the police report Detective Jorgensen left for me."

"Take it and go, no dogs allowed." Sommers was like a broken record, and while Ally could understand the rule, it wasn't as if she didn't have control of Roxy's leash.

Previous encounter with Domino aside.

"Thanks." Roxy's growls deepened, and the glass wall must not have been soundproofed because one of the cops turned to stare at her.

Officer Roberts.

The flash of anger in his eyes had her taking a step back. Holding the police report in one hand, she tugged on the dog's leash with the other. "Come on, Roxy. Time to go."

Roxy's growls continued until they were once again outside the building.

Ally stared down at Roxy, who'd finally stopped growling. "What was that about? Something you don't like about Officer Roberts? Or maybe cops in general?"

Although Roxy hadn't growled at Noah, other than that first day. Maybe Roxy didn't like or was afraid of men. Except for Noah, Marty, and Gramps . . . nah, that theory didn't work either.

The crowd at the Lakeview Café had thinned a bit and the scent of food made her mouth water. She'd skipped lunch and only had ramen noodles in her cupboard for dinner.

She should have kept Harriet's lunch leftovers, rather than insisting on taking them back. Although after the lasagna dinner and homemade garlic bread, she'd decided to cut back on the carbs, so she could once again button her jeans.

The Lakeview Café had plenty of delicious salads, so she turned in that direction. Roxy sniffed at several of the patrons as they went up to the hostess stand, without growling at any of the men.

Interesting. Ally was tempted to call Noah to let him know about her theory of Officer Roberts possibly being the source of Roxy's growling, but managed to refrain.

She had no proof of Roberts being involved in anything nefarious. And why would a cop like Roberts have it in for Marty Shawlin?

Unless Roberts had been one of Marty's clients too?

But that didn't really make sense, either. Cops had good pensions, and Roberts looked to be in his forties, likely close enough to retire with full benefits. Why would he bother to meet with Marty about a will and a trust?

"Is this okay?" The hostess had shown Ally to a table way off to the side, some distance from the others. Because of Roxy? Maybe.

"Fine, thanks." Ally truly didn't mind being separated off to the side, as the seat gave her a perfect view of the entire patio seating area.

Roxy stretched out at her feet, seemingly content to hang out. Ally ordered a cobb salad and lemonade and wished her grandfather were there with her.

"He'd be interested to know that you growl at Officer Roberts," she confided to Roxy. Then she frowned as another thought struck her. "Maybe it's the uniform itself, not the cop wearing it. As a detective, Noah doesn't wear a uniform."

Roxy rested her head on the ground between her paws.

"You're not helping," Ally complained. She took her time eating her salad, thinking about the case.

And her car.

As much as she missed Gramps, she didn't want him anywhere near the crosshairs of danger, where she'd somehow ended up.

Lost in her thoughts, it took a minute for her to clue into the conversation drifting over from the table closest to her.

"The food at Gino's is much better than this stuff," a woman said with derision. "Helen's a great cook, not sure why they don't have her name on the door instead of her husband's."

"Gino's sounds better than Helen's," the other woman pointed out.

"They could have gone with Ryerson Family Restaurant."

Ryerson? Ally took a bite of her salad and glanced over to see who was talking. Two women she didn't know were seated at the table. Wait a minute, she straightened in her seat. She did know one of them, the pink suit of the real estate agent, the one with the beautiful straight blond hair. Amanda's mother. What was her name? Oh yes, Ellen Cartwright.

She'd seen a sign advertising Gino's Family Style Restaurant but it had never occurred to her that the owners of the restaurant were the Ryersons, who also happened to be potential clients of Marty.

"Hmm, sounds like it's time for me and Gramps to head out to Gino's for dinner, Roxy. Maybe even tomorrow night, if I have my car back by then. What do you think about that?"

Roxy perked her ears forward.

Ally was just paying the bill when Roxy lunged to her feet, once again growling low in her throat. Ally tucked the cash in the billfold and glanced around, expecting to see Officer Roberts nearby, as she began unwinding Roxy's leash from the arm of the chair. "What is it, girl?"

Woof! Woof! Woof!

Roxy's staccato barks made Ally jump to her feet. Too late! The boxer lunged forward, taking the chair with her as she continued barking.

Ally's feet tangled in the leash and the chair legs, sending her face first onto the pavement. She let out a muffled oomph, and managed, just barely, to catch herself with her palms, rather than adding bruises to her face.

"Roxy, sit!" She still had Roxy's leash wrapped around her foot. The boxer continued to bark like mad.

From her supine position it wasn't easy to see, but there was a flurry of activity off to the side. Ally caught a glimpse of two people—a man and a woman, she thought, hurrying away from the café.

"Roxy!" She yelled at the dog with the same volume Gramps used during his cell phone calls. "Sit!"

Roxy sat, the barks giving way to low growling. Ally pushed herself upright, untwisted the leash from her foot and the chair legs, and tried to ignore the restaurant patrons gaping at her.

"Come, Roxy." She took off in the same general direction the two diners had gone. Roxy was eager to go yet didn't keep up the growling, barking alarm that had caused the hoopla in the first place.

Reaching the sidewalk running along Main Street, Ally looked right and left, but couldn't see anything unusual. There were plenty of people strolling around, but none that reminded her of the couple who'd hurried away from the Lakefront Café.

Had they really left because of Roxy's barking? And if so, was it just because they didn't like dogs in general or more because they were afraid of Roxy in particular?

Was Officer Roberts one of them? Maybe he was off duty by now—it was six thirty in the evening—and planned to take his wife or girlfriend to dinner.

Until Roxy chased him off.

She fumbled for her phone and called Noah's cell. No way were both of these episodes of Roxy's growling and barking a coincidence.

"Ally? Are you okay?" Noah's deep voice sent shivers of aware-ness down her spine.

"Yes, mostly." She glanced at the open hole in her jeans, where her knee had scraped the concrete. "Listen, I need you to meet me here at the Lakeview Café."

"I can be there in five." A pause, then Noah added, "You're sure you're not hurt?"

"I'm okay, just a few more bruises." To add to the colorful assortment she was already sporting. "But I think Roxy knows who Marty's killer is."

Another long pause before Noah repeated, "Be there in five."

She paced the sidewalk with Roxy at her side until Noah arrived. As tempting as it was, she resisted the urge to throw her-self into his arms again.

His gaze took in her torn jeans and bleeding kneecap. "What happened this time?"

"Roxy leaped forward and started barking like crazy." She flushed. "It was my fault I fell, because I had the leash wrapped around the arm of the chair."

Noah's expression turned skeptical. "Dogs bark for all kinds of reasons. Not because they're tracking a killer."

"I think it was Officer Roberts."

Noah blinked then scowled. "And what makes you say that?"

"You don't like him very much, do you?"

He looked taken aback by her comment. Then his gaze turned thoughtful. "I guess you saw how irritated I was with him at the scene of Marty's murder."

She nodded. "He doesn't seem to like you, either."

"It's nothing, just an old cop that doesn't like to be shown up by a younger guy." Noah folded his arms across his chest. "So again, why do you think Officer Roberts is the killer?"

"Roxy doesn't like him." As soon as she said the words, she knew they sounded lame. "I mean, she growls anytime he's nearby and that's happened twice now that I know of, and if this last time was really him, then that's three times she's growled at Roberts." Noah didn't say anything, so she added, "I told you, Roxy was in her crate when Marty was murdered. Why wouldn't she know who was responsible?"

"Ally." He sighed. "I appreciate your concern over Roxy and her ability to find the killer, but this isn't helping."

"But if you just talk to Officer Roberts, see if he or anyone he knows personally met with Marty Shawlin before he died . . ."

"I can't make him talk to me," Noah interrupted. "And it's not like I can give a dog's growl as evidence to justify a search warrant."

Her shoulders slumped. "Okay, tell me this. Is Roberts married?"

"Divorced, no kids." Noah frowned. "His mother lives here in town, he does yard work for her."

"Aha! So it's possible his mother might have been one of Marty's clients. And wouldn't Roberts be upset if his mother had been swindled by Marty?"

Noah didn't respond, but she could tell the idea intrigued him.

Ally reached down to pet the boxer. "You're a good girl, Roxy. I just know you're going to help Noah crack this case."

"I told you, she's not a K-9 cop," Noah said testily. "Trust me, I'll find the murderer by using good old-fashioned detective work."

Before she could offer an apology, Noah stalked away, clearly unhappy with her.

She glanced at Roxy. "We'll find a way to help him, whether he likes it or not. Deal?"

Roxy wagged her stubby tail in agreement.

Chapter Fourteen

Ally woke up early on Tuesday morning to Roxy licking her face. "No, girl." She gently pushed the dog away and swiped at her cheek. Sitting up, she blinked and brought the clock into focus. "Roxy, it's barely six o'clock."

Roxy didn't care, she clearly wanted to go out. Granted it wasn't the dog's fault that Ally hadn't slept well. Last night, after Noah had walked away, she couldn't get his woodsy scent—or the rest of him for that matter—out of her head.

She took Roxy outside, remembering how Sheila Young, Marty's ex-wife, was supposed to have come last night to pick up Roxy. Had she missed the woman because she'd been at the Lakefront Café? Maybe, but Sheila hadn't called, either, so she highly doubted it.

Keeping Roxy wouldn't be a hardship, especially if Sheila was going to be mean to Roxy.

After she'd showered, changed, and eaten her requisite oatmeal for breakfast, she headed down to the clinic. There wasn't a single appointment scheduled for the day, and that was more than a little depressing.

Maybe having Gramps helping out as her receptionist had been her good luck charm. And if that was the case, she needed to get him back there, ASAP.

But she couldn't do that without a car.

She decided to call the garage for an update. She had the police report, but still no clue about the amount of damage that had been done.

"Good news," the mechanic said cheerily. "The repair estimate turned out to be just under a thousand dollars."

That was the good news? It was the amount of her deductible, which meant more money coming out of her bank account. *Peachy.* "Okay, when will the car be ready?"

"I can have it ready to go by noon as long as you give me the authorization to do the repairs."

"Yes, please do. Thanks." She disconnected and contacted her insurance agent to provide him the information. Now that she knew the repair would be on her dime, she figured he wouldn't need the police report.

Surprisingly, he asked for it anyway. She scanned and sent it to him, then glumly looked through her client list. There had to be another animal who was overdue for their vaccinations.

Ten minutes into her second round of reminder calls to those who hadn't responded the first time, a woman walked in carrying a schnauzer.

"Erica?" Ally recognized her old high school friend. She jumped out of her seat, smiling broadly. Roxy came too, sniffing at the schnauzer. "It's great to see you!"

"Hi, Ally." Erica grinned and hugged her. "I wanted to come sooner, but I had to wait until I could arrange for childcare to run errands."

"Childcare?" Ally belatedly saw the wedding ring. "You're married with kids? Congrats!"

"Yep. A five-year-old and a two-year-old." Erica blew out a breath. "It's nuts but I like it."

"And who's this?" Ally bent to pet the schnauzer.

"Tinker Bell, name courtesy of my five-year old daughter, LeAnn." Erica shook her head. "We call her Tink."

"Tink." The name and the dog clicked in her memory. "I called to remind you about Tink needing shots. I never even put Erica Kirby together with the Erica Logan I went to school with."

Erica waved her off. "It's fine, we haven't seen each other in a long time."

Ally nodded. "Since freshman year at University of Wisconsin Madison."

"I left and never came back." Erica shrugged. "I was never as smart as you, Ally."

"Don't say that, you're plenty smart. But college isn't for everyone."

"You're right about that. I like being a hairdresser." Erica eyed her wild curls. "I work three days a week at the Bluff Salon, if you're interested."

"This"—Ally tugged on her hair—"is hopeless. But I could use a trim." She smiled again, thrilled to have a friendly face in town. "Seriously, Erica, it's really good to see you again."

"Agreed." Erica gestured to Tink. "Ready to vaccinate her?"

"This way." Ally led the way to the first exam room. Roxy tried to follow, but Ally made her sit, and closed the door. "Did you marry anyone I know?" She thought back to their high school days. Her eyes widened in surprise as she remembered one of the football players who'd laughed at her the night of the fire ant incident. "Jim Kirby?"

Erica blushed and nodded. "Yes. Jim works for his dad's construction business." Her gaze turned uncertain. "I know I should have invited you to the wedding . . ."

"Don't be silly," Ally interrupted. "I totally understand. When I headed off to college, I thought I'd left Willow Bluff behind for good. But now?" She thought of her grandfather, the widows, and the quaint town. Marty's murder wasn't great, but everything else was. "I like it here and can't figure out why I was so eager to leave in the first place."

"Well, I'm sure some of your high school experiences didn't help much. Between the chemistry lab fire and the fire ants, people weren't exactly kind to you." Erica paused and added, "You know Noah Jorgenson also came back about four years ago. He and Jim have been hanging out some."

"I've seen Noah, he's a detective with the Willow Bluff police department." Ally was surprised to hear Noah had only been back four years. For some reason she'd gotten the impression he'd been here since high school or maybe after college. Since she didn't really want to talk about Noah, especially her jumbled feelings toward him, she patted the table. "Bring Tink up here and give me a minute to get the vaccinations."

Vaccinating the schnauzer didn't take long, and soon they were back in the main area of the clinic.

Erica handed over her credit card. "We should have lunch together to get caught up."

Ally felt a little guilty charging Erica for the vaccinations, but business was business, and she wouldn't expect free haircuts. "I'd love that, but it sounds like your schedule is worse than mine. Tell me what's best for you and I'll make it happen."

"Yeah." Erica blew out a sign. "My mother-in-law has the little monsters now and helps out while I'm at work. My shifts are short, Tuesdays and Thursdays from four to nine and Saturday mornings from eight to noon. I can do lunch either Saturday after work or Sunday."

"Weekends are fine. Like I said, I can work around your schedule." Ally waved a hand at the clinic. "As you can see, I'm not bursting at the seams with clients at the moment."

"Yeah, I've heard some of the ladies saying how much they miss Greg Hanson; apparently several of the more mature single women had their eyes set on snagging him." Erica grinned. "I get all the good gossip while doing hair."

"I bet you do." Ally knew she'd been right about Hanson getting friendly with the pet owners. She crossed over and gave Erica another hug. "Is this coming Saturday too soon to do lunch?"

"That's perfect." Erica returned her hug. "Can't wait. See you then. Come, Tink. We'd better get home so I can finish my errands. Bye, Ally."

"Bye." Ally held Roxy's collar as Erica and Tink left the clinic. Amazing to find out Erica had not only married one of the football players from high school but also had two small kids, a dog, and worked in a hair salon.

Erica had acted as if dropping out of college had made her something less, but Ally knew her friend had everything. A home, family, career.

Enough. No need to wallow in a pity party. She liked being a veterinarian. And was generally good at it.

Most of the time.

She scheduled another grooming appointment for the following day, then decided to head over to the garage to pick up her car. It was almost a mile out of town, so it would take her a while to walk there. Good thing Roxy needed the exercise.

As she clipped Roxy's leash to her color, she thought again how she'd heard nothing from Sheila Young. It was becoming clear the woman had no intention of picking Roxy up, ever.

"I don't want to do it, Roxy, but I guess I'll give her a call."

Roxy ignored her, standing at the door, waiting impatiently to go out.

She opened the door and walked right into Noah. Roxy greeted him as if he were a long-lost friend.

"Hey, girl," he said, rubbing his hands over her coat. "Miss me?"

Ally just barely resisted responding in the affirmative. On Roxy's behalf, of course. "I was just heading out to pick up my car. Tell me you have good news."

"Nothing new, sorry." Noah straightened. "But I came specifically to drive you over to pick up your car."

"You did?" Why-oh-why did he have to be so nice? It was hard enough to keep her distance; these sweet gestures were so not helping. They only made her like him more than she should.

"Figured you'd need a lift." He stepped back and gestured to his SUV. "Hop in."

"Okay, but I'm bringing Roxy."

He nodded. "Not a problem. But I thought Sheila Young was coming to pick her up?"

"Yeah, that was the plan. I get the impression she's not interested in keeping her." She glanced back at the boxer. "Which is too bad, she's a great dog."

"You going to keep Roxy?" He sent her a sidelong glance.

"If Sheila never shows up? Yeah." She grinned. "Although you might want to think about taking Roxy off my hands, because I think she'd be an amazing police dog."

"K-9s are highly trained dogs. And Roxy is great, but I don't think she'd pass the K-9 requirements."

"She's not that old, might not be too late for her to learn." Ally knew a little about police dogs—they'd cared for several of the Madison PD K-9s at their clinic. Mostly Tim had, but she'd done her fair share. "I ran into Erica Kirby today, she brought Tink in for shots."

Noah let out a low chuckle. "Jim was the one who told me that Hot Pants was back in town. Meaning you, of course."

"Stop!" She held up her hand. "Enough with the nickname. That was a long time ago."

"But it was still funny," Noah protested.

"To you, maybe," she muttered. "Those ant bites hurt."

"I'm sure. Anyway, it's crazy to see how domesticated Jim has become since marrying Erica. They have two kids, a boy and a girl."

"I know, and don't forget the schnauzer named Tink."

"Tinker Bell." He shook his head with a sigh. "Pathetic name, but LeAnn wasn't interested in any other name. I'm her godfather, by the way."

Her jaw dropped. "Really?"

"Yep." He pulled into the parking lot of the garage. "Do you need me to hang around until your car is ready?"

"No need." She quickly pushed open her door and jumped down. "I have Roxy for company."

His green gaze clung to hers for a long moment, and she had to force herself to look away. Was she blushing again? Probably. She opened the back door. "Come, Roxy. Thanks for the ride."

"See you later, Ally," Noah said as Ally shut the door and led Roxy away from the SUV.

Whew. She resisted the urge to fan herself.

Not if I see you first, she thought.

*   *   *

Ally's Honda didn't look any worse for wear. She put the repair costs on her credit card, hoping that a month from now her business would be booming and making the payment a piece of cake.

One could dream, right?

Instead of heading straight back to the clinic, she detoured to the Legacy House. She had Roxy with her, but Harriet would just have to get over it.

Especially since it was looking more and more like Roxy was going to be her dog from now on.

Instead of knocking at the door, she took Roxy by the leash around to the patio. As she'd hoped, Gramps and Tillie were outside playing cribbage.

"Hi, Ally." Gramps greeted her with a broad smile. "You must have your car back."

"Yep. It's running great."

"Good timing, you showing up. Tillie's been kicking my butt."

She embraced her grandfather, pressing a kiss to his temple. "Great to see you, too. But don't let me keep you from your game. Roxy, sit."

Roxy stretched out between Ally and Gramps as if knowing that was her spot.

"Oh, Oscar will use any excuse to get out of a losing game," Tillie teased. "You missed lunch, Ally, but I can see if Harriet has any leftovers."

Tempting, very tempting. "No thanks, I'm fine."

"Okay, then. How about some iced tea? I was going to get some for Oscar anyway."

"Sounds good, thanks, Tillie." Ally waited until the widow went inside to lean toward Gramps. "Listen, how would you like to go to Gino's for dinner?"

"Anything for you, Ally, but you know Harriet cooks for free," Gramps pointed out. "No need to spend money going out."

"Do you know who owns and runs Gino's?" Ally kept an eye out for Tillie's return. "The Ryersons. Gino and Helen Ryerson."

"You wanna interrogate the Ryersons?" His blue eyes gleamed. "Sign me up."

"Well, I was thinking we'd take Roxy around the restaurant, see if she growls at their scent, then have dinner and talk to them."

"If we're taking the dog, we should just have dessert, instead of a full meal. But why do you want Roxy to growl?" Gramps asked with a frown.

There wasn't a lot of time, Tillie would be back any moment. "Roxy has growled at Officer Roberts twice now, maybe three times. I think it's her way of warning us that he's involved." Tillie appeared in front of the patio doors. Ally jumped up to help. "We'll do dessert then tonight, and I'll fill you in on the rest later."

Gramps took her cue and changed the subject as Tillie set their iced tea on the patio table. She drank her tea in record time, then stood. "I have to go, but I'll swing by to pick you up at say six thirty?"

"I'll be ready," Gramps promised. "Although if you come early, you could eat dinner with us."

She knew she shouldn't, but she'd used up most of her will-power in dealing with Noah. "Okay, as long as Harriet doesn't mind."

"She always makes plenty," Gramps assured her.

Yeah, that was the problem. Ally's waistline was suffering from Harriet's cooking. But getting the Ryersons checked off the list of suspects was important. And Gramps was right.

Why let perfectly great free food go to waste?

*   *   *

Harriet had a delicious Bavarian pot roast for dinner. It was so tasty Ally was having trouble believing Granny was a better cook than Harriet. Ally cut back on her portion, and thankfully didn't need to unbutton her jeans this time.

"We have hot fudge sundaes for dessert," Harriet announced when they finished.

"Um, we can't stay, sorry." Ally jumped up from the table, coaxing Roxy out from underneath. "Next time, okay? Thanks again for dinner, it was absolutely amazing!"

"Oh, but—" Harriet began, until Gramps interrupted.

"I'll have some before bed. Ally's right, we have to go." He struggled to stand. Ally tucked her hand under his arm, helping him up.

"It's not healthy to eat right before bed, Oscar," Lydia said with a frown.

"Bah." Gramps waved her off. "I'll be fine."

Once they were settled in her Honda, Gramps glanced at her. "Tell me more about Roxy's growling."

She kept a keen eye out for any sign of a truck following them. Then she filled him in on the incident outside the Lakefront Café and her subsequent conversation with Noah about Officer Roberts. "The only problem is that Anita didn't say anything about referring Marty to anyone named Roberts."

"Doesn't mean Marty didn't call on Roberts's mother on his own," Gramps said thoughtfully. "I like this theory, Ally. You did good work." He glanced back at Roxy. "You too, Roxy."

"Well, Noah isn't completely sold on this theory, but I think he's going to check it out." She pulled into the parking lot of Gino's Family Restaurant. There were a couple of trucks in the parking lot, but none that were dark red. "Ready? Let's see what Roxy comes up with."

"I'm ready. And after Harriet brought up hot fudge sundaes I'm surely in the mood for one. Think they have them here?"

"If they don't, we'll go back to the Legacy House," Ally promised. "Harriet would be thrilled."

"True."

She gave Gramps a hand up and out of the car, gave him his cane, then took Roxy's leash. "Come on, girl. Gramps, stay by the car, I'll walk her around the parking lot first."

"Why not just walk her around back—isn't that where most of the staff go in and out?" Gramps asked. "I guess you could try her around the front door, too."

Since he had a point, she headed first toward the front of the restaurant, staying off to the side as a young family came out. Roxy eagerly sniffed along the ground but never once growled.

Ally began to wonder if this was a waste of time, but since they were here, she headed around to the back of the restaurant. It wasn't easy going, as the sidewalk was cracked and there were high weeds along the pathway. Good thing she had left Gramps waiting at the car.

Roxy again eagerly explored the area but, as before, never once growled. Ally spent more time than she probably should have and eventually gave up and came around to the front.

"Nothing, Gramps." She pushed her wayward hair from her eyes. "Should we put Roxy in the car with the windows open and grab dessert? Shouldn't take long."

Gramps peered over her shoulder. She turned to see an SUV pulled into the parking lot. "Isn't that your detective?"

She scowled as Noah stopped the car and slid out from behind the wheel. Enough already. He was dancing on her last nerve. "What are you doing here?"

Noah lifted a brow. "Be glad it's not another officer from the Willow Bluff PD. A call came through on the scanner about a suspicious woman with a dog staking out the restaurant accompanied by an old man who was peering in car windows, and somehow I just knew it was the two of you."

Chapter Fifteen

"Are you the police?" a deep voice asked from behind them. Ally glanced over her shoulder to see a tall, very rotund man, completely bald, waving a spatula in the air. "I want these two and that dog arrested for trespassing."

"I'm Detective Noah Jorgenson from the Willow Bluff Police Department." Noah's smile told her he was enjoying this fiasco far too much.

"We're not here to trespass," Ally spoke up quickly. "I was just taking my dog out back to—um, you know, do her business."

"On my property?" The spatula punctured the air. "That's not right."

His property? "You must be Gino Ryerson," Ally said again, before Noah could jump in. "I've heard such great things about your restaurant. Gramps and I specifically came to check out your desserts."

"We did," Gramps agreed, coming up to stand beside her. He eyed Gino curiously. "Nothing wrong with that, is there?"

Gino waved the spatula at him. "Why were you looking into car windows? Planning to find one to steal?"

"While it's still light out?" Gramps countered. "Who would be so stupid?"

"Enough," Noah said in an authoritative tone. "Mr. Ryerson, I don't think they meant any harm. Mr. Winter, Dr. Winter, maybe you should head home? Stop in for dessert another day."

Gramps narrowed his gaze, and Ally knew he was furious about missing his chance to talk to Gino about Marty Shawlin. Sensing the alternative might be heading to jail, she put a hand on Gramps' arm.

"Sounds good, Noah. Come on, Gramps. Let's get our hot fudge sundaes at the Legacy House." She shot an annoyed glance at Gino. "They probably don't have them here, anyway."

"I got plenty of ice cream and other desserts, too." Gino swept the spatula through the air for emphasis, clearly unhappy she'd implied otherwise. "My Helen offers the best desserts in all of Willow Bluff!"

"Not as good as Harriet's," Gramps shot back. "See if I ever come back here!"

Ally groaned and tightened her grip on Gramps' arm. "Let's go," she repeated loudly. "Come, Roxy."

"You better go back and clean up after your dog," Gino said. "She has to, right, officer?"

"Detective," Noah corrected. His smile had faded and she wondered if that was a good or a bad thing. Deep down, she hoped Noah was getting just as frustrated with Gino Ryerson as she was. "If the dog made a mess, she would have to pick it up." Noah caught her gaze. "Did Roxy make a mess?"

"Nope." She lifted her hand, even though she'd never been a girl scout. "I promise."

"I believe you." Noah lowered his voice. "Get your grandfather out of here, Ally. I'll calm Ryerson down then follow you back to the Legacy House."

She was totally on board with getting Gramps out of there, not so much with Noah following. Oh, the having-him-there-to-keep-them-safe part was fine, but she sensed Noah wasn't going to take off and leave them alone once they arrived at their destination.

Urging Gramps toward her Honda wasn't easy, but soon she had him settled in the passenger seat, with Roxy tucked in the back.

"I can't believe the old fool called the cops on us," Gramps muttered.

"He has a right to call for anything deemed suspicious, which apparently Roxy and I were. But why on earth were you looking into car windows?" Ally asked. "That might be what pushed him over the edge."

"Not cars, trucks." Gramps looked chagrined. "It was a truck that sent you flying into the ditch."

"A dark red truck," Ally corrected. "There weren't any in the parking lot when we arrived."

"There was a burgundy one that showed up just after you and Roxy walked toward the back," Gramps said. "That was the one I was checking out, you know, just in case."

In case what? Ally decided it was safer not to ask. She pulled into a parking space in front of the Legacy House and was helping Gramps out when Noah pulled in beside her.

"You want to tell me what that was about?" Noah asked.

Ally barely glanced at him. "We wanted dessert."

"And you didn't intend to interrogate the Ryersons about Shawlin's murder?"

Noah knew full well they did, but she wasn't going to admit it. "That would be interfering with your investigation, and we agreed not to do that, right, Gramps?"

Her grandfather grunted.

Noah stared at her for so long she shifted beneath the intensity of his gaze. It was almost as if he could see right through her, which wouldn't be good, considering how attracted she was to him. "There's no need to talk to them, I've already done that."

She shrugged. "So?"

Noah scowled. "And why did you take Roxy to the back of the restaurant if she didn't have to go to the bathroom?"

She shrugged. "She might have had to go, I can't read Roxy's mind."

The muscle at the corner of Noah's left eye twitched. "You were trying to use Roxy as some sort of scent tracker, weren't you? Even though you know full well she's not a trained police dog."

Again, since he knew the answer already, there was no point in responding. "Here's a question for you, Noah. Did you check with Officer Roberts about whether or not his mother had any business dealings with Marty Shawlin?"

Noah's mouth thinned and, this time, he was the one who chose not to respond. She only wished she could see his eyes clearly in the twilight.

"Yeah, well, I hope you're able to rule him out as a suspect. Come on, Gramps. There are two hot fudge sundaes in there with our names on them."

Noah didn't say anything as she helped Gramps inside, but she could feel his green gaze boring into her back. Shaking off the encounter, she listened as Gramps informed Harriet they'd returned for dessert. Harriet was thrilled and quickly dished up the ice cream topped with thick hot fudge.

Gramps was right. No way could anything at Gino's possibly be this good.

"Need help at the clinic tomorrow, Ally?" Gramps asked. "I need to return a book to the library anyway."

How was it Wednesday already? "Sure, I'll pick you up in the morning."

"What about me?" Lydia asked with a frown.

Ally didn't want to put any of the widows in danger. It was bad enough that Gramps insisted on coming in. "Ah, maybe next week, okay? This one is almost half over anyway. And I don't have that many appointments scheduled."

"That will be fine." Lydia waved a knitting needle at her. "Don't forget."

"I won't." Her sundae finished, Ally headed back outside, stopping short when she saw Noah still standing next to his SUV, his arms crossed over his chest.

"Now what?" She wasn't in the mood for another round of twenty questions.

"Have you forgotten that a few short nights ago, you were run off the road after leaving here?"

"Of course not." She yanked open the driver's side door of her Honda. "What am I supposed to do, Noah? Stay at the clinic without coming to visit Gramps?"

"Visiting is one thing, taking him to Gino's is different."

"For your information, I've been keeping a close eye out for any trucks with square headlights, dark red or otherwise. The last thing I want is for my grandfather to be hurt."

Noah pinched the bridge of his nose, then let out a sigh. "I'll follow you home."

"Fine." She was about to slide in behind the wheel, but stopped to ask, "The Ryersons have an alibi for the day of the murder, don't they?"

Noah didn't answer, but something in the way he stared at her made her feel that she was on the right track.

"I looked up their restaurant hours, they're closed on Mondays but open Tuesday through Sunday, starting at six AM and staying open until nine PM. Marty was killed on a Tuesday morning."

Still Noah didn't say anything.

"Gino had a spatula in his hand, but I heard his wife Helen does most of the cooking. So you may want to be sure Gino didn't slip out the back to kill Marty."

"Gee, thanks. I wouldn't have thought of that all by myself," Noah said dryly.

"So you did clear them!" She felt certain he had. "Glad to hear it. Now you need to focus your efforts on Officer Roberts."

Noah sighed. Since she'd made her point, she got into the Honda and backed out of the drive. Noah's SUV stayed right behind her the entire way back to the clinic. She parked, took Roxy out from the back, and gave a half-hearted wave before heading inside.

Noah's judgment of her actions cut deep. Had she been careless in taking Gramps to Gino's?

Maybe, but at the same time, she knew Gramps wasn't going to let the murder mystery go. It was too much like having a *Dateline* episode happening right in his own backyard.

She needed to figure out a way to keep him safe, while allowing him to satisfy his insatiable curiosity enough to prevent him from going off on his own to do whatever he wanted.

Talk about walking a tightrope. Leaning too far one way or the other could be disastrous.

* * *

Wednesday morning was cloudy after a predawn early morning rain. She took Roxy outside and made a mental note to call Sheila Young again. If the woman wasn't going to pick up Roxy, fine, but Ally wanted to know one way or the other.

"It's not so bad here, is it, girl?" She asked, scratching the area behind Roxy's ears.

Roxy's answer was to lick her.

Forty-five minutes later, Ally was on her way back to the Legacy House to pick up Gramps. She'd figured they'd end up eating lunch on the patio at the Lakefront Café if it didn't rain.

Gramps was eagerly waiting when she arrived. She frowned. "Where's your library book?"

"Almost forgot." Gramps thumped his way into the living room to grab *The Evil Within*. "Got it."

She eyed it warily. "Was it any good?"

"Gruesome," he said honestly. "Yet I find it interesting how these criminals eventually slip up and get themselves caught."

She helped Gramps into the Honda. "So far Marty's killer hasn't slipped up."

"He or she will," Gramps assured her. "They always do."

She wished she could be as certain but let the matter drop. Keeping her gaze focused on the traffic around her, she was glad there were no more signs of a dark red truck with square headlights.

After Gramps was settled behind the desk, she set a slip of paper in front of him. "Remember, name of the owner, name of the pet, and a phone number, okay? No more t-po's shorthand."

Gramps squinted at the note. "I'll try."

Ally's first appointment of the day was grooming a Scottish terrier named, of course, Scotty. He was not happy with the entire process and nipped Ally's finger.

Still, she finished him up and went out to the front desk to make sure Scotty was caught up on his shots. Gramps eyed her bandaged index finger.

"He got you?"

"No, the Band-Aid is a fashion statement." She scooted behind him to use the computer, grateful to note that Scotty was up to date. His vaccinations were also due in a few months, so she made a reminder note to keep track.

It was nice to know some money would be coming in down the road.

The phone rang and Gramps answered it. "Yes, she's here." He handed over the receiver. "Some woman wants to talk to you."

So much for name of the client, their pet, and a phone number. Ally forced a cheerful tone. "This is Dr. Winter, how may I help you?"

"Do you realize that Brutus is the father of Patsy's puppies?" A shrill voice asked.

"Um, no, I didn't know that." She quickly placed the name of the caller. "Ms. Granger, I can't force pet owners to get their dogs neutered and spayed. I haven't met Brutus yet."

"He's a GREAT DANE!" Wendy's shrill voice rose an entire octave. "You have to do something! Having his puppies will kill her!"

Ally strove for patience. "Ms. Granger, I promise that Patsy will be fine. Dogs have mixed-breed puppies all the time, and Great Danes have been bred with Labs before, they call them labradanes. But if you're that worried, you can bring Patsy in for an ultrasound in a week. I can use that to estimate the size of her puppies."

There was a long pause as she digested that information. "Are you sure she'll be okay?"

"I'm sure. Would you like an ultrasound?"

"Yes." Wendy didn't sound happy about it. "I think it's best to know how big the puppies are."

Ally reached over to borrow Gramps' pen and paper. "What date and time works for you?"

"Tuesday at one."

Ally painstakingly filled out the information on the paper as a way to show Gramps how it was done. "Okay, I have you down with Patsy at one o'clock on Tuesday next week, and what's your phone number again?"

Wendy rattled it off.

"See you then." Ally hung up the phone and gestured toward the slip of paper. "See? All set for an appointment next week."

"Hmm." He didn't look impressed. "When do you want to head over to the library?"

She glanced at her watch. "We can leave soon. Now that the sun has started to peek out from behind the dark clouds, it would be nice to have lunch at the Lakeview Café."

"I was thinking we should go to the police station, see if we can find Officer Roberts," Gramps countered. "He's our top suspect at the moment."

"Yes, but that's only because of Roxy's reaction to him." She rested her hand on Roxy's head. "But we could be wrong, and Roxy might not like him for some other reason."

Gramps scowled. "That detective of yours isn't giving us enough information. For all we know he could have cleared half the suspects by now."

"Speaking of which, I think the Ryersons are in the clear." She recounted her brief conversation with Noah after leaving the Legacy House, and the restaurant hours.

"Even if they're not guilty, we still have Kevin Kuhn's temper, Ginny and Eli White's loss of sixteen hundred dollars, and Rosie Malone's lie about talking to Marty." Gramps summed up their investigation so far.

"And Roxy's growling at Officer Roberts." She glanced at Gramps. "Feels like Noah should have someone in custody by now, I mean whichever one of them has a dark red GMC truck must be a person of interest, don't you think?"

"Maybe, maybe not." Gramps blue eyes gleamed. "I've got an idea. Let's leave now and stop in at the police station."

She'd thought he'd been joking about going there to see if Roxy growls again at Officer Roberts, but why not? It couldn't hurt to try.

They walked down Main Street, with Roxy in tow. It occurred to Ally that if Sheila ever did show up to claim the boxer, their star witness would be taken far, far away.

Not good. She'd miss the dog. Ally would be willing to pay Sheila for Roxy, as long as the price wasn't too steep. If Sheila was willing to sell.

All the more reason to find a way to test her theory about Officer Roberts before that happened.

Gramps was walking better than last time, making Ally realize that working two days in a row was likely too much for him.

Ally opened the door of the police station, not surprised to find Barbara Sommers, the same clerk as last time, seated there.

"You again?" Sommers sounded cranky and her scowl deepened when she saw Roxy. "I told you no dogs are allowed."

Gramps stepped forward, flashing a winsome smile. "I need to report a stolen vehicle."

"Another one?" Sommers shook her head. "What is this town coming to? Okay, what's the make and model of the stolen vehicle."

"A GMC truck, dark red in color."

Ally sucked in a quick breath. What was Gramps doing?

Sommers frowned. "That truck has already been reported stolen. Are you George Harrisburg?"

Ally felt a surge of pride. Gramps had just proven the truck that ran her off the road was indeed stolen. No wonder Noah didn't have a lead on their suspect.

"No, I'm not George Harrisburg," Gramps said. "Sorry for the confusion." He turned away from the desk and winked at Ally.

"Wait a minute. How did you know the truck was stolen if you aren't the owner?" Barbara Sommers called out.

"An educated guess," Gramps shot back. Ally peered beyond Barbara Sommers, but there was no sign of Officer Roberts in the cubicles behind the glass. *So much for testing Roxy's growling theory,* she thought as they headed outside.

"I can't believe you did that," Ally said in a hushed tone. "You'd better hope Noah doesn't find out."

"Find out what?" The deep rumbling voice from behind them made her freeze. Dread washed over her as she turned to face Noah.

He was not the least bit happy to see them.

Chapter Sixteen

"Nothing, we were just walking by, right, Ally?" Gramps tried and failed to look remotely innocent. "We're having lunch at the Lakeview Café."

"Tell me what, Ally?" Noah repeated, glaring at her. He was so mad, he completely ignored Roxy wagging her stump of a tail as she nudged him, seeking attention.

"N—nothing. As Gramps said, we're having lunch at the Lakeview Café." She tugged Roxy away from Noah, doubting she pulled off the innocent look either. Lying was not something she did well.

Unlike her cheating ex.

"You're carrying a library book, but came out of the police station," Noah pointed out.

She stared stupidly at the book in her hand, having completely forgotten about it. She gave herself a mental head-slap. "Right. We were going to return this book to the library first, then have lunch."

"Yep," Gramps added helpfully.

"You know I'm going to find out why you were inside the police station," Noah said in a warning tone. "You may as well tell me what you're up to."

Since it was all too easy to imagine Barbara Sommers repeating their brief conversation, she let out a sigh and caved under the pressure. "We learned a dark red GMC truck was reported stolen."

"I pretended to be the owner, George Harrisburg," Gramps added helpfully. He smiled with satisfaction. "Worked like a charm."

The eye twitch was back. "Just because a dark red GMC truck was stolen doesn't make it the one used to run you off the road, Ally."

She scoffed. "Nice try, Noah. How many dark red GMC trucks are there in town, anyway? The entire population of Willow Bluff is barely four thousand people. I mean there can't be that many of them, and the coincidence of the truck of the same make, model, and color being stolen and involved in a crime?" She shook her head. "No way."

The muscle twitched faster. "I told you I'm investigating the vandalism and you being run off the road. I need you to trust me."

That made her feel bad. "It's not that I don't trust you, Noah, because I do. But you're not filling us in on what's happening, either." She gestured to include Gramps. "Which is why we're digging for information on our own."

"Because you don't trust that I'll get to the bottom of it!" Noah's sharp tone caused her to wince. "In fact, your constant interference is getting in the way of my ability to solve Marty's murder!"

He'd never yelled at her before. She felt bad that she and Gramps had pushed Noah to his breaking point.

"Don't you yell at my granddaughter!" Gramps waved a finger in Noah's face. "She's been a victim twice now, and if you ask me, with your resources you should already have Marty's murderer in custody."

Noah's face reddened with anger. Ally grabbed Gramps by the arm, urging him forward. "He didn't mean that, sorry, Noah. Come on, Gramps, time to go to the library to return your book. See you later, Noah. Have a great day."

Gramps took the not-so-subtle hint and went along with her toward the library. Noah didn't say anything more, but she knew he was still furious with them.

Although really, all they did was ask about a stolen dark red GMC truck. Why couldn't Noah have shared that information? How confidential was it, anyway?

If she was one of those who listened to police scanners, she'd have known that already.

Hopefully Gramps wouldn't decide to get one. Thankfully, he wasn't tech savvy.

And she wasn't planning to help him out in that regard, either.

Returning the book didn't take long, but Rosie Malone's cool greeting was an indication she was still upset with Gramps. Which made Ally wonder again about the lie Rosie had told them about not knowing Marty or even speaking to him.

Gramps was right about it being a silly lie. As a librarian Rosie must speak to half the population of Willow Bluff. Her talking to Marty wouldn't necessarily mean anything.

So why the lie?

Roxy trotted meekly at Ally's side as they headed to the Lakefront Café. The same hostess was there, eyeing Roxy with disdain, but went ahead and showed them to the same table Ally had used the night Roxy had growled and tried to go off after the couple, one of whom Ally still suspected was Officer Roberts.

"My treat today, Gramps." Ally gave him a stern look.

He waved a hand. "Fine, but we need to come up with a plan."

"A plan for what?" She should have known Gramps wouldn't listen to anything Noah had said. "If we keep pushing, Noah will make good on his threat to arrest us both. And I have a veterinary business to run."

"Bah. I don't believe he'll do any such thing." Gramps peered at his menu for a moment, then set it aside. "We need a way to draw out Officer Roberts."

She ignored him, inwardly debating between the salad or the less healthy cheeseburger. The memory of downing Harriet's hot fudge sundae made her determined to stick with the salad.

After their server took their lunch orders—of course Gramps had the cheeseburger—and brought their glasses of lemonade, Gramps tried again. "Maybe we can stage a break-in at the Legacy House, forcing Officer Roberts to come check things out."

"Noah would be the one to come, not Roberts." Ally sipped her tart lemonade. "And we're not staging any such thing. Bad enough real crimes are happening, no need to make up additional ones."

"What's your plan, then?" Gramps asked in exasperation. "We need some way to get him near Roxy."

She suppressed a sigh. "Gramps, why don't we have a nice lunch and leave the investigating to Noah?"

"Your detective hasn't solved it yet, has he?" Gramps countered.

"For all we know, Noah has Roberts in his sights. He might even be investigating the guy's background, checking to see if his mother was indeed one of Marty's clients." And why was she sticking up for Noah? "Besides, we don't have a lot of time to dawdle, I have a vaccination coming into the clinic at one thirty this afternoon."

Gramps fell silent, his expression resigned. He sulked, remaining quiet throughout their lunch.

"Come on, Gramps. You're killing me here." Ally paid their lunch tab, closing the billfold with a snap. "If you're going to give me the silent treatment all day, I'll just drop you back at the Legacy House."

"I'm not giving you the silent treatment, I'm thinking." Gramps avoided her gaze and struggled to his feet, shaking off her attempt to help.

Yeah, but Gramps spending his time thinking was exactly what she was afraid of.

* * *

Ally had just finished vaccinating a chocolate Lab named Moose, when she heard the phone ring. It had been inordinately quiet again, but as she'd tallied up her business income the past two weeks, things were definitely looking up.

"Ally? It's someone named Sheila Young."

Roxy's mom. Ally smiled at Marianne, who was still soothing Moose after his shot. "Excuse me a moment."

Ally hurried around the counter so she could take the phone from Gramps' outstretched hand. "Ms. Young? I'm assuming you're calling about Roxy?"

"I'm still in Chicago," Sheila announced.

"Okay, does that mean you're returning to Willow Bluff soon?" Ally wasn't sure what the woman was getting at.

"No, I'm not. I mean, I was there briefly to talk to that detective, but this trip wasn't exactly a business trip, the way I told Marty. I met a man and have decided to relocate to Chicago permanently. I'm sorry, but I'm not going to be able to bring Roxy with me. Marty was supposed to keep her in the divorce, not me," Sheila added, as if that explained everything.

Had Noah cleared Sheila as a suspect? Otherwise, why had he let her return to Chicago? Either way, Ally couldn't help but smile and reached down to pat Roxy, sitting tall beside Gramps. "Just so I'm clear, you're telling me you're not coming to get Roxy, ever?"

"Exactly. You'll just have to send her to the pound. Oh, and I'm not paying for boarding, either." Sheila didn't wait for a response but disconnected from the call.

Ally had forgotten about telling Sheila she'd have to pay for boarding Roxy. She hung up the phone and did a quick little dance. "Guess what? Roxy is mine, Gramps. All mine!"

"Congrats." Gramps' features softened into a smile. "At least now we can keep using Roxy to help solve the case."

"Gramps . . ." Ally shook her head. She gave Roxy another quick rub, then walked back over to the exam room. Marianne had put Moose on the floor, no easy task as Moose was, well, the size of a baby moose. "Any other health concerns about Moose?" Ally asked.

"Nope." Marianne held Moose's leash as the dog tried to squirm out of the exam room. "He's been fine. Thanks again for the reminder about his shots."

"Not a problem." Ally couldn't seem to keep the silly grin off her face, one that had nothing to do with the success of her reminder calls and everything to do with Roxy.

They walked over to the counter. Ally handed Marianne the invoice and was relieved when the woman's credit card went through without a problem.

Moose strained at the leash in an attempt to get around the counter to Roxy, and Roxy whined in response. Marianne tugged Moose outside. Roxy pressed her nose near the crack in the glass and continued whining as she watched them leave.

"You might need to get Roxy a playmate," Gramps said without any sign of his earlier crankiness. "She's lonely."

"One dog is plenty." Ally gazed fondly at the boxer who was now hers forever. "Especially a great one like Roxy."

"Marty's ex is still in Chicago, huh?" Gramps asked.

Trust Gramps to get back to the murder. "She was in town briefly to talk to Noah, which makes me wonder if he's cleared her as a suspect, but according to what she just told me, she's staying in Chicago with some guy she met."

"A man?" Gramps raised a brow. "Maybe he was the one who did Marty in? Who gets the house now that Marty is dead?"

"I have no idea. But it sounded like their divorce was final before the murder, so he could have left the house to anyone."

"Unless he hadn't gotten around to changing the beneficiary in his own will." Gramps smacked his hand on the table. "This could be a real clue! We need to get a look at who gets what's left of Marty's estate."

She eyed him wearily. "Don't you think if Sheila was going to kill her ex-husband, she'd have done the deed before he became an ex?"

"Not if she didn't meet the new guy until after they got divorced. Hear me out. Sheila divorces Marty, finds a new guy, then realizes how much better off she'd be with Marty dead, so arranges to have him killed while maintaining her alibi of being in Chicago." Gramps was warming to his theory. "Could be that she was banking on the fact that he wouldn't have changed his beneficiary so quickly. They didn't have any kids, right?"

"How should I know?" Although she felt certain if there had been kids, Roxy would have ended up somewhere other than with her. "It's a stretch, Gramps."

"Stretch? I think it's a perfect setup. Who would suspect the ex-wife who was in Chicago during the murder?" His expression turned thoughtful. "Wonder if we should let that detective of yours in on this new theory."

"No, we should not." Ally wasn't planning to see Noah Jorgenson again until after he'd solved the various outstanding crimes. "Let it go, Gramps. And stop watching so much TV."

"If only we knew her new boyfriend's name," Gramps mused, completely ignoring her comment. "You could try calling her back to ask?" Gramps suggested.

"No." Ally narrowed her gaze. "Even if I did attempt such a crazy thing, there's no reason for her to tell me the name of her new boyfriend."

"You could say you need a formal agreement to transfer ownership of Roxy to you permanently, signed by both Ms. Young and her new guy."

Where did Gramps come up with this stuff? "Is that something you saw on *Dateline*?"

"No, but it's a good idea for several reasons." Gramps began ticking them off on his fingers: "You have the agreement in writing, so she can't come back and change her mind, you also have both of their full legal names on record and lastly you'll have their address." He spread his hands. "What more could you ask for?"

Ally stared at him, at a loss for words. Was she crazy to consider his suggestion? Probably, but there was no denying that having a formal agreement in writing about Ally taking custody of the dog would be a smart idea. What if, a few months from now, Sheila broke up with the new boyfriend and changed her mind about wanting Roxy?

Roxy got up from her spot next to Gramps and stretched. Then the boxer padded over to nudge Ally's hand, no doubt needing a trip outside.

"Will you be okay here for a few minutes, Gramps?" Ally took Roxy's leash. "She needs to go out."

"I'll be fine. But think about what I suggested. Knowing more about Sheila's new boyfriend might be the key to solving the crime."

"Or just an invasion of privacy," Ally pointed out wryly. "Come, Roxy."

"Think about it," Gramps called after her.

She ignored him. Outside, she took Roxy on their usual walking route.

"I shouldn't encourage him by going along with his latest scheme," she told Roxy as they found a grassy area for the dog to do her business. "But now that I've gotten to know you over the past two weeks, I can't bear the idea of letting you go."

Roxy pooped and Ally used the plastic bag as a glove to pick it up.

"Especially not after the way she's treated you," Ally added. "You deserve better, Roxy."

Roxy wiggled her stubby tail in agreement.

She took Roxy around to the back of the building to drop the bag in the garbage, then went inside through the back to wash up.

Gramps was on the phone when she entered the main reception area of the clinic. He waved her over. "Dr. Winter just walked in." He held up the phone. "It's for you."

Yeah, I gathered that much. Ally took the phone, sighing when she heard the familiar panicked voice of Wendy Granger.

"I think the puppies are coming early!"

"Okay, try to remain calm. What makes you think that? What symptoms is Patsy displaying?"

"She's just lying around not doing anything, which is not like her. I'm telling you, those Great Dane puppies are going to be too much for her to handle!"

They were clearly too much for Wendy Granger to handle. "I understand your concern, but pregnant dogs get tired out easily, just like pregnant women do. Patsy resting more than usual is very normal."

"But—how will I know when the puppies are coming?" Wendy wailed.

Didn't they just have this conversation? "You have a couple of weeks yet, so try not to worry. And Patsy will likely make a soft bed someplace to have her pups. Maybe you could make one for her now, so she feels comfortable when the time comes." And would give the woman something constructive to do.

"Are you sure she's not about to give birth?"

"As sure as I can be without seeing her." Ally rubbed her temple. "Please know that dogs give birth without our help all the time. And we'll know more after next week's ultrasound."

"Okay, thanks." Wendy didn't sound reassured.

Ally dropped the phone back in the cradle. "This is why it's important to get your pets neutered."

Gramps glanced at Roxy. "Do you know for sure Roxy is?"

"Yes." It was one of the first things she'd checked amidst Hanson's notes. "And her shots were up to date. After talking to Sheila, I'm sure Marty was the one who took care of Roxy."

"Which is why you need an agreement," Gramps insisted.

"Fine." She threw up her hands. Why did she bother trying to fight with him? She pulled the computer keyboard over and pulled up a Word document. She wasn't a lawyer, and Marty wasn't there to ask for assistance, so she did her best to draft the agreement. When she was finished, she picked up the phone and dialed Sheila's number.

To her surprise the woman answered. "Yes?"

"I'd like you and the new man in your life to sign off on an agreement that states you're formally granting me custody of Roxy," Ally said bluntly. "I'll email it, have you both sign it, then scan it back to me."

"But—I don't have a scanner." Ally noticed she didn't balk at signing the agreement. "Hang on a sec. Nick? Can you access a computer scanner at the precinct?"

Precinct?

"Okay, fine," Sheila said. "Nick can scan it and send it back to you from the police station."

"Nick is a cop?"

"Yes. He works second shift and we live in a small apartment, which is why we can't have a dog. Send me your agreement and I'll return it as soon as possible."

"I'll need your email address." Ally wrote it down, then said, "Should show up in a few minutes."

After she disconnected from the phone, she sent the agreement via email, then glanced at Gramps. "You heard?"

"That he's a cop and they live in a small apartment? Yep." Gramps looked down at Roxy. "You know what I think? Living in that small apartment makes the idea of killing Marty to get the house a motive for murder. Housing is very expensive in the big city, so it makes sense that they'd want something more. And maybe Roxy doesn't like police uniforms."

"You might be right about that." She frowned at Roxy. "We should tell Noah about this." The thought wasn't a cheery one.

"Let's wait until we get the agreement back." Gramps rubbed his hands together with glee. "That way we'll have everything your detective needs to look into this guy's alibi. If he has one."

Chapter Seventeen

Sheila returned the agreement within an hour, and they had Nick Calderone's full name and address. Gramps was thrilled to have another possible suspect, but Ally hesitated, not at all convinced she should present this new information to Noah.

Roxy growling at cop uniforms was one thing, but if Nick had murdered Marty, why would he wear a uniform to do it? As a way to throw off suspicion? Would a Chicago police uniform even look the same as the Willow Bluff police uniform? Maybe, but the more she thought about it, the less likely it seemed that Nick Calderone was involved.

One phone call from Noah to check his alibi could clear the guy. But she felt certain Noah wouldn't appreciate Gramps' latest theory.

"Ready?" Gramps asked, leaning on his cane near the door.

She blew out a breath. "I don't think this is a good idea." With reluctance, she led Roxy toward Gramps. "All we're going to get is another lecture."

"Who cares? The important thing is to crack the case. It's already been over a week. Your detective is falling behind if he wants to solve this."

Ally opened the door for Gramps, then locked it behind them. She prayed for a veterinary emergency call the entire walk down Main Street.

No such luck.

As they approached the police station, Ally could see two men standing outside talking. One was in uniform, the other was in dress slacks and a collared shirt. Even from here, she recognized Noah.

On cue, Roxy began to growl.

Ally quickened her pace, hurrying over to where Noah and Officer Roberts were talking. "See?" She gestured to Roxy, who bared her teeth and growled at Roberts. "I told you Roxy doesn't like him."

To his credit, Noah didn't raise his voice. "Ally, I need you to take Roxy and your grandfather away from here. Roberts? Let's go inside to talk."

"I can't believe you think I'm guilty of murdering someone!" Roberts said, taking a step back from Roxy. "It's not my fault the dog doesn't like me."

"I didn't accuse you of anything," Noah pointed out, shooting Ally a dark look. She knew he wanted her gone, but she wasn't moving. "All I want to do is talk to you, *inside.*"

In other words, discuss the crime away from curious ears, like hers and Gramps'.

Gramps huffed a bit as he came up beside her. He glared at Roberts. "Roxy doesn't like you because you murdered Marty. Don't even try to deny it."

"I didn't!" Roberts insisted, taking another step back from the dog. "Okay, maybe I did go see Marty the morning he died, to

201

warn him away from my mom, but I'm telling you he was alive when I left!"

Noah appeared surprised by his confession. "Listen, Roberts, you don't have to say all this. Remember, you have the right to remain silent, a right to an attorney . . ."

"I didn't kill him," Roberts repeated empathically. "In fact, he was practically on his way out the door when I stopped by. Told me he had a meeting in town." Roberts sent another wary glance at the dog. "We stood in the kitchen while that dog was in the crate. All that thing did was bark and growl the whole time. So yeah, maybe I yelled at Marty, told him to stay away from elderly ladies like my mom, but I didn't kill him!"

Reading people wasn't Ally's strong suit—wasn't Tim proof of that? However, her gut sensed Roberts was telling the truth.

"I haven't accused you of anything," Noah repeated. "All I asked was to talk to you, inside, about whether your mom was Marty's client." The tick at the corner of his left eye was back and she felt a little guilty for the way she, Roxy, and Gramps had disrupted his discussion with Roberts. "Come on, Roberts, you know the law as well as I do. You shouldn't be talking to me with civilians present and without a lawyer."

Roberts pointed at Roxy. "I want you to know that I'm innocent, and I have no idea why that dog hates me."

"I understand," Noah said in a soothing voice. "I'll need to talk to your mother, though, to hear her side of the interaction she had with Marty Shawlin."

"Go ahead," Roberts muttered. "I have nothing to hide."

Noah sighed and waved him off. "Get back to work, we'll talk more later."

Roberts slithered away, giving Roxy a wide berth. When Noah turned to face her, Ally could see the frustration etched on his features. "I'm this close," he said holding up his thumb and forefinger less than an inch apart, "to tossing you and your grandfather behind bars."

"We're just trying to help," Ally protested weakly. "It's not my fault Roberts is afraid of Roxy. Or that Roxy doesn't like him."

Noah pinched the bridge of his nose in an attempt to rein in his temper.

"And it's also not our fault that Roberts ignored your attempt to talk to him inside," Gramps added. "But look on the bright side, we learned he visited Marty the day of his murder. That's a break in the case, isn't it?"

Noah opened his mouth, then closed it again. Without a word, he spun on his heel and walked away.

Ally put a hand on Gramps' arm to prevent him from following. "No need to bring up Sheila's cop boyfriend now. Seems as if Roxy was growling at Roberts specifically."

"You never know," Gramps protested. "Could be that Marty's meeting in town was with Nick Calderone. That detective of yours should make the effort to cross him off the suspect list, just in case he did show up here in Willow Bluff."

"I'm not going to push Noah any more today." Ally reached down to pet Roxy, who'd stopped growling as soon as Roberts left the area. "Let's head back to the clinic. It's almost time for me to drive you back to the Legacy House."

"Bah." Gramps didn't look happy. "We were on a roll today, Ally. We learned the dark red GMC truck that ran you off the road was likely stolen, that Marty's ex is dating a cop and might still be a beneficiary to his estate, and that Officer Roberts met with Marty the day he died. If we keep going, we have a good chance of solving the crime."

Or messing the case up worse than they already had, Ally thought wearily. "More than enough action for one day, Gramps."

When they arrived at the clinic Ally's phone rang. "Hello, this is Dr. Winter, may I help you?"

"Smoky ate a dishtowel this time!" Ally easily remembered Rachel Turks and her black Lab named Smoky. "Dad's gonna kill me!"

"Can one of your parents come with you and Smoky to the clinic?" Ally asked. "We need to get that dishtowel out right away, or he'll need surgery."

"My dad is home, but he's gonna kill me," Rachel repeated tearfully.

"The sooner you get Smoky here the better." Ally unlocked the clinic door, holding it for Gramps.

"Okay, we'll come right away." Rachel disconnected the call.

Ally shook her head, wondering how Smoky had gotten a chance to eat the dishtowel. Had it been on the floor in Rachel's room? For the girl's sake, she sincerely hoped not.

"Will you be okay here for a while longer, Gramps?" Ally asked, getting him settled behind the desk. "This may take a while."

"Of course I'll be okay." He looked relieved to be sitting in the chair. "I was in 'Nam, I'm not made of fluff."

Ally quickly took Roxy upstairs to her apartment, knowing she'd need to concentrate on Smoky. She'd never had a dog come in after eating an entire dishtowel. An entire pumpkin pie? Yes. Socks, yes.

But a dishtowel was large enough to require surgery. And if that was the case, Rachel was right to fear her father's wrath.

Richard Turks hadn't been happy paying the previous bill, and surgery would be far more expensive.

Even though her bank account could use the boost, Ally sincerely hoped she wouldn't need to perform a surgical procedure on Smoky.

The poor Lab didn't deserve it.

She prepared the apomorphine so the medication would be ready to go. When Rachel, her father, and Smoky arrived, the young girl's eyes were red from crying. Thankfully, Richard Turks didn't look too upset.

"Let's get Smoky into the first exam room, okay?" Ally led the way inside. "Rachel, can you tell me what happened? Are you absolutely sure Smoky ate a dishtowel?"

"I'm sure, because I—I left it hanging over the edge of the counter and saw Smoky grab it." She sent her father a guilty look. "I kept telling him to drop it, but he wouldn't listen. And when I chased him, he ducked into the bedroom and began chewing it up."

Ally was encouraged by this news. "So he didn't eat the entire towel?"

"Most of it." Richard Turks held up what was left of the dishtowel. More than half of it was missing. "He's not going to need surgery, is he?"

To his credit, he looked more worried about the dog than his wallet.

"I hope not. I'm going to take Smoky in the back and use the same medication as last time. Hopefully it will work."

"Thanks, Dr. Winter," Rachel said, sniffing loudly and wiping her eyes.

"Why don't you both have a seat in the lobby?" Ally took Smoky's leash from Rachel's fingers. "We'll be back soon."

Ally lifted Smoky into the washtub and tied him in place. "Sorry, buddy, but this will be the same drill as last time." She held him tightly and injected the apomorphine.

As before, it didn't take long for Smoky to begin to retch. At first, nothing came out of his stomach, which was worrisome. If the towel had already gotten into his small bowel, she'd have no choice but to operate.

But then a few small pieces came up, then a larger one. Along with yet another sock. Ally shook her head and stroked Smoky's fur. "Hang in there, buddy. You're doing great getting that nasty stuff out of there."

The rest of the shredded dishtowel came out in a clump. Since it appeared most of the towel had been expelled, she decided against surgery.

She gave him a quick bath, then injected a small bolus of saline into the scruff of Smoky's neck, since the poor animal seemed dehydrated. When he'd recovered, she lifted him out of the tub and set him on his feet.

Smoky's tail thumped weakly against her leg as he gazed up at her with eyes that asked why she was torturing him like this. Her heart went out to him.

"I'm sorry, big guy. I'll give Rachel another lecture about keeping clothing off the floor and out of your reach so maybe you won't need to come back on a weekly basis."

Smoky gazed up at her, seemingly on board with that plan.

Ally led Smoky out to the reception area. Rachel jumped up from her seat. "He's okay?"

"He's fine," Ally assured the girl. She glanced at her father, then back to Rachel. "The rest of the towel came out, but so did a sock. You really have to keep all clothing items off the floor and out of his reach, Rachel. Smoky is a puppy, he's depending on you to watch over him."

"I know, I'm sorry." Rachel knelt on the floor beside Smoky, hugging him close. He licked her cheek in forgiveness. "Thanks for saving him from surgery."

"You're welcome." Ally couldn't help smiling at them. Whatever Rachel's faults, she clearly loved the black Lab.

"Yes, thank you," Richard Turks added. "I'm hoping this is our last trip here for a while."

"Understandable." Ally went around the desk to the computer. She pulled up the invoice she'd issued last time and made a duplicate copy.

Richard Turks handed over his credit card without complaint. The dishtowel incident had been a close call, and he knew it.

"Take care of Smoky," Ally said as she handed Richard the receipt.

"We will." He sent his daughter a stern look. "We're going to head over to the store to buy a very large clothes hamper, right, Rachel?"

"Right," the girl agreed.

"I appreciate you using less invasive techniques before going straight to surgery," Richard Turks said. "Willow Bluff is lucky to have you, Dr. Winter."

Ally blushed. It was the nicest thing any of her clients had said to her since she'd taken over the business. "Thank you, but it's the right thing to do."

Richard and Rachel Turks left with Smoky. When the door closed behind them, Gramps squeezed her hand. "See? I knew the people in Willow Bluff would come around."

"Yeah, guess you were right about that." Ally had to admit this was a great way to end the day. "Let me get Roxy and I'll take you home."

This time, Gramps didn't protest. He looked tired, and it was well past five thirty. Harriet was likely ready to pitch a fit over how late they were.

Getting to the Legacy House didn't take long. Ally helped Gramps out and left Roxy in the Honda as she walked him up to the door.

"Oscar!" Harriet must have been watching and waiting for them to get there. "We were getting worried about you!" She frowned at Ally. "You should have called."

"My fault, I had an emergency case come in at the last minute." Ally stepped back as her grandfather made his way inside. "See you later, Gramps."

"You're not staying for dinner?" Harriet's frown deepened. "I already set a spot for you at the table."

Ally wavered for a split second before she caved. "Just let me get Roxy."

Harriet pressed her lips together in disapproval but didn't complain.

"Roxy belongs to Ally, now. Marty's ex-wife gave the dog up."

"Really?" Harriet looked dismayed by the news. "How . . . unfortunate."

"Not for Roxy," Gramps said, the twinkle in his eye betraying how much he enjoyed needling the widow. "Ally is a much better dog owner than Marty's ex by a mile."

"Thanks again, Harriet." Ally tried to smooth things over. "Something smells great!"

"Beef stroganoff," Harriet announced.

Ally thought it was a wonder Harriet's arteries hadn't clogged up from all the rich food she cooked, but hey, who was she to complain? Harriet's meals tasted delicious, no reason to refuse them now that all the widows seemed to be involved in her life. She nudged Roxy under the table, telling her to lie down, as Harriet filled their plates.

"What time are you picking me up tomorrow, Ally?" Lydia asked.

Gramps scowled, and for a moment Ally thought he might insist on coming instead, but he didn't.

"Nine o'clock, if that's not too early," Ally said.

"I'll be ready." Lydia beamed with excitement.

After dinner, and somehow finding the willpower to refuse Harriet's cherry pie, Ally insisted on heading home. She took Roxy outside and into the Honda.

She'd only gone a block when she caught a glimpse of a green sedan.

But it didn't sound loud, like the muffler was bad. Because it had been repaired? Or because the owner was innocent?

Ally wrenched the steering wheel to the left, making a last-minute decision to find the car. It wouldn't hurt to catch a glimpse of the driver.

The green Ford disappeared around another corner, but she could still hear the engine.

Then it abruptly stopped.

No! Ally ground her teeth together and slowed her speed, searching for where the green sedan might have gone. Was it already inside a garage?

She searched frantically for any sign of a garage door still coming down.

There! Not a garage door, but a green Ford sedan sitting in the driveway of a yellow house.

Ally drove slowly past in an attempt to glimpse the driver but didn't see anyone. She drove around the block, and then parked her Honda on the road two doors down from where the green Ford was parked.

Now what? It was tempting to call Noah, but she quickly decided against it. Sliding out from behind the wheel, she opened the back door and let Roxy out.

"Let's take a short walk, Roxy."

The W-word had Roxy jumping around with excitement. Ally walked with Roxy toward the green Ford, and the dog abruptly began to growl.

Yes! She was onto something! Roxy growled and tugged against the leash in an attempt to get closer to the car.

"What is it, girl? Do you know the owner?" Ally risked taking a few steps up the driveway so Roxy could get a better whiff of the scents around the car.

If the owner called the cops, she felt confident Noah would toss her in jail for trespassing.

Roxy continued to growl low in her throat until Ally decided there was no point in continuing the test. Roxy had made it clear she didn't like the owner of the green Ford.

Not that she understood what that meant for the case. Unless the driver of the green Ford was some sort of accomplice? Nah, she was letting her imagination run wild, just like Gramps.

"Come, Roxy," she said, pulling the dog from the house. Then she glanced back over her shoulder to make note of the house number. Wouldn't hurt to find out who the owner was, just to satisfy her curiosity.

Twenty-one-zero-three. Ally repeated it to herself as she half dragged Roxy back to the Honda.

Once she was behind the wheel, she pulled out her phone and wrote herself a note about the address and the license plate number for the Ford. When that was finished, she dialed Noah's personal number. With an actual address and license plate, he could run a trace on the owner.

"Not a good time, Ally," Noah said abruptly.

"But it's important," she started, only to realize she was talking to dead air.

He'd hung up on her! Fuming, she punched his number again, only this time he didn't answer at all.

She tossed her phone into the passenger seat. Great. The first solid clue she had, and he was too mad to hear it.

Noah was treating her like the little boy who'd cried wolf.

And deep down, she knew she had only herself to blame.

Chapter Eighteen

B ack at the clinic, Ally pored through Hanson's client list, searching for an address that matched the house with the green Ford parked in the driveway. She searched by house number and street name, without luck.

She tried a basic internet search, but couldn't find a name associated with the property. Instead, she was directed to a site requiring a fee before releasing the information. She frowned. Was it worth it? Maybe, but not now. Bleary-eyed from staring at the monitor, she pushed away from it, shut the machine down, and took Roxy outside one last time before heading up to the apartment. She'd been taking care of Roxy for so long, it was difficult to remember what her life in Willow Bluff had been like without the boxer.

"Feeling guilty I don't have a nice yard for you to run around in," she said, scratching Roxy behind the ears. "But at least you're not in a crate all day, right?"

Roxy rested her chin on Ally's thigh as if content.

When she finished brushing her teeth, her cell phone rang. Noah? But no, it was the number from the Legacy House.

"Hello?"

"Ally? It's Lydia. I'm afraid I've twisted my ankle." The widow sounded as if she might cry. "I won't be able to come to the clinic. And Tillie's daughter is coming up to take her to lunch, so she won't be available either."

"Oh Lydia, it's okay, truly. I'm sorry to hear about your ankle, but I'll be fine."

"Oscar said to tell you he's willing to come in. Here, he wants to talk to you."

"Ally?" Gramps was speaking in a normal voice, likely because he was using the Legacy House landline. "I told Lydia not to call you this late, but she insisted. I'll be ready to go by nine o'clock tomorrow morning."

"Are you sure it won't be too much for you?" Ally suspected that Gramps wanted to come in solely to interact with potential suspects. "You can come on Friday, instead."

"I'm sure, I'd like to help out tomorrow." He said something to Lydia, then continued, "See you in the morning."

"Goodnight, Gramps." Ally disconnected the phone and connected it to her charger. Then she patted the bed, inviting Roxy to jump up.

The dog stretched out beside her, and Ally smiled in the darkness.

Then her smile faded. Noah wasn't speaking to her anymore? Fine. She'd figure out who owned the house on twenty-one-zero-three Terrace Lane on her own.

And if that house was owned by one of their suspects, then Noah would have to listen to her.

* * *

Ally brought Roxy along as she headed to the Legacy House to pick up Gramps the next morning. Her first grooming appointment wasn't until ten thirty, so there was plenty of time to stop and watch the house.

She filled Gramps in on Roxy's behavior outside the green Ford sedan. After taking a slight detour down Terrace Lane, she gestured to the house. "That's the one."

Gramps leaned forward to peer out the window. "But the Ford isn't in the driveway, so that means the owner has already left for the day."

"I know." She blew out a frustrated breath. "But there's a garage, too. Could be two people live there, and one of them is still home."

"Hrmph," Gramps grunted.

Ally drove past the place, turned around, then parked on the opposite side of the road where they would have a good view of anyone coming out. "Can you think of anyone you know that owns a green Ford?"

Gramps shook his head. "Trust me, I've been trying to remember. Most of the time, people walk around town, so I don't often see their vehicles." He grinned. "Except when Marty showed up at the Legacy House."

Ally draped her wrist over the top of the steering wheel. "We can sit here for a little while, but I can't be late for my grooming appointment at ten thirty." It was interesting that her appointments were split about fifty/fifty between grooming and veterinary services.

Thank goodness she'd learned how to groom animals during summer breaks while attending college.

After sitting there for fifteen minutes, Gramps grew antsy. "The Ford isn't there, I say we drive around town to look for it."

"You think we're going to stumble across it the same way we found Marty's car?" Ally asked.

"Why not?"

She couldn't argue his logic. They headed into town, and slowly drove through the large parking lot outside the municipal building.

"What if Officer Roberts owns the car?" She frowned at Gramps. "We already know his side of the story, about his concern over his mother."

"Yeah," Gramps agreed.

"I tend to believe him." It occurred to her that Roberts owning the car would explain Roxy's dislike of the scent around the vehicle. And if that was the case, the green Ford wasn't a clue to the crime after all.

She'd gone up and down several aisles before Gramps shouted, "Stop!"

She slammed on the brakes and peered through the steering wheel. "Where?"

"You went past it. Back up about six feet."

She did and saw a green Ford. "Hang on, I wrote down the license plate number." She thumbed through her phone, then held it up toward Gramps. "It's the same car."

"Okay, then." Gramps nodded thoughtfully. "So the owner of the car either works somewhere in the municipal building or is here visiting."

"I'm leaning toward the former," Ally noted. "It's fairly early to be visiting the library, City Hall, or the police station. It really might belong to Roberts."

"Maybe. Or it could belong to someone else. The library opens at eight AM in the summer, and parents bring their kids to the library all the time."

Taking her foot off the brake, she let the Honda roll forward. "This is a dead end, Gramps. We need to get to the clinic."

"I know." But Gramps twisted in his seat, watching the car as she drove out of the parking lot and down Main Street. "I wish I knew who owned the car, though."

I wish for a lot of things, she thought with a sigh.

Gramps didn't argue as she pulled up in front of the clinic and helped him from the car.

She'd barely unlocked the clinic and helped Gramps get settled behind the counter, when the door opened.

A familiar young girl stood there, cradling yet another wild animal against her chest. Roxy lifted her head, clearly catching the animal's scent.

Great. Ally suppressed a sigh. "Hi, Amanda, what did you bring in today?"

"I found a baby bunny," Amanda looked as if she might cry. "She's bleeding, you have to help her."

At least it wasn't a bird. Still, this craziness had to stop. "Amanda, honey, you can't keep bringing wild animals in for me to fix."

"But—she'll die."

No matter how much she wanted to, Ally couldn't resist the girl's big pleading eyes. A glance at her watch confirmed she had roughly thirty minutes before her grooming appointment arrived. "Fine. Roxy? Sit. Stay." When Roxy obeyed, she gestured to Amanda. "Bring the bunny into exam room number one."

Amanda Cartwright nodded and carefully crossed the clinic to the exam room. Ally followed, hoping the animal wasn't hurt too badly but fearing the worst. Only the strong survive in the wild, and in her experience the baby bunny had been attacked by either a dog or a coyote. And there was always the possibility of wild animals having rabies.

Wouldn't Ellen Cartwright have a fit about that?

For Amanda's sake, she hoped the bunny wasn't diseased or too far gone to be helped. Ally dutifully donned protective gear, then gently took the baby bunny from the girl's arms.

It was bleeding from teeth marks and sat motionless in the palm of her hands with its eyes closed. Rabbits sometimes remained motionless in a play-dead attempt to avoid predators, but Ally didn't think that was the case. She felt for a heartbeat but found nothing.

Amanda was gazing down at the rabbit with a rapt expression on her face. Ally could tell the girl wanted to make a pet out of the baby bunny.

Not happening. Even if the animal was alive, it wasn't a good idea to make pets out of wild animals.

"Looks like she has several cuts I'll need to clean up." Ally held the dead baby bunny against her abdomen. "I'll take care of her in the back and will probably have to keep the bunny here for a few days, okay?"

"Okay," Amanda agreed.

Ally didn't like lying to the child, but she couldn't bear to tell the little girl the rabbit was dead. The phrase frightened to death came from situations just like this. Baby animals in particular could get so scared they died.

Teeth marks hadn't helped. She figured the dog had carried it for a while before dropping it.

A coyote would have eaten it.

Best Amanda not know about that possibility.

She carried the baby bunny into the back and found an empty supply box to put it in. Maybe Amanda would forget about it, but if not, she'd explain the poor thing had died and she'd given it a proper burial.

"Will you call me when the baby bunny is all better?" Amanda asked when she returned to the exam room.

Frankly, it was the last thing Ally wanted to do, but she nodded. "Let's go out to the counter, I'll need your phone number."

When she picked up a paper and pencil, Amanda rattled off her number. The door flung open, revealing Ellen Cartwright.

Roxy barked and got to her feet. In Ally's opinion, the boxer had good taste when it came to people. Today Ellen was dressed in robin's egg blue. Blue suit, blue pumps, perfectly straight blond hair.

Ally was keenly jealous of Ellen's straight blond hair.

"Amanda, what have I told you about leaving while I'm in the middle of an open house?" Ellen demanded.

"I found a bleeding baby bunny and brought it to Dr. Winter. She's going to fix her all better."

A flash of anger from Ellen speared Ally. "You don't have my permission to treat a wild animal."

It was on the tip of Ally's tongue to respond she didn't need Ellen's permission, but decided to try smoothing things over. "I understand, Ms. Cartwright. You won't be held responsible for any bills associated with caring for the rabbit."

218

There wouldn't be any bills as the rabbit was dead, but she wasn't going to say that in front of Amanda.

"Why do you keep doing this?" Ellen asked Amanda, true bewilderment in her gaze.

"I dunno," Amanda muttered, staring down at her shoes.

"Amanda loves animals, and I'm sure she's just looking out for the injured or lost ones because she doesn't have a pet of her own," Ally offered.

Ellen scowled. "We can't have pets. Who would look after it while I'm at work and Amanda's at school?" She shook her head. "No, this has to stop. Amanda, go wash your hands, there's no telling what diseases that thing might have."

The girl's shoulders slumped, but she nodded. "Okay."

"This way." Ally steered Amanda to the public restroom. She stood by, making sure the girl actually washed her hands. "Your mom is right about one thing, Amanda."

"Like what?"

"Wild animals, like that baby bunny, can carry diseases. Very bad diseases. Have you heard about rabies?"

Amanda finished washing and drying her hands. "Yeah, but I didn't see the bunny foaming around her mouth."

"Not all animals with rabies foam at the mouth—they might act goofy, or be easily caught by other wild animals because they can't run as fast." She knelt down so she was at eye level with the girl. "Rabies is very bad for humans, Amanda. The treatment is really painful, lots of shots which don't feel good. You need to stay away from injured wild animals like birds, bunnies, raccoons, mice, anything that doesn't come from a pet store or animal adoption. I wouldn't want you to get sick, okay?"

Amanda slowly nodded. "Okay. But you heard my mom. We can't get a pet."

"I know." And that was sad in its own way. Not that she had any right to pass judgment on Ellen Cartwright's reasons for not having a dog or a cat. "Maybe you can come by and help me with Roxy once in a while. That way, you can still be near pets without having one of your own."

"Really?" Amanda's entire face lit up. She threw her arms around Ally's neck and squeezed tightly. "Thanks, Dr. Winter. You're the best."

She hugged the girl back. "It's not a problem. And you may as well call me Ally."

Amanda released her and stepped back, ducking her head shyly. "Okay—Ally."

She took Amanda's hand and walked her back to her mother. Ellen was tapping her pointy-toed shoe impatiently. "Let's go, Amanda."

Amanda obediently followed her mother out of the clinic, glancing one last time back and waving at Ally.

She waved back and waited for the door to close before murmuring, "Poor kid."

"Are you really going to treat a wild animal?" Gramps asked.

"No, the bunny is dead, so I'm going to bury it and hope Amanda forgets all about it. But later. My grooming appointment should be here any minute."

Gramps tapped a slip of paper on the desk. "Took a call from another pet owner needing immunizations. Looks like the Furry Friends Veterinary Clinic is in business."

"Yeah." Ally smiled. It was a good feeling. A smaller clinic like this might never be as busy as the one she and Tim had run in Madison, but as long as she could make enough money to pay the bills and buy groceries, she'd be fine.

Her grooming appointment was a mixed breed, some terrier, poodle, and maybe bichon frise thrown in.

Cooper nipped and yipped, but overall it wasn't too difficult to wash and cut his fur. She'd cleaned out his anal glands, too, her least favorite part of the job.

She tied the Fourth of July bandana around his neck, thinking she needed to find more material as she was running low. And pick up some fall swatches, too.

Since Cooper's mom wasn't coming back until after lunch, Ally placed him in one of the crates, wincing as the volume of his yips increased. "Sorry, little guy."

Upon returning to the desk, she heard a loud sickening thud, followed by someone shouting, "Hey! You can't leave!" After a quick horrified glance at Gramps, she whirled and ran out of the clinic.

"What happened?" Ally caught a glimpse of a dark-colored car careening around the corner, leaving the scene of the crime. She focused her gaze on a beautiful golden retriever lying at the side of the road. It was struggling to get up, but one of its hind legs was clearly broken.

"She hit the dog!"

Ally dropped down beside the injured animal, quickly assessing the retriever for other signs of injury. A broken leg was one thing, but internal bleeding could be life threatening. "Is the owner nearby?" she called.

"I don't think so." A young boy in his early teens knelt beside her. "I can't believe the driver didn't stop."

Unfortunately, Ally could. "Call the police," she instructed the boy. "I'm taking the dog inside."

The kid had his cell phone out and was already dialing 911. The golden was easily seventy pounds, but Ally's adrenalin had kicked in and she managed to cradle the animal in her arms and stagger to her feet.

The kid was talking to the police dispatcher but noticed her struggle and ran to open the door.

She hurried inside and set the golden on the table of the exam room. In Madison she'd taken care of several trauma injuries, but this was her first in Willow Bluff. The dog had a collar, his name was Amos. She finished her exam, then carried the dog into the back for X-rays.

The left hind leg was broken, but thankfully it wasn't too bad a break. The speed limit on Main Street was only twenty-five miles per hour; if the dog had gotten hit on the highway, he'd be in worse shape.

Her treatment of choice for this kind of fracture would be to apply an external fixation device. Amos would have to get medication to relax him, so she could insert pins into the bones to set them properly. Not as expensive as doing a full-blown surgery, but not cheap, either.

Using her cell phone, she called the number on the tag.

No answer. Great. She left a message, but decided not to wait, figuring if the owner put up a fuss, she'd reduce the charges. She didn't want to wait any longer.

Amos was clearly in pain.

She placed the animal in her small operating room suite and went to work. After medicating him, she quickly placed the pins and secured them to a long pole. The contraption looked a lot like an erector set, but when she finished, she felt good about how the post X-ray looked.

He might need to wear a cone of shame to keep him from licking the pin sites, but otherwise he should do well. Placing the animal in a large crate to sleep off the meds, she washed up and returned to the clinic. The kid who'd called the police was there, and so was Noah.

"The owner called back," Gramps informed her. "Said to go ahead with the procedure."

That was good news. Avoiding Noah's gaze, she looked at the teen. "Did you get a good glimpse of the car that hit Amos?"

The boy nodded. "I was just telling the detective here that it was a green car, a Ford I think."

A green Ford? The same one she'd followed the night before and found this morning?

What were the odds?

Chapter Nineteen

"**D**id you get the license plate number?" Ally asked. She pulled out her phone. "I have one here to a green Ford and if they're one and the same, then I know where the owner lives." She was more upset about the dog being hit than the owner's possible involvement in the murder.

"No, sorry." The kid's shoulders slumped. "By the time I tried to look, the car was too far away."

"Thanks for your help, Billy," Noah told the kid. "If I need anything else, I'll call, okay?"

"Yeah, that's fine." Billy looked at Ally. "You're sure the dog is going to be okay?"

"I set his leg, and he's sleeping off the medication now. Amos should recover without a problem."

"Good." Billy looked relieved. "I better go, or my mom will come looking for me."

Noah waited until the kid left before turning toward Ally. "What license plate number do you have in your phone?"

It was the first question he'd directed at her since refusing her call the night before. She wanted to be mad, but always found it difficult to hang onto a grudge. "One from a green car I followed to a house located on Terrace Lane." She held up the phone to show him the license number and address. "This is what I was trying to call you about last night."

Noah leaned forward to check the information, then pulled out his own phone. "Read it off to me."

She did as he asked. "I'll be honest, the muffler wasn't loud, Noah. We may have been wrong about that part. But you should know Roxy growled when I took her around the vehicle."

His green gaze flashed with impatience. "Why would you take Roxy around the car like that? I already told you I can't depend on a dog's growl to help solve a crime."

"You'd be foolish not to use every tool available to you," Gramps said tartly. "The dog didn't like Officer Roberts, and turned out he was in the house the day Marty died. It's logical to believe Roxy knows who the killer is, too."

"Maybe, but she can't testify at trial," Noah said wearily. Ally took some comfort in the absence of an eye twitch. Maybe Gramps' theories were growing on him.

"We found the same car in the parking lot of the municipal building," Gramps added helpfully. "Not far from where Marty's car was found. You know how some criminals like to return to the scene of the crime."

"The scene of the crime was in Marty's house, not the parking lot," Noah said dryly. "And it doesn't matter where the car was parked but who owns it. But now that I know the location of the green Ford, I can head over to question the owner about Marty's murder and hitting the dog."

"Amos," Ally said. "The golden's name is Amos, and he's a sweet dog. He didn't deserve to suffer a broken leg by being hit by a car."

"There's no indication the driver hit the dog on purpose." The muscle twitch was back as Noah scowled. "And where is the dog's owner? A better question is why is the dog roaming around town off leash?"

It was a good point, but she still felt bad for the animal. "I don't know, but if hitting the dog was an accident, why take off? Most normal people would stop and check to make sure the animal was okay."

"I agree," Gramps chimed in. "Pretty heartless to keep going."

Noah sighed. "Anything else you'd like to share before I leave?"

"Were you able to verify Roberts's story?" Gramps asked.

Noah remained stubbornly silent.

"Does Roberts own a green Ford?" Ally added.

Noah didn't answer, but the annoyed expression in his eyes made her think the cop was not the Ford's owner.

"I see, so this chatting is a one-way street." Gramps looked irritated. "I don't have anything else to share, do you, Ally?"

While she understood Gramps' frustration, she knew Noah was trying to maintain a professional distance in solving this crime. Personally, she thought he'd be better off including Gramps, but clearly that wasn't happening.

"No. And I need to check on Amos." She turned, hearing the door shut firmly behind Noah as he left.

Amos was still sleeping it off. She stayed for a moment, petting his sleek fur. Poor guy would be hurting once the meds wore off, so she crossed over to her locked medicine cabinet and filled a small bottle of pain pills adjusted for his weight. She added a muscle relaxant too, just in case. Finally, she grabbed a cone and brought everything out to the front counter.

"Any idea when the owner will get here?" she asked Gramps.

"A guy named Mitch said he'd be here as soon as he could." Gramps shrugged. "He didn't give a time frame."

"Okay." She propped her elbows on the counter. "Noah was right about the dog running loose around town. Makes you wonder how that happened?"

Gramps looked down at Roxy. "Not all dogs are well trained."

"I'm pretty sure if I let Roxy run around off leash, she'd take off after a squirrel or some other small animal without hesitation." It was bugging her that Amos had been out on Main Street. "Although the difference being that I'd be out there too, chasing after her."

"True." Gramps glanced down at his notes. "Oops, forgot to tell you about a boarding request. A woman named Renee Kramer is going to be out of town over the Fourth of July, wants to know if you'll board her dog, Coco."

"That's not a problem." Ally was glad that all aspects of her business were attracting customers.

No job too small was beginning to pay off.

Mitch Hanover arrived wearing a construction hat and a tool belt around his waist. He was younger than she'd anticipated and looked truly worried about Amos. "Is he okay?"

"Yes, come with me. Amos is starting to come around." She led Mitch back to the crate area. "You didn't realize he'd gotten out?"

"No." Mitch dragged a hand over his face. "I have a fenced-in yard, and there's shade and water for him. He's never gotten loose like this before."

No wife or kids apparently. Not that she was interested. "Well, I'm sorry to hear he managed to escape the yard."

"Amos." Mitch looked heartbroken to see his dog wearing an external fixator on his leg. He reached in to pet him. Amos lifted his head, looking groggy, but thumping his tail in recognition. "What does this mean? Will I need to stay home with him until it heals?"

Ally hesitated. "I wouldn't say he needs care twenty-four seven, but he shouldn't be alone for long periods, either. Any chance you could stop over to see him a few times a day?"

"Yeah, I can make that happen." Mitch looked determined, and she liked him all the more for it. "My boss, Mr. Kirby, is pretty easygoing. As long as I get the work done, he won't care if I take a few breaks throughout the day."

Kirby? As in Erica's husband? It made her smile to hear Mitch describe Erica's husband as a decent guy. "Good. If something happens and you can't do it, just call me. I can always drop in to check on him too." No way could she ignore Mitch and Amos's plight.

"Thanks, Dr. Winter, I appreciate the offer." Mitch stared at Amos for a moment, then shook his head. "I sure wish I knew how he got out of the yard."

Ally hoped it wasn't a kid's idea of a prank, but kept her thoughts to herself. Mitch paid for the procedure without hesitation, then lifted his dog and carried him out to the truck.

"He seems like a nice guy," Gramps observed. "I think I like him better than your detective."

"Noah has no interest in being *my* detective," she pointed out. "And I don't need a boyfriend. My life is complicated enough, thank you very much."

"Just saying." Gramps shrugged. "Mitch works construction the way I did. You could do worse, you know."

"I know."

"You don't have any other scheduled appointments coming up," Gramps continued. How about we take a drive out to Terrace Lane? See what's happening?"

Her grandfather was incorrigible, but Ally couldn't deny she was curious, too. "Okay, but then we'll grab something for lunch too, okay?"

"Fine with me." Gramps reached for his cane. "Let's bring Roxy. I'm curious to see her reaction to the owner of the Ford."

To be honest, Ally wanted to see it too. She led the way through the clinic and out back to where her Honda was parked. Minutes later, they were on their way.

"Do you think your detective is still there questioning the owner?" Gramps asked. "Could be the person responsible has already been arrested and taken to jail."

"We'll find out soon enough," Ally replied. She kept a wary eye out for stray pets as she navigated the streets. As she approached house number twenty-one-zero-three, she saw Noah's dark SUV parked in front of the place.

But there was no sign of the green Ford. And when she pulled up alongside Noah's SUV, he was sitting behind the wheel.

"No one has shown up yet?" she asked, lifting a brow.

"What are you doing here?" Noah scowled.

"Trying to find out who lives here." She smiled sweetly. "I need to let the dog's owner know the name of the person who hit his dog."

"The dog he left running loose?" Noah countered.

"The dog that somehow got free from his fenced-in yard," Ally corrected. "Now, are you going to tell me who owns this place or not?"

There was a long pause as she and Noah regarded each other through their respective open windows. Finally, he sighed. "Kimberly Mason."

"Kimberly Mason?" Gramps echoed with a frown. "Who is she?"

"But that doesn't make any sense," Ally argued. "She's not on our suspect list."

"I've tried to tell you that a growling dog isn't proof of a crime," Noah said. "And you said yourself the car's muffler wasn't loud."

She hated to admit Noah was right. "So why did Roxy growl near the car?"

"Ally." Noah shook his head. "You and your grandfather absolutely need to leave the investigation to me. I'll figure out if Kimberly is the one who accidently hit the dog, and verify she's not Marty's client. There's nothing more for you to do here."

"You already know Kimberly Mason isn't one of Marty's clients?" Gramps latched onto Noah's words. "Why didn't you just tell us that?"

Noah's left eye twitched but his tone remained calm. "Leave the investigation to me."

"We're going," Ally said, quickly lifting the window to prevent Gramps from saying anything more. Pressing on the accelerator, she drove away.

She tried to look on the bright side. At least they had one less suspect to worry about.

* * *

By the end of the day, Ally was more than ready to drive Gramps home. She buried Amanda's bunny, and tried to ignore Gramps' fixation on Kimberly Mason. "Noah pretty much told us she's not a suspect, Gramps," Ally said wearily.

"I guess." Gramps didn't look happy as they headed outside. Ally tucked Roxy's leash under her arm as she locked the clinic door. "But Roxy growled at the car for a reason."

"Dogs growl, Gramps." She understood Noah's frustration with her idea that Roxy could find the killer. "But it doesn't matter anyway, so let it go, okay?"

"Fine." Gramps paused, then said, "How do you feel about stopping for a quick bite at the Lakefront Café?"

"Why?" Ally was immediately suspicious. "What are you planning now?"

"Nothing." Gramps grinned. "It just might be nice to see if we can find anyone else that makes Roxy growl."

"Gramps . . ." she sighed. "You're seriously killing me."

"What's killing you? To share a meal with your own grandfather?" He thumped his cane. "How many more dinners out do you think I have left?"

She hated when he played up his age to get what he wanted. "Fine, we'll have dinner. But we are not going to use Roxy as a bloodhound, taking her through the patio in an attempt to sniff out a suspect."

"Who, me?" She didn't for one minute buy his innocent act.

231

"You want me to drive over there?" She offered. "I know it's been a long day."

"Nah, I can walk."

She shortened her pace to match his, Roxy trotting along eagerly beside them. "I wonder if Noah has found out who hit Amos."

"As a detective, he should be able to solve at least one mystery," Gramps said with a snort.

Time to change the subject. "How is Lydia, by the way? Will she be okay at lunchtime without Tillie?"

"She should be fine with Harriet." Gramps shrugged. "Although I'm not sure why Tillie's daughter didn't take Harriet with them. Harriet is her aunt, after all."

From what Allie could tell, Harriet barely left the Legacy House. The widow could work wonders in the kitchen, but Ally didn't think she liked walking very far, despite wearing her support hose. "Maybe Harriet stayed specifically to keep Lydia company. Besides, I wouldn't want to be the one to serve Harriet at a restaurant. I think her cooking tops anything out there."

"True. Just like Amelia," Gramps said loyally.

"Aw, you're sweet."

"Whoo-hoo! Oscar!" A woman in her forties wearing a yellow summer blouse over white capri slacks and a large floppy hat waved from one of the Lakeview Café's tables. It took Ally a moment to recognize Virginia White. "Do you have a minute to chat?"

"Hey, Ginny." Gramps recognized her too and nodded. "Sure, we'd be honored to join you."

Ally listened carefully for Roxy to growl, but the boxer was sniffing the air with curiosity, maybe enticed more by the varying scents of food rather than the people seated around them. She followed Gramps over to where Ginny White stood.

"Sit, please," Ginny invited with a smile. "I told Eli about your idea of getting a lawyer to get our money back, and he was very intrigued by the idea."

"Glad to hear it," Gramps said. He sat across from Ginny and hooked his cane over the edge of his chair. "Where is your husband, anyway?"

"Oh, he should be here soon." Ginny sighed and fanned herself. "No matter how hard he tries, Eli always runs late. My, it's certainly warm today, isn't it?"

"No breeze off the lake," Gramps said wisely. Oddly enough, her grandfather never seemed bothered by the weather one way or the other. He leaned forward. "Did you meet with any of Marty's clients about joining the lawsuit?"

"Oh, well, I wouldn't want to intrude." Ginny glanced up as a server approached. "These two are joining me, but we're still waiting on one more."

Ally and Gramps gave their drink orders; raspberry lemonade happened to be one of her favorites, while Ginny sipped a Coke.

"But Marty's other clients deserve to have their money returned as well," Gramps pointed out. "Helping them accomplish that is hardly an imposition."

They fell silent as their server returned with their drinks. Only after she left, promising to return when Eli White arrived, did Ginny speak up.

"I tried, Oscar, but no one wanted to talk to me." Ginny looked put out. "I wasn't trying to be nosy, just mentioned the possibility of getting our money back, but some people were downright rude."

"Like who?" Gramps demanded.

"Kevin Kuhn, for one." Ginny set her Coke aside. "He accused me of snooping into his business."

Gramps flashed Ally a knowing look, no doubt remembering their interaction with him. "He was pretty upset when I happened to mention his dealings with Marty. In fact, he yelled at me, thumped his fist on the counter, and left Ally's veterinary clinic in a huff."

"See?" Ginny waved a hand. "That's what I'm talking about. Kevin saw my question as an invasion of his personal life." She sniffed. "As if I care what he does and when."

"Who else did you talk to?" Gramps' tone sounded casual, but Ally could tell he was having trouble restraining himself. "Anita Jones by chance?"

Ginny's eyes widened comically. "How did you know?"

Ally tried not to roll her eyes. The woman was playing right into Gramps' ego.

As if he needed any help from that perspective.

"I spoke to her right after Marty's murder, and she claimed she wasn't doing any business with him." Gramps pinned Ginny with an intense gaze. "But I gotta tell you, I didn't believe her. I think she was doing business with him, which is why she agreed to refer him to her friends and neighbors."

Ginny nodded sagely. "Exactly. She told me the same thing, that there was no reason for her to be a part of any lawsuit because she hadn't done any business with Marty. That her only goal was to help out a new neighbor by giving him referrals."

Gramps took a long gulp of his lemonade. "What did your husband think of the idea? Is he on board with the plan?"

"Eli was hesitant at first, but he's all gung-ho now. He'll be happier once we get our money back, with interest."

"Sure, sure." Gramps nodded.

Roxy began growling low in her throat. Ally sat up and raked her gaze over the patio, trying to figure out who the dog was growling at.

Ginny frowned and gazed around the restaurant. "Where is he? This is late, even for Eli."

Roxy's growls grew in volume. Gramps turned to her. "Maybe you should take Roxy for a W-A-L-K?" He tipped his head to the side. "See what's bothering her."

Despite her earlier determination not to take Roxy through the sea of tables to sniff out a bad guy, she stood and unwound the leash from the chair. "Roxy? What is it, girl?"

She heard the thudding of footsteps but couldn't see who they belonged to. Ally gave Roxy the lead, doing her best to follow the dog through the convoluted pathway around the patio tables.

There! Someone disappeared through the narrow opening between the Lakefront Café and the municipal building, not far, actually, from the spot where she'd been sitting that first night Roxy had growled at someone's scent. Without glancing back at Gramps, Ally continued in Roxy's wake.

When she reached the dark area between the two buildings, she hesitated, tugging on Roxy's leash. "Wait, girl."

Roxy stood on all fours, her nose pointed at the other end of the alley. Suddenly, Ally heard a car engine roar, the sound echoing loudly through the alley.

The Chevy truck with a bad muffler? Ally hurried forward with Roxy, but it was too late.

The loud vehicle was nowhere in sight.

Chapter Twenty

By the time Ally and Roxy made it back to the table, Ginny's phone was ringing.

"Where is that stupid phone?" She dug around in her massive straw purse that matched her straw hat. "Oh, it's Eli. Hello, where are you?"

Ally dropped beside Gramps, listening to the one-sided conversation. Gramps raised a brow, but she shook her head, indicating she'd found nothing.

"Well, that's a shame, okay, then. I'll see you when I get home." Ginny disconnected from her phone and dropped it into her purse. "Eli isn't feeling well, so he won't be joining us after all."

Wasn't that interesting? Ally glanced over to the other side of the patio, wondering if Eli had started over only to be outed by Roxy's growl. "His illness came on rather suddenly, didn't it?"

Ginny frowned. "Well, you know how it is with these summer bugs. One minute you're fine, the next you're not."

"Are you sure he's at home?" Ally persisted.

"Yes, he has no reason to lie. Besides, I heard the cuckoo clock chiming in the background." Ginny craned her neck searching for their server. "I'm ready to order if you are, Oscar."

"Sure," Gramps agreed.

Ally felt certain Ginny would have preferred to have Gramps all to herself, but she wasn't leaving. Why hadn't she considered Eli White as a suspect? For all they knew, Ginny was oblivious to what her husband might have done.

"What kind of car does Eli drive?" Ally asked.

Ginny and Gramps both stared at her as if she'd sprouted wings and declared her intent to fly.

"Why do you ask?" Ginny's tone was sharp.

Gramps lightly kicked her under the table, as if annoyed with her lack of subtlety.

"Oh, um, I thought I saw Eli the other day." Ally took a hurried sip of her raspberry lemonade and then began coughing and choking when it went down the wrong pipe.

"You okay?" Gramps thumped her on the back. Roxy stared up at her, wide brown eyes full of concern.

"Fine," she managed between hacking coughs. "Water?"

No water had been set on the table. Ally took a tentative sip of raspberry lemonade, slower this time.

"I didn't realize you'd met Eli," Ginny commented, when Ally finally managed to stop coughing.

"I ran into him at the sandwich shop," Ally replied.

"The sandwich shop? Why on earth would that make you curious about his car?" Ginny demanded.

Good question. Ally sent a panicked glance at Gramps. She wasn't cut out for this kind of thing. Her interrogation skills sucked. If she'd been smart, she would have found a way to get Gramps to ask about the car.

Gramps would have gotten the information without choking to death or breaking a sweat.

"No reason," Ally murmured. "I was just curious."

Their server approached, so they spent the next few minutes ordering dinner. When the woman left, Ginny had eyes only for Gramps.

"Oscar, I heard you visit the library every week, do you have any recommendations for me?"

This time, Ally poked him beneath the table in an attempt to prevent him from recommending Ginny read *The Evil Within*.

"Oh, you must have spoken to Rosie," Gramps said with a smile. "I read a lot of true crime stuff, you might not be interested in those books. But I did read the latest David Baldacci. Have you tried the Amos Dekker series? It's great."

"No, I haven't." Ginny was at least twenty-five years younger than Gramps, but she actually batted her eyelashes at him. "Sounds intriguing."

"I used to listen to some of his audiobooks, back when I was doing more driving between construction sites," Gramps added.

It was all Ally could do not to gape in surprise. Audiobooks? The man who couldn't use his cell phone without yelling in her ear? No way.

"I haven't tried listening to audiobooks," Ginny admitted.

"My son used to get them for me. I guess he listened to them often during his commute from here to the university."

Understanding dawned. Gramps didn't listen to audiobooks. This was just his way of getting back to the type of car Eli White drove. Ally smiled at Ginny. "The newer cars have it so that the book plays right off your smart phone and through the speakers. It's pretty cool technology." Ally sighed dramatically. "My Honda is too old to have that feature."

"Our cars are too old, too, I'm sure," Ginny said, waving her hand. "Eli drives them until they're beyond repair."

"Speaking of which, do you need a ride home now that Eli is sick?" Ally asked. "I can give you a lift."

"Oh, that won't be necessary. We live just a few blocks behind the municipal building."

"Close to Marty Shawlin, then?" Gramps said idly.

"Not close enough to have heard the commotion, but not far." Ginny frowned. "I still can't believe we had a murder here in Willow Bluff."

"Me either," Ally agreed.

"It's the first one we've had in the past few years, since old Benny Halloway pushed his wife down the stairs." Ginny tsk-tsked. "And he confessed right away, so there was no real investigation by the police needed to solve that one."

"I remember that. You know, Ally here found Marty's body," Gramps confided in a low voice. "How long would he have been lying there if she hadn't agreed to take Roxy for a walk every day at lunchtime, I wonder?"

"It's crazy." Ginny didn't look the least bit surprised at the revelation. The way news traveled around here Ally wondered if everyone in town had a secret phone number they used for updated gossip. "That must have been dreadful."

"It was." Ally wanted to get back to the subject of Eli White's car but couldn't find a good transition.

Gramps seemed to have run out of ideas too. A few minutes later, their food arrived and conversation lagged as they ate. Ally picked up the check, feeling it was the least she could do.

"We insist on driving you home," Gramps announced. "Ally, why don't you run back and get your car? We'll wait here."

"Okay." Ally wasn't sure why Gramps wanted her out of the way, but she stood and unwrapped Roxy's leash. It didn't take more than five minutes for her to get back to the clinic. She put Roxy in the crated hatchback, then drove back toward the Lakefront Café.

"See? I knew that wouldn't take long." Gramps grinned and gestured for Ginny to precede him. "You can sit up front if you like."

"Okay." Ginny slid into the passenger seat while Ally helped Gramps into the back.

Ginny gave her directions to the house, which indeed was just two blocks from Marty's place. As she pulled into the driveway, she noticed a red and rather rusty Chevy truck parked in the garage.

The same one they'd seen a few nights ago? Up close, it looked older and in worse shape than the one she remembered.

Then again, she'd only gotten a quick glimpse.

Ally couldn't seem to tear her gaze away. Was it possible Eli had thrown the rock at her clinic, then escaped in his old rusty Chevy? Then took things a step further to steal the GMC truck to run her off the road? Had Eli White murdered Marty Shawlin? Had he taken off earlier, despite what Ginny had said about his being home, due to her hearing the cuckoo clock? This all seemed to be a stretch, just like most of Gramps' theories.

"Thanks for dinner and the ride," Ginny said cheerfully, unaware of the tumultuous thoughts running through her mind. "Don't be a stranger, Oscar."

"I won't," Gramps assured her.

Ginny got out of the car, waved, and walked toward the house.

"Do you see it?" Gramps asked from the back seat.

"Yeah. Think it's the same one we saw near the Legacy House? And the vehicle that was heard after the rock slammed into my clinic?" Ally backed out of the driveway.

"I don't remember it being in such rough shape, but maybe. If so, that detective of yours should already have the guy behind bars," Gramps muttered in disgust. "What's taking him so long?"

Ally didn't have an answer for that. It was all so confusing. Noah had asked them to trust him, and she was trying. Yet Willow Bluff didn't have a high crime rate, especially related to murder.

It could be that Gramps was right about Noah's inability to solve the crime.

And it was distressing to think that Marty's murderer might get off scot-free.

*　*　*

Ally dropped Gramps off at the Legacy house and dredged up the willpower to refuse Harriet's offer of hot fudge sundaes for dessert. She took a moment to check on Lydia's twisted ankle, relieved to see that it wasn't too badly swollen.

"I'll be ready to help next week, Ally," Lydia promised.

"I don't mind working for you, either, Ally," Gramps added, as if she could possibly forget.

"I know, thanks to both of you." As she left, she hoped that one day she could afford to hire a real vet tech to relieve the widows from their duty.

She was about to head home when she decided to take a quick swing past the house with the green Ford on Terrace Lane. Had Noah questioned Kimberly about hitting Amos?

If he had, she doubted he'd let her or Gramps know.

Really, Noah should be working *with* them on this. Especially if he didn't have much experience in homicide. Not that she and Gramps were experts, but the more minds working the details, the better, right? The more she thought about that, the angrier she became.

Annoyed, she returned to the clinic. After opening the hatch and letting Roxy out, she took the dog for a short walk before going inside. Roxy's nails were loud against the hardwood floor, so she made a mental note to clip them in the morning.

She filled Roxy's food and water dishes, then ran down to clean the clinic. Tomorrow was Friday and she only had one appointment scheduled, but it was bright and early at eight o'clock.

Pungent bleach filled her nose as she wiped down all the surfaces. Why had Gramps set an appointment for eight o'clock? Maybe she should post regular hours for the Furry Friends Veterinary Clinic. At first, there'd been no need as there hadn't been many clients to care for, but now that business was picking up, Ally didn't want to work at the whim of the local pet owners.

But she was working, which was the point.

Staying flexible during the summer hours might be smart, and once she found some sort of routine, she could post regular hours.

Except of course she'd always be available on call for emergencies.

Like poor Amos being hit by a car.

She made another mental note to check with Mitch on Amos's progress the next day, then went back upstairs. Roxy wanted out one last time, then she settled down to sleep.

*   *   *

The loud BEEP BEEP BEEP of her alarm had Ally skyrocketing out of bed. She groaned and stared at the time. Six o'clock. "I hate mornings," she muttered, hitting the snooze button with more force than was probably necessary.

But getting another ten minutes of rest was impossible. Roxy was up and licking her face for attention. Ally gently pushed her away. Roxy whined and licked again. Ally groaned and rolled out of bed. "Fine, I'll take you out."

She used the bathroom and decided not to change out of her baggy shorts and ratty T-shirt she used as sleepwear. She slid her feet into flip-flops, hooked Roxy's leash, and took the stairs outside.

Because she was dressed like a bum, Ally stayed along the back of the building. Roxy wasn't having it, though, and strained against the leash in an effort to go farther.

Ally stumbled after Roxy, letting the dog take the lead. She had a baggie in her pocket and was more than ready for Roxy to finish her business so she could shower and change.

Roxy turned the corner, still pulling at the leash. Ally frowned when she realized Roxy was taking her toward Marty's house.

She hadn't been there since that first day she'd stumbled across Marty's body.

"What is it, girl? Are you missing Marty?" Ally gave up fighting the dog, letting the boxer lead her down the street toward her previous home.

The white Cape Cod with black shutters looked the same, with the exception of the crime scene tape still crisscrossed over the door.

Noah hadn't released the house yet? Interesting. They must have gotten all the evidence out of there by now, hadn't they? Too bad she hadn't taken the time to look through the papers around Marty's briefcase. Certainly, Noah must have garnered a decent list of suspects from those.

Had Noah crossed Sheila off the list? She remembered now Gramps' theory about Sheila Young potentially being Marty's beneficiary, despite their recent divorce. If Ginny and Eli White could be considered suspects over a measly sixteen hundred dollars, imagine how much Sheila stood to gain from the property.

From the little Ally knew about the woman, Sheila seemed to be the type to pester Noah to release the house if she was entitled to the property. Now that she'd relocated to Chicago, Sheila would no doubt want the place listed with the colorfully annoying Ellen Cartwright ASAP.

Roxy used Marty's front lawn to do her business. For a split second Ally toyed with the idea of leaving Roxy's gift for Sheila, but the responsible pet owner in her couldn't do it. She scooped the poop and looked around for a place to dump it. Along the side of Marty's one-car garage, she could see two large containers, one for garbage the other for recycling.

With a shrug, she walked up the driveway to the side of the garage and used the garbage can. Roxy sniffed the air, making

Ally wonder if she could still pick up Marty's scent all these days later.

Personally? She thought it was likely Roxy could. "Better, girl?" She asked. "Can we go home, now?"

Roxy looked up at her, wagging her stumpy tail.

Ally bent over to scratch the softness behind Roxy's ears, feeling bad she hadn't come by this way before. "Wow, Roxy. All this time you were missing Marty and I never noticed. What kind of vet am I, anyway?"

Roxy licked the back of her hand.

"I guess that means I'm forgiven." Ally straightened and was about to turn away when she caught a glimpse of a house two doors down.

She frowned. Anita Jones's house? She took several steps to get a better view of the back side of the home. As she watched, the door opened, and a figure eased out. It took a moment for her to realize it was a man with brown hair, someone she didn't recognize from the back, who was leaving Anita's house through the back door. What in the world was he doing? As the question flashed through her mind, Roxy began to growl.

Not again. The man must have heard Roxy's growl, because he jerked and smacked his head against the edge of the door.

She heard a muttered curse, then the guy began to run.

A burglar?

"Hey! Stop!" Ally called out. Roxy strained against the leash, and following the guy seemed like a good idea.

She let Roxy take the lead, although keeping up while wearing ridiculous flip-flops wasn't easy. The damp grass made her slip and slide. "Hey!" she shouted again. "Don't make me call the police!"

Why wasn't she calling the police? Oh yeah, because she hadn't brought her phone with her. This was just supposed to be a quick bathroom break for the dog, not a cross-country marathon in inappropriate footwear.

The brown-haired guy was dressed in jeans and a short-sleeved tan polo shirt. That was all she could tell from the back, and she hadn't gotten a good look at his face from the front.

He darted between two houses, disappearing from view.

Roxy and Ally followed, but when they came out from between the two properties, she stopped abruptly upon reaching the street.

There was no sign of the guy.

"Which way, Roxy?" Ally asked between gasping breaths. Her toes ached from trying to keep the stupid flip-flops from flipping and flopping right off her feet.

Roxy lifted her head, her nostrils quivering as she tried to pick up the guy's scent.

"Well?" Ally asked, feeling impatient. "We don't have all day."

Roxy looked up at her, then back at the last place they'd seen the brown-haired man.

They'd lost him. And worse, Ally couldn't even say for certain who he was and why in the world he'd been leaving Anita Jones's house through the back door at six thirty in the morning.

A weird coincidence? A hot affair? Or was this all related in some bizarre way to Marty's murder?

Chapter Twenty-One

Ally took Roxy back to the clinic, hobbling a bit as a stone had gotten between her bare foot and the bottom of her sandal, impaling itself in her arch. "We shouldn't have come this way, Roxy."

The dog trotted happily beside her, clearly thrilled with the extra time outside.

Who had the brown-haired guy been? And why on earth had he snuck out the back door like that? Okay, maybe she'd read books or seen TV shows where men having illicit affairs escaped because a spouse had come home early, but Anita didn't have a spouse.

A burglar? That might explain it, except for the fact that it was six fifteen in the morning. Who burgled houses that early? Wasn't that a nighttime activity?

The whole thing made no sense.

By the time she'd showered, eaten breakfast, and made it down to the clinic, it was ten minutes to eight. She donned her white lab coat and headed over to unlock the door.

Ten seconds later, it opened.

"My name is Mary Baker and I'm here for Toby to get his shots." The woman looked to be Ally's age, but Ally couldn't place her from high school. Not that her memory was perfect by any means. Mary could be a more recent transplant to the area, although the younger crowd tended to leave small towns like Willow Bluff for the bigger cities of Madison, Milwaukee, and Green Bay.

"Of course, come on in." Ally smiled at Toby, a white shih tzu that couldn't have weighed more than four pounds dripping wet. Ally gestured to the exam room. "We can use the first room."

"Great." Mary stroked Toby's white fur. "He hates coming to the vet," she confided.

"Most animals do," Ally said with a wry smile. "But it's important to keep their immunizations up to date."

"I know." Mary gently set Toby on the table. The dog wasn't trembling the way some did, and Ally hoped that meant he wasn't as afraid of shots as his owner believed.

"Any problems or concerns?" Ally asked as she prepared the medication.

"No, he's doing very well." Mary lifted her hand to shield Toby's eyes, explaining, "I don't want him to see the n-e-e-d-l-e."

Roxy knew the word walk, so it was possible Toby understood the word needle. Rare, but possible. Ally nodded. "Okay, hold him steady, and this will be over in a minute."

She gave the injection and Toby let out several high-pitched yips, turned his head, and sank his teeth into Ally's hand.

"Ouch!" Ally snatched her hand out of the way.

"That's a good boy," Mary crooned, oblivious to the blood welling from the bite marks on Ally's skin. "Yes, you were such a good boy."

Not that good, Ally thought, glancing at her injured hand. She disposed of the needle, then went over to wash her hands in the sink. It wasn't her first dog bite and wouldn't be her last, but usually animal owners apologized when their pets bit the vet.

Not this time.

"Okay, do you need anything else?" Ally asked with a forced smile. "Flea and tick medication?"

"No, I think we're good there." Mary was cradling Toby against her chest.

Ally led the way back out to the counter and went around to print the invoice. Mary's credit card worked fine, and the woman was gone in a matter of minutes.

She slowly headed up to the apartment, needing more coffee. Between her sore foot and injured hand, this was turning out to be a less than stellar day.

Two cups of coffee and nearly an hour later, she was feeling better. She'd brought Roxy down to the clinic for company, since the place was empty.

Her phone rang and she quickly answered. "Furry Friends, this is Dr. Winter, may I help you?"

"Ally? It's Erica. Listen, Tommy is sick so I'm not going to be able to do lunch today."

"Oh, I'm sorry to hear Tommy is sick." Ally smacked her palm against her forehead. She'd forgotten all about lunch with Erica. She'd been looking forward to reuniting with her friend.

And pumping her for information about Noah.

"Rain check?" Erica asked.

"Of course. Take care of Tommy." Ally had no sooner hung up when the phone rang a second time. With a sigh, she braced herself when she recognized Gramps' cell phone number. "Hey Gramps, what's new?"

"YOU FORGOT TO COME GET ME!"

"Please don't yell, and I thought we agreed that three days in a row was too much. I only had one appointment so far today and she's already been here and gone."

"WE NEED TO TALK ABOUT THE CASE."

His shouting was giving her a headache. "Okay, how about Roxy and I come visit with you later this afternoon?" Ally planned to close early, especially if she didn't get any additional calls. "We can talk more then."

"WHY NOT COME FOR LUNCH? HARRIET WON'T MIND."

Very tempting, but Ally refrained. "I'll stop by after lunch, Gramps. I need to run a few errands, anyway. I'm out of people food and dog food."

There was a long silence as he digested that bit of information. She could tell her grandfather didn't like the idea of her going off on her own. He wanted to be there with her if she stumbled across any clues.

Although she wasn't sure why he was worried. Gramps was the one who managed to get suspects to talk, not her.

All except for Kevin Kuhn.

"SEE YOU LATER, THEN." Gramps thankfully disconnected.

Ally sat back in the chair. Later, she'd have to fill Gramps in on how she and Roxy had chased after the guy they'd seen leaving through Anita's back door. Sure, Roxy had growled at the guy, but lately she seemed to be growling at several people. Cars, too.

Making it difficult to believe the dog actually knew who'd killed Marty.

As much as Ally hated to admit it, Noah might have been right about that. Roxy wasn't a trained police dog, and maybe there was a certain category of men she just didn't like in general. Like smokers, or those who wore a certain kind of cologne.

Now that she thought about it, Ally remembered smelling smoke last night as she approached the narrow opening between the two buildings. That might be an interesting clue. Did Sheila's boyfriend, Nick, smoke? And what about Eli White or Kevin Kuhn?

"I wish you could talk, Roxy." She smoothed her uninjured hand over Roxy's soft fur. "At the rate this case is going, we're never going to figure out who killed Marty and why."

After another hour had passed without a single phone call or walk-in, Ally decided to lock up and go to the grocery store. It had been two weeks since she'd bought any food, but thanks to the recent uptick in clients, she had enough cash to get something other than mac and cheese from a box and ramen noodles. Not to mention top-of-the-line dog food for Roxy.

"Sorry, Roxy, you can't come with me this time." She took the dog outside briefly, then left her in the apartment.

The grocery store wasn't far, but it was more crowded than she had anticipated. Ally took her time going through the store, choosing meats and veggies she could make into simple meals.

Cooking was not her forte, certainly not like it was Harriet's.

The fifty-pound bag of dog food barely fit along the bottom of the cart. She went through her mental list, then took her place in line. Ally was surprised to find Rosie Malone standing in front of her. For a moment, Ally wondered again about Gramps' claim that Rosie had lied about knowing Marty.

"Good morning, Rosie," Ally said in a cheerful voice. "How are you?"

Rosie turned and looked flustered. "Oh, uh, Ally, right? Oscar's granddaughter? I'm fine, thanks."

Ally couldn't think of a subtle way to ask about Marty, more proof she hadn't inherited Gramps' interrogation techniques. "Remember when Gramps and I stopped at the library and asked about Marty?" She blurted.

Rosie stiffened. "Yes, but I already told you I never spoke to him."

"Yeah, but the thing is that Gramps remembered seeing you talking to him at the library counter less than a week before the murder."

Ally's blunt statement caught Rosie off guard. Her hand fluttered to her throat. "I'm sure Oscar was mistaken."

"Really? That's your story?" Ally shook her head. "You know as well as I do that Gramps is as sharp as a tack. If he says he saw you and Marty together, then that's what happened."

"I'm sorry, but that's impossible. Oscar is wrong," Rosie insisted, her gaze darting around the grocery store. "Excuse me, I seem to have forgotten the ravioli."

Before Ally could say anything more, Rosie left the line and walked briskly to the noodle aisle. Ally briefly considered following her but figured the woman would just continue to deny everything.

Interesting, though. Rosie's odd behavior convinced Ally that the woman had indeed spoken to Marty before he died.

But why? Ally knew people only lied to cover up something they didn't want anyone else to know.

What was it about her meeting with Marty that Rosie didn't want anyone to discover?

* * *

Ally and Roxy arrived at the Legacy House just after the widows had finished eating lunch. Lydia was sitting in the living room with her injured ankle propped up on the ottoman, while Gramps, Ally, and Roxy made their way outside.

Harriet hadn't said a word about Roxy being in the house, but Ally thought it best not to push her luck.

"Hey, Gramps." Ally embraced her grandfather and then took a seat beside him. Roxy greeted him enthusiastically, too, wagging her stumpy tail as Gramps scratched behind her ears.

"Slow day at Furry Friends, huh?" Gramps asked. Then he frowned. "What happened to your hand?"

"Toby." She rubbed the bite marks, hoping she wouldn't need to go on antibiotics. "A white shih tzu I immunized this morning."

Gramps shook his head. "You get bit a lot, don't you?"

More than she should. "Yeah, but I'm fine. Things at the clinic have definitely been looking up." She paused, then added, "What do you know about Anita Jones's private life? Is she seeing anyone? A particular guy she's been spending a lot of time with?"

"Not that I know of, but we could ask Lydia. She talks to Anita more than I do." Gramps' keen blue gaze narrowed. "Why do you ask?"

Ally filled Gramps in on her early morning walk that ended up taking her to Marty's house and the man she'd seen escaping out the back door of Anita's house.

"Curious indeed," Gramps murmured.

"I also ran into Rosie Malone at the grocery store. I flat-out called her a liar, but she still insists you were mistaken and that she never spoke to Marty."

"I'm not wrong, I know what I saw," Gramps said firmly. "But that's not nearly as interesting as a man sneaking out of Anita's house. What do you think that was about?"

"No idea."

"You didn't get a good look at him?" Gramps asked.

"No. Brown hair, not as tall as Noah, medium size, on the thin side." She shook her head. "I hate to say it but could have been anyone."

"I should have been there."

She shook her head. "I'm telling you, if it wasn't for Roxy half dragging me to Marty's place at six in the morning, I would have missed seeing him coming out through the back door." She rested her hand on Roxy's head. "Poor girl misses Marty more than I realized."

"Hrmph." Gramps clearly held no such sentiment toward Marty Shawlin.

"What do you think, Gramps? Is Anita having a hot fling? Or were the two of them talking about how to continue covering up Marty's murder?"

"Good question." Gramps nodded thoughtfully. "I'm going with covering up murder."

No surprise there.

"Lydia?" Gramps called loudly.

"What do you need, Oscar?" Lydia shouted back from her perch on the living room sofa.

"Don't yell back and forth, I'll go inside and ask about Anita." Ally opened the screen door and stepped inside. "Hi, Lydia, sorry to bother you, but do you happen to know if Anita Jones has been seeing anyone recently?"

Lydia's fingers wielded her knitting needles like tiny swords. Her brow furrowed. "No, dear, not that she's mentioned. Why?"

"I was just curious. Thought I saw a man leaving her place early this morning."

"Really? I'd think if Anita had a man in her life, she would have confided in me. We used to volunteer at the hospital together and became quite friendly." Lydia's brow furrowed, and her snow-white curls bounced as she bobbed her head. "I'll have to check with my sources, see if I've missed something along the way."

"If you do find out she has a new man in her life, will you let me know?"

"Of course, dear." Lydia frowned. "But surely you don't think Anita had anything to do with Marty's murder?"

"Probably not, but you never know." Ally flashed a smile and was about to leave, when she turned back to Lydia. "You mentioned you and Anita were friends. Was she also close to Marty? I'm just trying to figure out why Anita referred Marty to you and the others around town."

"Anita had a kind heart," Lydia said with a hint of defensiveness. "I believe she truly wanted to give Marty a helping hand since he had financial troubles after his divorce. If Marty's business wasn't legitimate, that was hardly her fault."

"Yet Anita insisted she wasn't a client of Marty's," Ally pointed out.

"Yes, she was, dear," Lydia corrected. "She specifically told me she was impressed with Marty's work."

Really? Ally didn't remember Lydia mentioning this information during her conversation with Noah, but Anita being Marty's client was exactly what she and Gramps had suspected. She nodded and headed back out to the patio to sit beside Gramps. "Lydia's going to see what she can find out. Oh, and she confirmed that Anita *was* Marty's client."

"I knew it." Gramps rested his hand on Roxy's back. "We'll need to question her again. Not just about Marty's business dealings, but about the guy who snuck out of her house this morning."

"We can't ask her that, Gramps, she'll kick us out." She shook her head, knowing all the charm in the world wasn't going to help Gramps get the information he wanted from Anita. Especially if the woman was having some sort of hot affair.

Her cell phone rang. Seeing Noah's name on the screen made her stomach do a funny little flip. She ignored it. "Hi, Noah, what's up?"

"Where are you? I'm at the clinic, but it's locked up tight."

He'd come to see her? Her stomach did another flip. "I'm at the Legacy House sitting on the patio with Gramps, why?" She straightened in her chair. "Do you have a break in the case?"

There was a moment of silence, almost as if Noah was debating the wisdom of including Gramps, but then he said, "I'll drive out to meet with you and your grandfather. Be there in a few."

Before she could ask another question, he disconnected.

"Your detective is heading this way?" Gramps asked with a gleam in his eye.

She was too intrigued by what Noah wanted to tell them to be annoyed with the way Gramps kept referring to Noah as if he belonged to her. "Yeah. You think there's been a break in the case?"

"Could be he's made an arrest." Gramps looked almost disappointed by the possibility. "Maybe someone else saw the guy leaving Anita's house and reported it." Gramps tipped his head to the side. "Which is what you should have done."

"I didn't have my phone with me. Besides, he left the house through the door, not a window." And the thought of Noah showing up and seeing her in ratty sleep clothes, her hair a wild mess, and no makeup made her shudder.

"Still." Gramps stroked his chin. "If he *has* made an arrest, I think Kevin Kuhn is our perp."

"Perp?" Ally rolled her eyes. "You sound like a TV show detective."

"Short for perpetrator," Gramps added.

"I know what it means." She considered secretly tampering with the TV in Gramps' room but knew he'd only read more books then. *Dateline* had to be less gruesome than a book called *The Evil Within*.

"What about Ginny's husband Eli?" Ally couldn't seem to get her mind off the murder either. "Last night was strange, wasn't it? Roxy growling at someone, then Eli White suddenly calling off sick. And don't forget his beat-up red Chevy."

"True," Gramps conceded. "Although if Ginny was right about the cuckoo clock and wasn't covering for him, he's probably in the clear. Either way, you need to fill your detective in on everything that's happened over the past twenty-four hours."

"Maybe." She wasn't so sure Noah wanted to hear their theory. At some point, both his eyes might start to twitch. She didn't want to be responsible for bringing on a full-blown seizure. "But it won't matter if he's already arrested Marty's killer."

"Kevin Kuhn," Gramps repeated.

Had the guy leaving Anita's house that morning been Kevin Kuhn? Very possibly. Kevin and Eli both had brown hair and the same general build. It was difficult to imagine Kevin and Anita engrossed in a passionate affair, but then again, what did she know?

Roxy leaped to her feet, her stubby tail wagging with excitement, moments before Noah strode into view. Ally hated to admit he was as handsome as ever, dressed in black dress slacks and a bright green polo shirt that matched his eyes.

"Oscar, Ally." Noah bent down to greet Roxy, running his hands over her golden-brown fur. "Hi, Roxy, have you been behaving yourself? No growling, I hope."

It was a less than subtle dig at her. Ally waved toward the empty chair. "Have a seat. I'm guessing you've arrested Marty's murderer?"

"What? Oh, no, not yet." Noah actually looked discomfited by having to admit his failure in that area. "But I did get a chance to talk to Kimberly Mason. She admitted to hitting the golden retriever, Amos, and feels terrible about it. She's more than happy to pay the vet bill."

"That's a nice offer, and Mitch is the one she'd have to work with on that, but why did she take off after hitting him?" Ally asked.

"Fair question. Apparently Kimberly used to work as the administrative assistant for Mayor Martha Cromlin. That morning, the mayor terminated Kimberly's employment."

It was hard to be mad at someone who'd just lost her job. "I guess I can understand," Ally agreed. "Although if it were me, I still would have stopped to make sure the animal was okay."

"I'm with Ally," Gramps said. "Why did she lose her job, anyway?"

"Apparently the mayor has a niece who needs a summer job." Noah shrugged. "Family first, as they say. And Kimberly claims she didn't realize she hit the dog at all. She was crying as she was driving, upset about being replaced by some fresh-faced college kid who doesn't know the first thing about being an administrative assistant. She didn't hear the thud, which is why she kept going."

Again, difficult to argue that.

"Kimberly was working both the day the rock was thrown at Ally's clinic and the day of Marty's murder," Noah continued. "Despite your concern about Roxy growling at the green Ford while it was in her driveway, I've taken her off the suspect list."

"One down, several more to go," Gramps quipped.

Noah scowled, and Ally hid a grin. It was reassuring to know Kimberly Mason hadn't hit poor Amos on purpose, was innocent of throwing the rock at her clinic, and of murdering Marty.

But from where Ally was sitting? Without Gramps' help, Noah would never solve the mystery around Marty's untimely demise.

Chapter
Twenty-Two

No one spoke for a long moment. Surprisingly, Noah didn't seem anxious to be on his way.

He'd either mellowed in the past few days or was waiting for them to spill what they'd uncovered about the suspects.

"You better fill him in on what we know," Gramps said, as if reading her mind.

Noah looked interested and, for once, there was no sign of the twitchy eye. "Yes, please do fill me in."

Where to start? Ally had to think back to the last time she'd given Noah any information. Oh yeah, it was when Amos had been hit by Kimberly's car and she'd completed the procedure to set his hind leg. "We had dinner with Ginny White at the Lakefront Café last night."

"You and your grandfather had dinner with Ginny White?" The way Noah asked, she could tell he was wondering how they'd finagled such a thing.

"Yes, it was actually Ginny's idea. She flagged us over. Her husband, Eli, was supposed to join us, but he was running late. A man tried to make his way over but did a one-eighty when

Roxy began to growl. The dog led me across the patio, through the opening between the buildings, in the direction the guy had gone. It was hard to get a good look at him, because there were so many other people sitting around tables, obstructing the view. As we approached the opposite end of the patio, I caught a glimpse of him leaving through the alleyway between the restaurant and the municipal building."

The earlier interest in Noah's gaze faded. He opened his mouth, no doubt to lecture her once again on the fact that Roxy's growls weren't evidence, and she lifted a hand to stop him.

"Hold on, let me finish. The guy disappeared and as I turned to head back to the table, I heard a loud car driving from the area. Within two minutes of me sitting beside Gramps, Ginny gets a call from her husband Eli, claiming he feels too sick to attend dinner."

Noah's green gaze was skeptical. "You think Eli White is the guy Roxy was growling at? And he took off when he realized the dog caught his scent?"

"Why not?" Ally waved at Roxy. "She doesn't growl at everyone, Noah. Oh, and I caught a whiff of cigarette smoke too, which makes me wonder if Eli White is a smoker."

"Yeah," Gramps added for emphasis. "Now tell him about the guy leaving through the back door of Anita's house."

"What?" Noah's gaze bounced from Gramps back to her. "When?"

"Early this morning." She went on to describe what had happened, leaving out the details of her ensemble and forgetting her phone at home.

"I think the guy who left Anita's house is Kevin Kuhn," Gramps said, leaning toward Noah. "Kevin has brown hair, just like the guy Ally saw, and he was very angry when I tried to talk to him about Marty."

"So you said," Noah responded dryly. "I thought Eli White was your latest suspect? He has brown hair, too."

"I know," Ally confirmed. "I met him at the sandwich shop. He's also the same general size and build as Kevin Kuhn."

"Isn't that interesting?" Gramps pounced on that tidbit of information. "Does Kevin Kuhn smoke? If not, that might help us narrow down our suspect."

Noah groaned and lifted his gaze toward the sky as if seeking divine intervention.

"Look, Noah, now that we know either one of them could be involved, we need more information. Like which one of them might not have an alibi for the time frame of Marty's murder," Ally pointed out.

Noah continued to avoid her gaze.

It was frustrating that he wouldn't talk to them about the case. Sure, she understood why he didn't want to, but it wasn't as if Noah couldn't use a little help.

"Let's assume that neither one of the two men has an alibi for the murder," Gramps said. "We have Roxy growling at the man at the café and growling at the man leaving Anita's place through the back door. Eli White could be having an affair, but it seems unlikely that he'd be heading home at six in the morning without Ginny noticing. I think it could just as easily be Kevin Kuhn who left Anita's house and was the same guy on the patio."

"But that would make Eli's calling off sick at the last minute a big fat coincidence," Ally protested.

"True." Gramps stared at Noah. "And we all know cops don't believe in coincidences, right, detective?"

Ally checked Noah's face. No sign of the eye twitch.

Yet.

"Okay, so you're leaning toward Eli White as being the suspect," Ally said since Noah was still staring up at the sky. Maybe sky gazing was a new technique to ward off the eye tic.

"I am," Gramps agreed, even though it hadn't been more than a few minutes since he'd declared Kevin Kuhn the culprit.

She put a hand up to her face. Was her own eye starting to twitch?

"I have a question," Gramps announced. "Who is the beneficiary to Marty Shawlin's estate?"

Noah drew in a slow deep breath and brought his gaze back to them. "His ex-wife, Sheila Young." Noah held up a hand. "Before you ask, she was in Chicago when Marty was murdered, and I verified her alibi."

"Did you know she has a new boyfriend who's a cop on the Chicago Police force?" Gramps asked.

Noah scowled. "And what, you think she sent the cop boyfriend up here to kill Marty so she can get the house?"

"Why not?" Gramps was warming up to his theory. *One of many*, Ally thought with a sigh. "The house and whatever cash is in Marty's bank account is worth more than what most of Marty's clients lost in his goofy will/trust scheme."

"I have his name and number, if you're interested," Ally chimed in. "Nick Calderone." She frowned. "Maybe Nick is of medium build and has brown hair, too."

And the eye twitch was back. "How did you get that information? Or don't I want to know?"

263

Ally grinned. "It was Gramps' idea to ask them both to sign off on a transfer of ownership agreement, giving Roxy to me. If Sheila thought it was strange that I included her new boyfriend, she didn't argue about it."

"I see." Despite the eye twitch, Ally could tell Noah was impressed. "Any other theories of the crime you've been holding back from me?"

"You weren't interested in hearing them, remember?" Ally narrowed her gaze. "And, no, the only other oddity is the way Rosie Malone lied to us about speaking with Marty. Which I asked her about earlier today when I went to the grocery store. She claims Gramps must be mistaken."

"But I'm not," Gramps interjected.

"I know," Ally assured him.

Gramps leaned forward. "Rosie's lie really bothers me. I get that she might be trying to avoid getting dragged into a murder investigation, but it doesn't make much sense to lie about something so innocuous." Gramps glanced at Noah. "Do you know why she'd lie?"

Noah simply sighed.

"Maybe she was embarrassed to have given Marty money and wanted to pretend it never happened." Ally could understand the motivation; she'd wanted to pretend Tim and Trina hadn't had an affair right under her nose.

And then left the country, leaving her with a pile of wedding debt and a partnerless clinic.

"You should let us review Marty's client list," Gramps said, still looking at Noah. "After talking to some of the Willow Bluff residents, we might be able to find something you missed."

Ally coughed, to hide a snicker.

"Not happening, Oscar." Noah's expression turned impatient. "Besides, the client list isn't foolproof. Marty could have taken money from someone without getting around to recording it before his death."

Ally remembered the open briefcase. "Or the killer took the paperwork with them, so it's missing from the client list altogether."

"Right." Noah rose to his feet. "Thanks for the criminal minds brainstorming session, but I need to get back to work."

"Who are you going to talk to next?" Gramps asked. "Are you going to check to see if Nick Calderone has an alibi, like Sheila? Or are you going to head over to talk to Anita Jones? It would be good to get the identity of the man who snuck out through her back door."

The corner of Noah's mouth quirked in a lopsided smile. "As much as I'd love to do that, Anita's love life isn't relevant to the murder investigation."

"You can't know that until you ask!" Gramps shouted as Noah walked away.

Noah didn't respond.

"You know," Gramps said thoughtfully. "The two main motives for murder are sex and money. We've been focused on the money side, but maybe an illicit affair is something to consider."

"Good point," Ally agreed, her gaze on Noah's retreating figure. The only new information the detective had given them was that Kimberly Mason wasn't a suspect because she had an alibi for the murder and the day of the rock incident.

So why had Roxy growled? Unless maybe Kimberly Mason was a smoker too, and the scent had upset Roxy.

She'd have to ask Noah, not that she expected to get a straight answer. She and Gramps had given Noah everything and then some. And now that their little chat was over, she was left with the distinct impression that both Kevin Kuhn and Ed White were ranked high on Noah's suspect list. And personally, she would have added Nick Calderone, as well.

Gramps would become even more addicted to true crime if he ended up solving this murder.

And if that happened? Noah Jorgenson would never live it down.

Which gave her a tiny sliver of satisfaction, retribution for him calling her *Hot Pants* back in high school.

* * *

Ally left Gramps and the WBWs shortly after Noah did. She returned to the clinic and decided to do inventory. Thanks to the past two weeks of increased business, she had money in the bank, so it was a really good time to replenish her supplies.

She'd just finished making a list of medications she'd need to reorder when she heard the clinic door open. Entering the main lobby area, she smiled when she saw Noah standing there.

"Long time no see," she joked.

He nodded but didn't return her smile. "Do you have a minute? I need to ask a few more questions about what happened this morning."

A shiver snaked down her spine. "Um, sure. I only have one chair behind the counter, but we can sit in the waiting room area, unless you'd rather go upstairs to the kitchen in my apartment? Although I should warn you, I don't have central air."

Noah hesitated, then shook his head. "No need for that. Why don't you take a seat behind the counter, Ally. I can stand and take notes as you describe what happened."

"Okay." Ally went around to sit behind the counter. She eyed him warily, as he was acting very strange. "What's going on, Noah? Did something else happen?" She thought about her burglar idea. "Did Anita Jones get robbed?"

"Ally, please." Noah gave her a stern look. "I need you to focus, okay? Tell me the story about how you ended up being at Marty's house this morning and where you were when you saw someone leaving Anita's house through the back door."

"It might be better if I show you." Ally spread her hands. "It's kinda hard to explain."

"Okay, let's take a walk. Oh, and bring Roxy," Noah instructed.

She didn't need to be asked twice. Given how she preferred pets over people, she'd much rather bring Roxy along than leave her behind.

"Come on, girl," Ally said, clipping the leash to Roxy's collar. "You're going to like this." She purposefully avoided the W-word.

"Start at the beginning," Noah suggested as she met him back in the clinic. "You were up early, right?"

"Right." She gestured to the clinic. "Gramps had scheduled an immunization for eight o'clock, and I got up around six." She went through the clinic and out the back door to the small landing at the bottom of the stairs. "We came down this way, and I went out the back." As she spoke, she went through the doorway, with Roxy at her side.

"Okay, then what?" Noah asked.

"Well, I didn't really intend to take Roxy far, I was only wearing flip-flops, shorts, and an oversized T-shirt, but she was on a mission. Kept tugging me in the direction of Appletree Lane." Ally paused, then said, "At some point, I realized that's where Roxy wanted to go. I think she must miss Marty more than I thought."

"I can understand that." Noah swept his gaze over the area. "Did you see anyone?"

"No. It was just after six in the morning, and the streets were deserted." She didn't add that she'd been glad about that since she'd just rolled out of bed and wasn't fit to be seen in public.

"And this is the route you took this morning?" Noah pressed.

"Yes, why?"

Noah didn't answer.

Ally continued until they reached Marty's front yard. "When we got here, Roxy did her thing."

Noah looked confused. "Her thing?"

"You know, went number two." Ally wasn't sure why she was embarrassed to talk about the dog's elimination habits with Noah. "I always carry baggies with me, so I picked up the mess and then carried it over to Marty's garbage bin."

"Along the side of the garage?" Noah asked, although he was looking right at it.

"Yes." Ally moved forward until she was parallel with the garbage bin. "I was right here, when Roxy started growling."

"And what time was that?"

She shrugged. "I don't know, maybe six fifteen?"

Noah jotted the time in his pocket-sized notebook. "Then what happened?"

"I turned to see what had caught Roxy's attention." Ally demonstrated. "I couldn't see anything right away, so I took a few steps and that's when I saw the brown-haired guy slinking out through Anita's back door."

"Slinking?" Noah asked dubiously.

"It wasn't like he just opened the door and walked out," Ally insisted. "He eased the door open and slid through, as if he didn't want to make any noise. I figured he didn't want Anita to know he was leaving, like maybe it was a one-night-stand type of deal." Ally gestured with her hand. "Do you want me to walk over there to show you?"

"Not yet, keep going with your story."

Ally had to think back. "Roxy's growl startled him, and he bumped his head against the side of the door. I'm pretty sure I yelled out, *hey, stop.* And then added, *don't make me call the police.*"

"And why didn't you call the police?" Noah lifted a brow.

"I didn't have my phone." The excuse sounded lame, but it was the truth. "But even if I had, I'm sure he would have been long gone by the time anyone arrived."

"Maybe," Noah reluctantly agreed.

"I ran after him, but it was pretty hopeless. I mean, I was sliding all over the wet grass with my flip-flops, and then I stepped on a rock that got between my foot and the sole of the sandal. He moved fast, I'll say that for him." Thinking back, she remembered Kevin Kuhn had the lean shape of a runner.

"Which way did he go?"

"Through that backyard, between the houses that way." She retraced her earlier steps, showing Noah the route. "By the time Roxy and I got to the street, there was no sign of him."

269

Noah looked both ways, running his gaze up and down the road. For several long moments he didn't say anything.

"Are you going to tell me what's going on?" Ally asked exasperated. "I mean, something must have happened for you to come out here like this."

"After you lost the guy, you headed back to the clinic?" Noah asked, ignoring her question.

"Yes, although I didn't go back through people's yards. I stayed on this street, went up to the corner and turned down the side street toward the clinic."

"And what time did you get back?"

"About six fifty, give or take a minute." She gestured to the road. "For one thing, my foot hurt. And staying on the street took us a little out of the way."

Noah nodded, his expression thoughtful. "What was he wearing?"

"Tan polo shirt and blue jeans." Ally sighed. "I saw his brown hair, but really wish I had gotten a good look at his face."

"Me too." Noah offered a crooked smile. "He never said anything either, right? You have no way to recognize his voice?"

"Not a word." Ally knew something must have happened at Anita's place for Noah to be this specific in his questioning. She turned and went back between the houses, to the spot where she could glimpse Anita's home.

"That's all I need from you, Ally." Noah tucked a hand beneath her elbow and urging her forward. "Let's get back to the clinic."

"Why the rush, Noah? Afraid I'll find out what happened over there?" Ally asked irritably. "I think I have a right to know if I caught a glimpse of a burglar."

Noah still didn't respond but dropped his hand from her arm when they reached Appletree Lane.

"Gramps will find out what happened sooner or later," Ally said persistently. "You know he and the widows have connections all through Willow Bluff."

"I'm well aware of their impressive communication network," Noah said dryly. "But I can't say anything yet."

Ally glanced back toward Anita's house. It wasn't as visible from this angle, but she did see a squad sitting on the road directly in front of the place.

Okay, so for sure some sort of crime had been committed by the brown-haired guy. But what? Robbery?

Or something worse?

Her cell phone rang, and she quickly answered when she recognized Gramps' number. "Gramps? Are you okay?"

"HAVE YOU HEARD THE NEWS?" Gramps' voice boomed so loudly, she knew Noah, and maybe the entire town of Willow Bluff, could hear every word.

"No, what news?" Ally kept her gaze locked on Noah's. The eye twitch was back, and in that second she knew it was bad.

Very bad.

"THERE'S BEEN ANOTHER MURDER!"

Ally sucked in a quick breath. "Who, Gramps? Who was murdered?"

"ANITA JONES. I WANTED TO WARN YOU SINCE YOU SAW THE GUY SNEAKING OUT HER BACK DOOR EARLY THIS MORNING. THE POLICE WILL WANT TO TALK TO YOU!"

"You think?" She drilled Noah with a narrow glare. "I'm here with Noah right now, Gramps. I just walked him through my route this morning."

"I CAN'T BELIEVE YOU SAW THE MURDERER!" Gramps voice rose even higher. "YOU BETTER BE CAREFUL."

"I will, Gramps. Talk to you later, okay?"

"OKAY! LOVE YOU."

Ally lowered her phone, never taking her gaze from Noah. "Anita was murdered and now I'm the only witness, along with Roxy?"

Noah blew out a breath. "Yes, I'm afraid so."

Great. Wasn't that just peachy? Ally shifted her gaze from Noah to Roxy and back to Noah. "You better find him, and soon."

He surprised her by taking her hand and giving it a gentle squeeze. "I will, but you need to be careful, too. No more walks alone."

"I'm not alone, I have Roxy." Ally tried not to give in to the wave of fear. Should she ask Noah to have an officer stationed outside her clinic? "And from the way Roxy growled at the guy, I'm pretty sure she'll protect me." She swallowed hard. While she knew Roxy would protect her, it was difficult to comprehend that she'd caught a glimpse of a *murderer.*

Noah needed to find this guy before he decided to do something more drastic than throwing a rock at her clinic or running her off the road.

Like trying to kill her and Roxy.

Chapter
Twenty-Three

A lly's intent had been to cook her own meals, making healthy choices like grilled chicken breasts and steamed broccoli, so that her jeans wouldn't be so snug around the waist. But after hearing about Anita's murder, she packed Roxy in the back of her car and headed over to the Legacy House.

Comfort food and being with other people was important in times of crisis.

And she desperately wanted to talk to Gramps about this latest news.

"Ally, it's great to see you." Harriet's greeting was a little less enthusiastic when she saw Roxy. "Come in, dear. You're just in time for dinner."

"Thanks, Harriet." Ally went inside, the coolness a welcome relief from the summer heat. She was glad Gramps had central air. What would the widows think if she asked to sleep on the sofa?

"What's for dinner?" Ally asked. The mouth-watering scent was a new one.

"Another of my mother's famous recipes," Harriet said with a broad smile. "Jägerschnitzel with mushroom sauce."

"Smells great." Ally had no clue was jägerschnitzel was, but anything that smelled that enticing had to taste good.

"It's just a fancy way of saying breaded pork chops," Tillie said in a sarcastic tone. "Harriet likes to make herself sound like a famous chef."

"It's not my fault that our mother taught me to cook better than you, Tillie," Harriet shot back. She lifted her voice. "Oscar? Ally's come for dinner."

Ally heard the thump of Gramps' cane as he made his way in from the living room. He surprised her by coming over to give her a hug.

"Good to see you, Ally."

Ridiculous tears pricked her eyes. "Back at you, Gramps."

"Such terrible news about Anita," Lydia said after they'd all taken their seats. "I couldn't believe it when Rosie Malone called to tell me."

Ally choked on a mushroom. "How did Rosie Malone hear about it?"

Lydia frowned. "Let me think. I believe Rosie heard it from one of Anita's neighbors, Evelyn."

"Who is Evelyn?" Ally asked. There were so many people in town she didn't know on a first-name basis.

"Evelyn Rawson lives next door to Anita," Gramps said.

"Yes, and apparently she grew concerned when she hadn't seen Anita come out to tend to her garden. Anita is crazy about flowers and normally comes out first thing each morning before the temperature gets too hot."

The jägerschnitzel congealed in Ally's stomach at the thought of the brown-haired guy running away from her and Roxy after murdering Anita. "She called the police because Anita didn't water her flowers?"

"She waited until later in the day, but when Anita still didn't show up and the flowers were wilting badly in the heat, Evelyn tried calling her. When Anita didn't answer the phone, she called the police."

"They can do what's called a wellness check," Gramps offered. "Make sure Anita wasn't lying on the kitchen floor with a broken hip or something."

Ally stared at her pork chop for a moment. "Did Rosie know how Anita was killed?"

"No, just that the police came, broke into the house, and then began stringing up crime scene tape." Lydia leaned forward. "Imagine two murders two houses apart on the same street!"

"Yeah," Gramps echoed. "What are the chances of that?"

Ally didn't want to know.

As the conversation turned away from murder, Ally managed to finish eating.

"Who wants dessert?" Harriet asked with a beaming smile. "I made strawberry cheesecake."

No dessert, no dessert, Ally told herself. But when Harriet brought out the beautiful cheesecake topped with fresh strawberries, she caved.

"I'd love some, thanks." Ally ignored the pinch at her waist as she took a bite.

It was the most incredible cheesecake she'd ever tasted.

After dinner, Ally insisted on helping clear the table, then took Roxy outside to sit with Gramps on the patio.

"You're right, Gramps. I should have called the police earlier today."

Gramps waved her remorse away. "Keep in mind, we both thought she was having an affair, not that she'd been murdered."

"But they would have found her much sooner if I'd reported it." It bothered Ally to know that Anita had been dead all day with no one knowing because of her.

"I wonder if Noah ever headed over to talk to her the way I suggested?" Gramps asked. "He should feel guilty, not you."

"Maybe he did head over. And maybe that was about the same time they heard from the neighbor about Anita not watering her flowers." Ally stroked Roxy's fur. "I can't believe we chased a murderer."

"One good thing about that is the guy ran away because he was afraid of Roxy." Gramps smiled at the boxer. "Probably knows Roxy would take a piece of his hide if she could."

"That's a good point." Hadn't she basically told Noah the same thing? Still, being a witness made her very uneasy. "I want you to be careful too, Gramps. We don't know anything about why Anita was murdered—it could be this guy has more than a couple of screws loose."

"I was wondering about the motive myself." Gramps gazed off in the distance. "I go back to the way Anita gave Marty a list of people to talk to about his will/trust services. If the motive for killing Marty was about the scheme, then maybe the motive for killing Anita runs along the same lines."

Ally tried to follow Gramps' twisted logic. "You mean some-one, either Kevin Kuhn or Eli White, found out after the fact that Anita was the one who sent Marty to talk to them? That would make the motive to kill her nothing more than simple revenge."

Gramps nodded. "Which takes me back to the anger expressed by Kevin Kuhn that day in the clinic."

Ally was having trouble seeing it. "Revenge alone doesn't seem enough to kill over."

Gramps reached over to pat her knee. "You should watch an episode of *Dateline* some time. People have killed for far less."

"When I relocated to Willow Bluff, I'd assumed I'd left the big-city crime in Madison behind." Ally shook her head sadly. "Now we've had two murders in two weeks? In a town of about four thousand people? It's crazy."

"Crazy kills," Gramps pointed out.

"Hardly the motto we want for Willow Bluff."

"True."

"I guess this means Nick Calderone isn't our murderer," Ally mused. "It isn't likely he'd come all the way up here from Chicago to kill Marty anyway, but if this is really about Marty's client list, then Nick and Sheila probably had nothing to do with it. And Nick would really have no reason to kill Anita."

"I wouldn't take Calderone off the list yet," Gramps protested. "Unless your detective has already cleared him."

"You can ask Noah yourself, the next time we see him." She forced a smile. "I need to get going. I appreciate you having me over this evening, Gramps."

"Anytime, Ally. You're always more than welcome."

She leaned over to give him a hug and a kiss. Then she took Roxy's leash and stood. "If Lydia or anyone else hears more about Anita's murder, will you let me know?"

"Of course." Gramps eyed her thoughtfully. "But being a witness and all, you'll likely hear more from that detective of yours before we do."

She wasn't sure she agreed with his logic. "Later, Gramps."

Ally walked Roxy to the car and drove back to the clinic, where she parked and took Roxy upstairs. The apartment was warm; the only window air conditioner she had was in the master bedroom to help her sleep. She crossed over to open the living room windows, to encourage the lake breeze.

It wasn't that late, barely eight o'clock in the evening, but she was exhausted from being up early. Still, she thought she might watch some television before heading to bed.

Not *Dateline*. Something light, funny.

Nothing that would give her nightmares.

Roxy stretched out at her feet, seemingly content.

At the end of the comedy she'd picked at random, she clicked the television off. "Okay, Roxy, we should head out one last time before going to bed."

Roxy lifted her head, looking around with interest.

It occurred to Ally that she should take up jogging if she was going to keep eating meals and desserts at the Legacy House.

Either that or find the willpower to resist going there in the first place.

Before she took two steps toward the kitchen where she kept Roxy's leash, her phone rang. She glanced at the screen with a frown. A transferred call from the veterinary clinic? She quickly answered. "This is Dr. Winter, can I help you?"

"Ally? It's Erica." Her former high school friend sounded tearful. "Tink was attacked by a coyote. It was awful, and she has several bite marks. She's shaking and scared, and so am I. Can you please see her?"

"Of course, bring her in right away."

"Thanks, Ally." Erica didn't waste a second disconnecting from the call.

Ally realized she should have taken Roxy out earlier, but it was too late now. "Sorry, Roxy, I have to take care of Tink. Behave yourself up here, okay?"

Roxy wagged her stumpy tail as if understanding there was a four-legged emergency.

Ally left the boxer upstairs and hurried down to unlock the clinic door and to wipe down the exam room. How awful that her friend Erica had to go through something like this. Coyotes have been known to kill small dogs like Tink the schnauzer, but at least Tink was still alive.

When Erica arrived, her face was red and splotchy, her eyes puffy from crying. She carried Tink close to her chest as if she couldn't bear to let the dog go.

"Are you okay?" Ally asked.

"Not really. It happened so fast! I mean, I had her on a leash and we were walking along the lakefront, which has always been safe enough. But tonight the coyote came out from beneath a willow tree and attacked her!"

"I'm so sorry. Bring her into the exam room so I can check her out." Because of the late hour, Ally locked the clinic door before following Erica inside.

"It's okay, Tinker Bell. You're going to be okay," Erica whispered.

The poor dog was trembling with fear, clearly traumatized by the attack. Ally felt bad for both Tink and Erica. She donned gloves and filled a stainless steel basin with water to clean the cuts.

There were several lacerations made by the coyote's teeth, mostly smaller in nature, but one was long enough to require closure, either with sutures or maybe glue. Thankfully, the laceration was long, but not very deep.

"What do you think?" Erica asked. "Will she be okay?"

"Yes, Tink will be fine," Ally assured her. "None of these cuts are too deep. After I clean them all, I'll glue this one here." She pointed to the open gash on Tink's flank.

"Glue?" Erica looked surprised.

"Wounds actually heal better with glue than sutures," Ally said with a smile. "And Tink will need to take a ten-day course of antibiotics to ward off infection."

"Poor Tink," Erica murmured, stroking the schnauzer's fur.

"Antibiotics aren't that big a deal. I'll inject her first dose here, the rest can be given via pill." Ally heisted, then added, "Oh, and she'll need to wear a cone for a few days, but after all of this, she should recover without any long-term problems."

"Thank you," Erica closed her eyes for a moment. "I wasn't sure who was more upset by all this, me or the dog. I have to tell you, Tink fought back, probably in an attempt to protect me, which scared the coyote off." Erica shivered. "I'm not sure what would have happened if the coyote had stayed to fight."

"Try not to think about it," Ally suggested. The way Erica was talking, she was bound to suffer nightmares after this.

"I'll try, but it was the scariest thing that has ever happened to me."

Ally could understand, although seeing what turned out to be a murderer escape through the back door of a house was a close second.

"I wonder if it was a young coyote." Ally frowned as she continued cleaning Tink's cuts. "They normally travel in packs, so having just one is unusual. Unless it's infected with rabies." She met Erica's gaze. "Good thing you brought her in for her shots when you did, or I'd have to treat her for a possible exposure."

"I know. Imagine if her rabies vaccine wasn't up to date?" Erica shuddered. "I need to do a better job of staying on top of things."

"Cut yourself some slack, Erica. You're juggling kids, a dog, and a job. You're doing fine."

Erica's eyes teared up. "That's the nicest thing anyone has said to me in weeks."

Really? That about broke Ally's heart. "What about Jim? I'm sure he understands." When the cleaning was finished, Ally took a device not unlike a hot glue gun, but one that was for medical use rather than art projects, to close the laceration on Tink's flank.

"He does, but he's too busy with his construction business to worry about how I'm managing at home." Erica grimaced. "And since I only work part time, he thinks I should have everything under control."

"Men. What do they know?"

"Right?" Erica echoed. "Jim is a great guy, truly, but he has no idea how fast two young kids can wear you out. Having Tink just adds to the chaos. Not that I'd give Tink up for anything, you understand. She's a great dog. It's just more things to juggle, that's all."

"I hear you." Ally finished with the laceration and stepped back from the table. "Okay, hold onto Tink while I get the antibiotic ready."

Erica nodded. Ally went into the medication cabinet for the meds, then grabbed a small cone and returned to the exam room.

"Hold her tight," Ally directed. She injected the antibiotic. Erica winced when Tink let out a tiny yelp. But then it was over. Ally threaded the cone in place, which Tink clearly didn't like one bit. "Sorry, Tink, but this is necessary for at least five days."

"She'll be fine," Erica said. "I'll make sure of it."

"I know you will." Finally, she handed Erica the bottle of antibiotics. "I want you to start the antibiotic first thing tomorrow morning, okay? Give her a pill twice a day until all the medication is gone."

"Is it okay to hide it in peanut butter?" Erica asked. "She'll eat anything if peanut butter is involved."

"Of course, that's not a problem. But if Tink starts to act funny, like she stops eating, or has vomiting and/or diarrhea, I need you to call me right away. That could be an indication the infection has gone into her bloodstream."

"Okay, I understand." Erica offered a watery smile. "You're a great vet, Ally. Thank you."

"You're very welcome." Ally led the way back to the main area. She tallied the care she'd provided, then took off a ten percent discount before printing out the invoice.

Erica paid, but frowned and tapped the invoice where the discount was noted. Ally had to keep her prices stable for accounting purposes. "You didn't have to do the discount," she protested. "I know this is your livelihood, and if you weren't here, I'd have paid Hanson or whoever else bought the place."

"I know, but I have no idea when I'll get into the Bluff Salon for a cut, so wanted to do something for you as my friend." At the moment, Erica was the only real friend she had in town, if you didn't count her grandfather and the WBWs. "I only listed the discount because my fees are all preset for tax purposes. The last thing I need is to get audited."

"Thanks again, but next time, don't worry about adding a discount." Erica gave her a quick hug. "Let's make sure to reschedule our lunch date, okay? I miss having a girlfriend like you."

It was Ally's turn to feel choked up. "I'd like that, Erica. Very much. I could use your advice on a few things, too."

"Great. I'll call you." Erica picked up Tink. "Thanks again for being here for me when I needed you."

"Anytime," Ally assured her. This was the best part of her job, helping pets when they needed care the most. Ally unlocked the door, waited for Erica to leave, then closed and locked it again.

Despite her slow day, June was looking to be a great month for Furry Friends. And for the first time since she'd returned home, Ally was beginning to feel like a real member of the community.

Ally forced herself to clean up the messy exam room, just in case she had another emergency in the near future. When that was done, she went to get Roxy from the apartment.

"Sorry, girl," she said when the dog greeted her with enthusiasm. "I'm sure you need to get outside, right?"

Roxy jumped excitedly and bolted down the stairs to the landing area. Ally clipped on the leash, thinking of the coyote Erica
had encountered.

At least Roxy was big enough to scare them off, but coyotes
were also known to hunt in packs, and a pack of coyotes could
easily bring down a dog Roxy's size.

Since she'd taken longer than anticipated in caring for Tinker
Bell, Ally figured Roxy deserved a good walk and took her down
Main Street. Knowing the coyote had hidden beneath the weeping willow was enough to avoid the lakefront. It was a beautiful
night and relatively peaceful despite the earlier events of the day.

Ally still couldn't believe Anita Jones had been murdered. She
shortened Roxy's leash, keeping the dog close to her side.

Better to be safe, right?

Roxy sniffed the air but didn't growl at the couple of pedestrians they passed along the way. Ally couldn't help but remember
how Roxy had growled at the man leaving Anita's house.

No matter what Noah thought, she was convinced Roxy had
the ability to sniff out Marty's and Anita's killer.

The murders had to have been committed by the same person.
What were the odds of two different murderers being in the same
town killing people in the same neighborhood?

The Lakefront Café wasn't very busy, maybe because it was
just after ten o'clock on a Friday night. The dinner rush was over,
and there was only a scattering of people still sitting outside.

When she reached the opposite end of Main Street just past
the grocery store, she stood for several minutes near a small grassy
area, waiting for Roxy to do the deed. Unfortunately, Roxy wasn't

interested. With a sigh, Ally turned to head home. "You better go number two pretty quickly here, Roxy. We are not having a repeat of this morning, understand? You can do your business in other places besides Marty's front yard."

Roxy glanced up at her, waving her stumpy tail, but then pulled on the leash as if anxious to move. Ally sighed, hoping the dog wouldn't hold off until reaching the clinic.

As they approached the municipal building, Roxy began to growl.

"Not now, Roxy," she said, tugging at her leash. Ally would have thought the dog simply didn't like the narrow alley between the municipal building and the restaurant, but the dog hadn't reacted like this on the first pass.

Roxy planted her large feet and continued growling, staring in the direction of the alley. Roxy was so intense, Ally couldn't ignore her.

"What is it, girl?" Since the dog wasn't going to leave the area, Ally moved closer to the narrow opening. Gathering her courage, she called out, "Who's there?"

No response.

Roxy's growls escalated in volume, and the boxer continued to pull at the leash. Ally wanted to run away, but Roxy didn't budge. Ally took one more step forward, trying to see if anyone was lurking in the darkness. The opening between the municipal building and the Lakefront Café was so narrow, it was impossible to tell.

She considered releasing Roxy's leash, so the dog could chase down whoever was bothering her, but feared that would only get her and Roxy in trouble.

"Who's there?" Ally called again, louder this time. She took one more step forward, reaching the narrow opening, when she saw the shape of a man along with the glow from the tip of a cigarette hanging low at his side.

Worse was the gun in his other hand pointed at the center of her chest.

Chapter
Twenty-Four

*T*he *murderer!*

Ally froze, her jumbled thoughts coming to a screeching halt. As she stared at the man mostly hidden in the shadows, she tried to get a clear look at his face. Kevin Kuhn? Or Eli White? She'd only met each of the men once. If this guy was Nick Calderone, she wouldn't recognize him at all.

Roxy's low-throated growls never let up. Ally gasped in horror when the muzzle of the gun dropped toward the dog. She drew Roxy closer to her side, trying to push the dog behind her legs, determined to throw herself in front of the animal to protect her if needed.

"I knew I should have shot the dog when I had the opportunity." The man's voice was low and flat, lacking any ounce of emotion.

Ally swallowed hard. "You mean the day you killed Marty Shawlin?"

The muzzle returned to her chest. "You and that dog have been nothing but a problem for me."

"That's because Roxy knows you killed both Marty and Anita Jones." *Say it*, she silently urged. Ally wanted to hear him admit to killing them.

"Marty got what he deserved, same as Anita. You and that stupid mutt are next. You'll need to come with me."

Yeah, that was so not happening. There were less than a handful of people sitting on the patio just a few yards behind her. If she started screaming, one of them would come running.

But what if this guy was able to get a shot off before anyone arrived? He could shoot twice and run, disappearing long before anyone could catch him.

Her instinct was to encourage him to keep talking. And to draw him from the shadows to get a look at his face. His voice sounded familiar, but she couldn't quite place it. "It's too late to kill me. I've already told the police about you sneaking out of Anita's house through the back door. I gave them a very detailed description for their file." That was a bold-faced lie as she hadn't gotten a good look at his face.

But he didn't know that.

The glowing tip of his cigarette dropped to the ground.

"Why did you kill Anita? After all, she covered for you the morning of the murder. Did you know that? She denied seeing anyone leave Marty's house that morning." Ally knew she was starting to ramble but couldn't seem to help herself. "Is that why she had to be silenced? Because you thought she'd eventually talk?"

"Take a step forward now, or I'll shoot you where you stand. And the mutt, too."

An empty threat, at least she hoped so. "Roxy isn't a mutt, she's a boxer. And you won't shoot me in front of witnesses. After all, isn't that why you want me to come with you?"

"Get over here, now," he demanded in a low hiss. He moved just enough that a sliver of light provided a brief glimpse of his face.

Eli White!

"By the way, does Ginny know you're a murderer?" Ally sensed someone coming up behind her and fought a surge of panic. What if Eli's accomplice had shown up? Kevin Kuhn? Was he armed, too?

But then she recognized a familiar woodsy scent.

Noah!

Before she could say a word, Noah rushed out from around her, pushing her back with one hand, and stepping in front of her. He'd placed himself directly in the line of fire as he faced the killer. Despite the bitter fear coating her tongue she was touched by his actions.

"Put the gun down, Eli," Noah said sternly. "It's over."

For a split second no one moved, then Eli whirled and ran.

Roxy lunged forward, straining at the leash in an attempt to go after him. Noah took off in pursuit, and Ally only hesitated a moment before releasing Roxy's leash. "Get him!"

The dog was fast and closed the gap quickly. Eli turned and looked as if he might try to shoot Roxy, but the dog's large jaws locked on his ankle, pulling backward and tripping him up.

Eli hit the ground hard. He dropped the gun, and the revolver skittered across the pavement far out of reach.

In a heartbeat, Noah grabbed him, wrenching his arms behind his back and placing cuffs around his wrists. "Eli White, you're under arrest for the murder of Marty Shawlin, Anita Jones, and the attempted murder of Dr. Ally Winter. You have the right to remain silent; anything you say can and will be used in a court of law. You have a right to an attorney. If you cannot afford an attorney, one will be provided free of charge."

Ally heard all of this as she caught up to Noah, Eli, and Roxy. "Good girl, Roxy," she praised, kneeling beside the boxer and giving her a huge hug. "You're such a good girl."

"Do you understand your rights?" Noah asked, pulling Ed White up to his feet.

"That dog bit me," Eli whined. "I wanna press charges against the owner."

Noah rolled his eyes. "I don't see any blood, so the injury can't be that bad. And of course, you can press charges, but I highly doubt the judge will be impressed when he hears you threatened the owner of the dog at gunpoint."

"And threatened to shoot Roxy too," Ally added, clipping the boxer's leash and rising to her feet. "He told me he should have killed Roxy from the beginning. And he said that Marty and Anita both got what they deserved."

"I heard," Noah admitted. He used his phone to call for backup. When the dispatcher promised to send a squad, he pocketed the phone. He grinned at a scowling Eli White. "It's always nice when the bad guy confesses in front of a detective and a civilian witness."

She hadn't realized Noah was close enough to hear everything that had transpired.

"I wanna lawyer," Eli said loudly. "I'm not talking until I get a lawyer."

"Okay, that's fine," Noah said in an affable tone. "But I'm going to warn you it's going to take a minor miracle to get out of this one. We have your confession and by the time we're finished matching DNA evidence? You'll be looking at life without parole."

The blood drained from Eli's face and he fell silent.

DNA evidence? Ally found the news very reassuring. "Why are you here, anyway?" Ally asked addressing Noah. "I thought I was all alone."

Noah sighed. "Because, despite what you and your grandfather think, I have been working the case. Eli White and Kevin Kuhn were both high on my list of suspects, especially after Anita's murder, so I've been following both of them, trying to catch one of them doing something illegal."

Her eyes widened. "You suspected Eli or Kevin all along?"

Noah looked sheepish. "Well, I have to say the tidbits of information you and Oscar provided were helpful. And you'll be happy to know Sheila's boyfriend Nick has an alibi for the time frame of both murders." Noah looked over as a squad pulled up. He pushed Eli toward the officer. "Get him processed and booked for the murders of Marty Shawlin and Anita Jones, as well as the attempted murder of Dr. Ally Winter. Oh, and let him call a lawyer."

"Will do, Detective," the officer said respectfully.

"I'll be in soon," Noah added, stepping back and watching as the cop guided Eli into the back seat. When the squad rolled away, he turned toward her. "I would like you to come in to give a formal statement, Ally, if you don't mind."

Dizzy with relief at knowing it was finally over, Ally nodded. "Can I bring Roxy?"

Noah's expression softened. "Yeah, you can bring her. After all, she helped save the day."

"I'm sure you would have caught Eli yourself in a foot race," Ally said, feeling the need to defend him. "You're several years younger than he is."

"Gee, thanks for the vote of confidence." Noah shook his head wryly. "I hate to admit you were right about Roxy knowing who killed Marty. When I heard her growling I was intrigued. Then I heard Eli's voice and knew she'd nailed it."

"Yeah." Ally rested her hand on Roxy's head. "Told you she'd make a great police dog."

"No lie," Noah admitted. "Come on, let's walk over to the precinct."

Ally fell into step beside Noah, flashing a crooked grin. "Gramps is going to be so upset he missed all of this."

Noah paused, then said, "I'm probably going to regret this, but if you need someone to be with you as you make your statement—you know, for support—you have that right."

Ally's heart swelled in her chest. "Really? You'd let me go get Gramps?"

"He can only be there for support," Noah cautioned, even though they both knew that her grandfather wouldn't just sit quietly through the process. "But yes, you can get him."

"Thanks Noah." She quickly leaned forward to kiss his cheek. "I'll be there soon. Come, Roxy."

On her way back to the clinic, she called Gramps to let him know what had transpired. She kept it brief, promising to fill him in on the way.

He yelled into the cell phone. "I'LL BE READY!"

Ally knew he wouldn't miss this for anything. What was better than watching *Dateline*?

Living it.

* * *

292

Ally helped Gramps inside the police station, thinking about how different it was now compared to the previous time they'd been in for questioning. Gramps had gotten a kick out of being considered a suspect nearly two weeks ago.

During the short drive over, he'd grilled Ally about her interaction with Eli White. "Good thing Noah was there to rescue you," Gramps said in an uncharacteristically serious tone. "You could have been seriously hurt, young lady."

Better me than Gramps, she thought. "I know, but I wasn't. And Roxy was the real heroine tonight. She grabbed Eli's ankle with enough force to bring him down. His gun went flying and Noah was able to handcuff him."

"If your detective was smart, he'd get himself a police dog," Gramps said. "Look at what a great job Roxy did in bringing a murderer to justice."

"I couldn't agree more."

Noah was waiting at the front desk for them. He nodded at Gramps. "Oscar, good to see you."

"I'm glad to hear you made an arrest," Gramps said, his gaze somber. "And I want to thank you for rescuing Ally."

Noah's expression turned serious. "You're welcome. I want you to know I had no idea she would end up in danger. Having her held at gunpoint is not something I ever want to see again."

The two men eyed each other for a long moment. "I believe you," Gramps said, breaking the silence. "But next time, maybe you should have more faith in a dog's ability to track a suspect."

"I will," Noah promised. He turned to Ally. "Ready to give your statement?"

"Yes."

Noah led them into the same interview room they'd used the day of Marty's murder. This time, the atmosphere was much more relaxed. Noah settled himself next to Ally, then gestured to the camera in the corner. "Just want to let you know this interview is being recorded."

"I understand." Ally pushed a strand of her wild hair away from her face, wishing she'd taken the time to refresh her makeup.

Which was a ridiculous thought.

"Start at the beginning," Noah suggested.

She frowned. "You mean the day I found Marty's body?"

"No, tonight," Noah corrected. "Start with why you and Roxy happened to be near the alley between the two buildings this evening."

"Oh, that." Ally rested her hand on Roxy's head. "I was home, about to take Roxy out for a walk, when I received an emergency call from Erica about her dog Tink being attacked by a coyote. The schnauzer had several lacerations that needed attention."

Noah looked surprised by that news. "Poor Erica and Tink, I'm glad to hear they're okay. Go on."

"I didn't finish that up until close to ten o'clock, so that's why I was out so late with Roxy. Since she'd been cooped up for several hours, I thought we'd take a longer walk, so I went down Main Street to the end, then turned around to come back when Roxy began to growl."

"And where were you standing when that happened?" Noah asked.

"Near the alley between the municipal building and the Lakefront Café. At first I was annoyed, but I took several steps closer, then I saw the shape of a man but couldn't see his face, as he was standing in the shadows. I did see the gun he had pointed directly at me."

Gramps put his hand on her arm for reassurance. She covered his hand with hers and tried to calm her racing heart. Reliving those moments wasn't easy. She'd been scared to death, but unable to do much except babble like an idiot.

"What happened next?" Noah pressed.

"He told me he should have shot Roxy when he had the chance." Ally continued, replaying their brief conversation to the best of her recollection. "I remember wanting to see his face and to hear him admit he'd killed them, both Anita and Marty."

"Okay, anything else stand out in your memory?" Noah asked.

"He finally moved enough for me to recognize him as Eli White, so I tried to keep him talking by mentioning his wife, Ginny."

"Any idea why he killed Anita?" Gramps asked.

Noah nodded. "I think you and Ally were right about the two of them having an affair, which is why Anita claimed she hadn't seen anyone leaving Marty's house the morning of the murder. And why she claimed she didn't pay attention to Roxy's barking."

"So he was afraid she'd talk, maybe turn him in," Ally murmured.

"Yeah. Anita was strangled but managed to get some of the killer's skin cells beneath her fingernails. There was also a partial fingerprint on the edge of Marty's briefcase, although Marty's car was wiped clean. They also found a partial print in the stolen GMC truck that we'll check for a match. And there's the fact that Eli's red Chevy needs a new muffler, which makes him the likely suspect of tossing the rock at the clinic. Once we get all the samples processed through the lab, the case against Eli White should be a slam dunk. Especially since I think he followed you tonight, Ally, with the specific intent of killing you."

Gramps nodded thoughtfully. "And the motive for killing Marty goes back to the sixteen hundred dollars they gave Marty to create a will and trust?"

"Yes. Turns out, there was no record of the transaction for the Whites in Marty's paperwork. Either because he hadn't gotten around to creating it or because the killer took it with him." Noah grinned. "We'll get a search warrant for the Whites' house and hopefully find what we need there."

"Poor Ginny," Gramps said shaking his head. "I can't imagine how she's going to feel about discovering her husband is a murderer. I guess she must have been covering for him last night, when he never showed for dinner."

"I'll find out for sure once I question Ginny again. Your idea about getting their money back was a good one, Oscar," Noah admitted. "That extra cash might help Ginny."

"Are you sure she's not in on it?" Ally asked. "I mean, she initially lied to us about giving Marty any money at all."

"We were able to verify that Marty was, in fact, simply pocketing the money, rather than actually creating the trust and will combo as promised. Creating a trust isn't illegal, but it sounds like Marty was talking people into doing more than they actually needed. And then he didn't follow through on his promises, which is why everyone began to get upset. Turns out that, other than the house, Marty didn't have any cash to his name."

"Does that mean Ginny and the others won't get their money back?" Gramps asked.

"We'll find a way to have Marty's estate pay all his clients back what they'd lost, even if that means taking money out from the sale of the house," Noah said firmly. He gave each of them a stern look. "Listen, while I appreciate what you did, it's over now. No more investigating anything— not even a parking ticket—on your own, you got that?"

"Who, me?" Gramps feigned innocence. "I just happen to ask a lot of questions, that's all."

"Yeah, and I'm the future king of England," Noah responded sarcastically.

"Well, I'm sure there won't be anything else to investigate anyway." Ally did her best to smooth things over. "I mean, this is Willow Bluff. The fact that we've had two murders in two weeks has to be an anomaly. Especially hearing the previous murder was five years ago."

"I guess that's true." Gramps looked acutely disappointed. "This town is fairly small." He turned toward Ally. "Maybe we should move to Madison?"

She rolled her eyes. "Nice try, but no way. I like Willow Bluff, especially the people who live here." The minute the words left her mouth, she wanted to take them back. Noah was looking at her with interest, maybe wondering if that included him, so she hastened to explain. "My clinic is doing better, Gramps. And I reconnected with my old friend Erica. Besides, we're not leaving so that you can get closer to a high crime area. You'll just have to get used to the quiet life here in Willow Bluff."

"I'm with Ally on that one," Noah added. "Okay, listen, I need to wrap things up. Thanks for coming in. Ally, I'm glad you and Roxy are okay."

"We owe that to you, Noah." She couldn't deny his timing tonight had been perfect. "Come on, Gramps. Time to get you home."

She assisted Gramps to his feet. "You know, I was wrong. I think your detective is pretty good at his job."

Ally winced and wished the floor would open at her feet as Noah flashed a lethal grin. "A high compliment from you, Oscar."

She considered trying to say something in her defense but knew it would only sound lame. "Bye, Noah."

"Ally." He winked at her. "Maybe we should get together with Erica and Jim, you know, talk about old times."

A date? Was he actually insinuating they should go out on a double date?

"Um, sure. Sounds fun."

They headed outside, Roxy sniffing the air curiously. There was no reason to worry about Roxy's growling any longer.

The murderer was behind bars, where he belonged.

"You know, there's still one thing I don't understand about all this." Gramps fastened his seat belt and sat back with a sigh.

"What's that?"

"Why did Rosie Malone lie about talking to Marty?"

Ally inwardly groaned. "That's a mystery for another day, Gramps."

"Don't you worry, I'll figure it out."

Yeah, that was exactly what she was afraid of.

Chapter
Twenty-Five

Ally slept in the following morning, waking only when Roxy made it clear she needed to go out. First by exuberantly licking her face, then jumping up on the bed, moving around and lying down on top of Ally.

"Okay, okay." Ally pushed Roxy aside, rolled off the bed and stumbled across the room. Where had she left the leash? The kitchen.

She was about to head that way but stopped short.

Uh-uh. No way was she going out in her ratty sleep clothes and flip-flops again. Even though the chance of witnessing a murderer escaping through the back door of a house was slim to none this time, she wasn't about to take any chances.

Especially if there was even a remote possibility she might bump into someone she knew. Now that her business had picked up, she was starting to recognize some of the local residents.

At least those with pets, anyway.

She quickly brushed her teeth, tried to tame her hair—why she bothered she had no idea—then pulled on a pair of white capri slacks and a blue sleeveless blouse that matched her eyes. She slid her feet into matching white sandals and was ready to go.

Feeling marginally more human, she took Roxy outside. The sun was already beating down, sending the temperature up to the high seventies while it was barely nine in the morning. It promised to be another scorcher of a day.

Maybe if her business continued to grow, she could afford to add central air to the upper apartment. Wouldn't that be awesome? Granted summertime in Wisconsin was short, but it was still pretty hot.

And they hadn't hit July and August yet.

"Hurry up, Roxy." Ally swallowed a wave of impatience as the dog took her along the same route to Marty's front yard. The minute they arrived, Roxy squatted to do her thing.

"Really? You had to wait until we got here?" Ally hoped the boxer would get over this fixation soon. She wasn't looking forward to taking this same walk every day in the snow and ice come winter.

Maybe later in the day, sure, but not first thing in the morning. She needed a minimum of two cups of coffee to function.

The crime scene tape was still strung across the front of Anita's house. It was creepy to realize that less than two weeks ago she and Gramps had sat chatting with the woman about Marty's murder and the list of clients she'd referred him to.

And why had Anita referred Marty to her friends and acquaintances anyway? Had it really been a nice gesture for a man who needed a boost after a nasty divorce?

It wasn't just Rosie Malone's lie that hadn't been resolved. She was curious what role Anita had played in all this. It seemed odd that Anita would send Marty to the Whites, when she was having an affair with Eli. Wouldn't it be smarter to stay far away?

Or was that a weird attempt to cover up their affair?

Maybe there wasn't an affair at all, although Noah seemed to think so.

The possibilities spun in her mind, making her crazy. She pushed them away with an effort. What did it matter? She wasn't Gramps, there was no reason to obsess over every detail of the murders.

She returned to the apartment and ate oatmeal for breakfast, splurging on adding raspberries she'd picked up at the store as part of her healthy eating plan. Thinking about the tightness at her waistband made her realize she needed to do a better job of getting exercise, both to look better and to get into shape.

Had Noah really mentioned a double date with Erica and Jim? Or had she imagined it?

Even if he had, she doubted he meant it as anything but a friendly get-together. Yeah, the more she thought about that the more likely it seemed that his focus was on being friends.

Nothing to get excited about. And she was through with men anyway. She had to concentrate on rejuvenating her business.

Ally went down to the clinic. It was Sunday, with no scheduled appointments on the books. Still, she ran a quick spreadsheet of her income and expenses, thrilled to see that she had more than enough for her July payments.

And that didn't include possibly getting her replacement door paid for by Eli White's insurance company.

She frowned. Whatever. At least she was in the black, which was all that mattered. As she finished doing her bills, her phone rang. She prepared herself when she saw Gramps' number on the screen.

"Hey, Gramps."

"ALLY? DO YOU HAVE TIME TO TAKE ME TO THE LIBRARY TODAY?"

"No need to yell," she reminded him. "Are you sure the library is open on Sundays?"

"SUMMER HOURS," Gramps shouted.

"Okay, that's no problem." She glanced at her watch. "I'll be there in fifteen minutes or so."

"I'LL BE WAITING!"

She rubbed her ear after he disconnected from the call. She really needed to show him how to use that blasted cell phone or take it away. More conversations like this and she'd need bilateral hearing aids before he did.

"Come on, Roxy. Let's go for a ride."

Roxy jumped up and down excitedly, making Ally groan. *Great.* Not only did the boxer know the word *walk*, but now she understood the word *ride*.

And she'd gone after Eli White when Ally had told her to *get him*. Not that Roxy needed much encouragement for that.

"You're too smart for your own good," Ally said as she clipped on the leash. "Maybe I should pay for some formal training sessions, huh? You're a natural."

Roxy bobbed her head as if in agreement.

She and Roxy arrived at the Legacy House in less than ten minutes. Ally left Roxy in the car before heading up to the door.

"Ally!" Normally, Harriet didn't show a lot of emotion, but today she grabbed Ally and pulled her against her buxom figure, wearing yet another brightly colored flowered dress, support hose, and sturdy black shoes. "I couldn't believe it when Oscar mentioned you were held at gunpoint!"

Ally patted Harriet's back in a soothing gesture. "I'm fine, nothing for you to worry about. Noah came rushing to my rescue."

"You really must stop encouraging Oscar's obsession with fighting crime." Harriet's gaze was reproachful. "Imagine if he'd been there with you?"

"Trust me, Harriet, I would if I could." She eased away and glanced around. "Speaking of which, is Gramps ready to go?"

"I'm here," he called, thumping in from the living room.

"Ally, it's so good to see you." Lydia hobbled behind him, wincing as she gingerly put weight on her sore ankle. Her gaze was full of reproach. "Honestly, we were so horrified to hear the news. Imagine Eli White a killer! And my sources did reveal a rumor about Anita seeing someone, but no one knew the name of the guy she was spending time with."

"Well, clearly you wouldn't advertise an affair with a married man like that," Tillie added. "But we're so grateful you're safe, Ally."

Ally looked at the Willow Bluff Widows and wondered why she felt like she had gained three grandparents?

"I'm really sorry to have worried all of you. But as you can see, I'm fine." She smiled at the three women. "Now things can get back to normal around here, right?"

"Right," Tillie agreed.

Gramps moved toward her, a book tucked under his arm as he wielded his cane.

"Here, I'll take that for you." Ally eased the book from him. "Did you finish this already?"

"Yes, of course." Gramps frowned. "Why wouldn't I finish it before returning it?"

"Okay, silly question." She helped Gramps out through the doorway and down the single step from the porch. Roxy was wagging her stubby tail in greeting as Gramps slid into the passenger seat.

As Ally drove toward the municipal building, she glanced at her grandfather. "So, what's your plan this time?"

"Plan? What plan?" He tried to sound innocent, but she wasn't buying his act.

"Come on, Gramps. I know you're dying to unravel the secret behind Rosie Malone's lie about Marty Shawlin. That's the only reason you asked me to take you to the library on a Sunday, isn't it?"

A smile broke across Gramps' weathered face. "You're right, it is."

She sighed. "Do you even know for sure Rosie is working today?"

"No, but we can always come back another day if she isn't." Gramps waved away her concern. "Besides, I was thinking we could also stop in to talk to your detective, see if he's learned anything new."

"No, Gramps." On this Ally would remain firm. "We are not going to keep bothering Noah. It was nice enough for him to fill us in on what he knew as of last night. Besides, the DNA evidence won't have been processed this quickly. It will likely be weeks before Noah finds what he needs to put Eli White away for murdering Marty and Anita."

Gramps scowled. "I hadn't thought about that, but you're right. The DNA always seems to get done faster on TV."

"Everything gets done quicker on TV," Ally pointed out. She pulled into the parking lot and began searching for a space. "And this is real life, Gramps. I don't see the harm in asking Rosie about Marty, but she's already denied lying about it several times now. I'm not sure that asking again is going to get you anywhere."

"You don't know that," Gramps said, wagging a finger at her. "I have a way of finessing a conversation to get results."

No argument there. Ally parked the Honda, grabbed Gramps' library book, then went around to free Roxy. The dog leaped down to the pavement.

"It's a hot one," Gramps muttered, squinting against the glare of the sun as he leaned on his cane.

"This was your idea, not mine." Ally shortened her stride to stay alongside her grandfather.

The coolness of the building was a welcome relief on the scorching day. Ally held the library door open for Gramps, inwardly groaning when she recognized Rosie Malone standing at the counter.

Here we go, she thought, as Gramps made a beeline toward the librarian.

"Rosie, good to see you!" Gramps flashed a warm grin as Ally hustled to keep up, reaching over to place the library book on the counter beside him. "Thanks for this," he tapped the cover. "Excellent read."

Rosie's smile again didn't reach her dark eyes. "Glad you liked it."

"Are you mad at me for some reason?" Gramps leaned forward, resting his elbows on the counter. "You look upset."

"I'm fine." Rosie avoided his gaze, focusing her attention on the book he'd returned. "I'm sorry, I haven't had time to find any new true crime stories."

"Rosie, please. Talk to me." Ally had no idea Gramps could look so compassionate. "You know, they arrested someone in connection with Marty's murder so there's no reason to lie."

"I didn't talk to Marty!" Rosie's outburst was loud enough to attract attention from other library patrons.

"Okay, that's fine." Gramps smiled gently. "But you should know that keeping secrets has a way of wearing you down. It's hard to remember who you said what to and when, isn't it? I promise you'll feel better if you let it all out."

Her eyes flashed with anger, then her hard expression abruptly crumbled, and two fat tears slid down her cheeks. "I loved him," she whispered.

Who? Marty? Dumbstruck, Ally could only gape in surprise.

"There, there, Rosie. It's okay." Gramps reached over to pat her hand. "Why shouldn't you love him? Everyone deserves to have someone special in their life."

"I—I didn't want anyone to know, because everyone was so mad at him." Rosie sniffled loudly and reached for a tissue. "They all acted as if he was some sort of criminal!"

"I know, that wasn't very nice," Gramps admitted, which also made Ally's jaw drop, since Marty had been taking money without providing his promised services, ones his clients likely didn't even need. And wasn't Gramps the one who'd booted Marty out of the Legacy House the afternoon before the murder?

"Th—then he was murdered. In cold blood. As if his life d— didn't matter." A sob erupted, and Rosie pressed the tissue to her

306

mouth in a vain attempt to muffle the sound. "It wasn't right that people were so mean, acting as if Marty deserved what happened to him."

"Everyone's life matters, Rosie," Gramps assured her. "And the police did their job in bringing Marty's killer to justice."

"Yes, I know." Rosie grabbed another tissue and dabbed at her eyes. She offered a watery smile. "It was silly to lie about talking to him, but I just didn't want anyone to know about us."

Ally could understand her reasoning. After all, Marty had soon become persona non grata around Willow Bluff. Being in a relationship like that would be difficult at best.

"I'm sorry for your loss, Rosie," Ally said. "And I shouldn't have brought this up at the grocery store yesterday. Please forgive me."

Rosie waved the tissue. "It's my own fault for trying to hide it. I always was a lousy liar."

"Well, I'm sure you'll feel better now that the secret is out," Gramps said.

"I do, thanks, Oscar." Rosie squeezed Gramps' hand. "I'll take a look through our new books and call you next week if I find anything I think you'll like."

"Appreciate that, thanks." Gramps turned toward Ally, a satisfied gleam in his eye. "Ready to go?"

"Sure." Ally tugged on Roxy's leash and walked alongside Gramps. When they were out of Rosie's earshot, she whispered, "I cannot believe you got her to admit she was seeing Marty Shawlin on the side!"

"I told you I'm good at interrogating people," he said smugly. "Hey, maybe you should convince your detective to let me interview his suspects from now on?"

Ally nearly choked on her own spit. "Um, I don't think so, Gramps."

"Why not?" He demanded. "Haven't I just proven how valuable my skills are?"

Ally simply shook her head, imagining the exasperated expression on Noah's face if she ever suggested such a thing. "You're great at what you do, but so is Noah. And we promised to leave the investigating to him from now on."

Gramps snorted in derision. "You promised that, I didn't."

"Yes, you did, Oscar," a deep voice said from behind them.

Ally caught the woodsy scent a second before recognizing Noah's voice. She glanced over her shoulder at him, sighing as Roxy greeted him with sloppy kisses. "Hi, Noah, what's new?"

"Did you know about Rosie having a fling with Marty Shawlin?" Gramps asked.

Noah smiled and nodded. "As a matter of fact, I did know. We found some emails and text messages between them when we dumped the information from his phone."

Gramps scowled. "I got Rosie to admit it. But you could have let us know that was why she was lying about talking to Marty. It was driving me crazy wondering why she'd do such a thing."

Noah flashed a smile. "I can't tell you all my secrets, Oscar. What fun would that be?"

"Well, I'm just glad it's over," Ally said. "That was certainly enough excitement for the week."

"I'm glad I saw you here, Ally. I wanted you to know that once Eli White knew about the forensic evidence we were compiling against him, he broke down and confessed everything, killing

Marty, throwing the rock at your clinic, and stealing the GMC truck to run you off the road."

"Really?" Ally brightened. "Does that mean he's going to pay for my broken door?"

Noah hesitated. "Maybe, although the damage was done in the course of committing a crime, so we'll have to work through that between his homeowner's insurance and yours. You might want to start with your insurance company first. Oh, and Eli admitted to having an affair with Anita, then killing her when she threatened to go to the police about seeing him leaving Marty's house that morning. Apparently the guilt over being complicit in Marty's death was eating at Anita."

"So it should," Ally said. "And what about Ginny? Did she know about the affair?"

Noah grimaced. "She admitted she suspected he was seeing someone because of his strange comings and goings."

"She lied about the cuckoo clock," Gramps said.

"Yes," Noah admitted. "But she was truly horrified to discover Eli had murdered two people."

"That's completely understandable. But I have one more question, Noah," Ally said.

"What's that?" His tone was wary.

"Does Kimberly Mason smoke?"

Noah looked surprised. "Yeah, but why does that matter?"

"I knew it! That must be the reason Roxy growled at her green Ford!"

"I can see how cigarette smoke might have set Roxy off, especially if she associated the scent with Eli White." Noah glanced at the boxer. "I guess she's smarter than I gave her credit for." He reached down and stroked Roxy's soft golden-brown fur. The animal sighed and rubbed against him, making Noah smile. "Anyway, you should know we're officially closing the case."

"Sex and money," Gramps said with a nod. "The root of all evil."

"You're right about that, Gramps." Ally was hit by an overwhelming sense of relief. "Well, thanks again, Noah."

"Oh, Ally? If you're free later this evening, Jim and Erica thought it would be nice to get together at the Lakefront Café."

"Um, yeah, sure," Ally stammered, trying to ignore Gramps' all-knowing grin and his not-so-subtle elbow jammed into her side. Where were her grandfather's manners now? Sheesh.

"Sounds good," she managed. "Should be fun to reminisce about old times."

"I'll swing by your place, say about six?" Noah offered. "It's not supposed to rain, so we can walk."

She hoped he'd think the redness in her cheeks was from the sun beating down. Now it seemed official . . . this was a date.

"Okay, see you then," she said weakly.

Noah gave Roxy one last rub before turning to walk away. Then he paused and turned to glance back at her. "Oh, and Ally? You're welcome to bring Roxy along."

"All right." As she watched him walk away, she found herself wondering who he really wanted to spend time with.

Her or the dog?

Yeah, probably the dog.

Acknowledgments

I'd like to thank my agent, Pamela Hopkins for her joyous excitement over this idea for a cozy mystery series. If not for her loving this so much, I may not have taken the time to write this book! I'd also like to thank the team at Crooked Lane Books, my editor Faith Black Ross and her production assistant Melissa Rechter for all the work they did making this book the best it can possibly be. What a fantastic team to work with!

For veterinary medicine insights, I've used a variety of sources, including Dr. Elaine Binor of Wauwatosa Veterinary Services. Thanks for your patience with me.

A quick shout out to my fellow authors in my critique group: Lori Handeland, Oliva Rae and Pam Ford. Thanks for letting me bounce ideas off you, no matter how crazy. I appreciate our brainstorming sessions.

Lastly, I'd like to thank my loving husband, Scott for being so incredibly supportive when I asked to retire from my day job as a nurse to write full time. I'm so blessed to have this opportunity to live my dream!